THE
TWELFTH
MAN

The Village Cricket Match
Tillingfold's Tour
Test Time at Tillingfold
Cricket Styles and Stylists
First Wicket Down

THE
TWELFTH
MAN

JOHN PARKER

ANDRE DEUTSCH

First published in Great Britain 1992
by André Deutsch Limited
105-106 Great Russell Street London WC1B 3LJ

Cataloguing-in-publication data for this title
is available from the British Library

ISBN: 0 233 98769 X

Printed in Great Britain by
Billings Book Plan Limited, Worcester

To Margaret

1

'Look out!'

My yell of warning carried away on the crashing swell of applause from 25,000 people as the ball, driven with merciless power from the Nursery End at Lord's, soared back over the bowler's head towards the pavilion. Half a dozen of us, packed on the old wrought-iron bench on the visiting players' tiny gallery, cheered with the crowd as the memorable six-hit from our captain, Persse Grace, hung in the blue air for an interminable moment before gaining speed like a heat-seeking missile and hurtling straight for our balcony. There's not much that even the best cricketers can do, crowded together, seated and standing in such a limited space, but I stuck out my hand instinctively and caught the ball an inch in front of the face of the man sitting on my right. The force of the trajectory smacked the back of my fist into his eye, but that didn't worry me as I tossed the ball down to the fielder to more applause from the assembled members and a chorus of raucous comments from the Tavern bar down on the right. Someone turned the television sound up in the dressing room behind us: '. . . Not bad for a twelfth man, that. Let's see it again . . . there's the ball from Carter . . . Grace's drive . . . What a hit! . . . and panic on the players' balcony as they realise they're the target . . . and young North's got it safely . . .'

'It's all right for you, you lucky young sod,' said Smithson, the Surrey opening bat. 'Sit on your backside doing sweet nothing and get yourself on telly all over the country. Some of us have to work for a living.'

I could understand his sourness. His first-ball duck – the one cricketers call 'golden' – had also been shown on national television, and so had the tricky little leg-slip catch he'd grounded. This new cricket channel that had come in with the satellite explosion of the nineties had much to answer for, with its daily coverage of the top county matches as well as the saturation reporting of Tests.

I couldn't complain. I was getting paid for handing round the drinks. I said nothing. There was no point in upsetting Smithson, who as senior professional had the ear of the captain and a disdain for younger players like me. I turned to my neighbour, who was holding his head in his hands and pressing a handkerchief to his eye. It occurred to me that I had failed dismally at the task entrusted to me by the captain as he left the dressing room on his way to the wicket; to take special care of Mr Pravisar, his friend from Pakistan.

'Sorry, sir, I couldn't quite take the force off the ball. Are you okay?'

The handkerchief was removed slowly. The dark skin around the eye was already turning a deep purple-black, while the white of the eye itself was shot with blood. It looked painful – and malevolent. His English was slightly accented but pedantically correct and just as supercilious as it had been during our few minutes of conversation on the balcony.

'Do not be absurd, young man. Had you performed your function correctly as a cricketer I would not now be so severely inconvenienced. Fetch me some ice.'

I thought both the tone and the comment were out of order, considering that I had just saved him from possible death and certain injury, but I held my tongue and fetched the ice-bucket from the dressing room table and a clean towel from my cricket bag. Pravisar took them from me without a word of thanks and lapsed into a haughty silence to watch the cricket, pressing the towel packed with ice against his face. None of my team-mates moved to help me. I did not expect them to; Surrey under Persse Grace was not that sort of team. The twelfth man did what he was told. At all events the action out on the field was of far greater interest than the minor misfortunes of a rather unpleasant interloper, even if he was the captain's friend. For Grace was playing the sort of innings his namesake would have been making on this same ground over one hundred years ago; indeed, the sort of innings for which both were equally famous in their time.

It was mid-afternoon on the Saturday of the traditional early-season four-day 'derby' match at Lord's between Surrey and Middlesex, and we, the visitors, at least until Grace went in to bat, had been on the end of a thorough thrashing from the powerful Middlesex side from the moment we lost the toss on the Thursday and batted first. By three o'clock that day we were all out for 124. Exactly twenty-four hours later Middlesex had scored 387 for three, with Stewey Baker unbeaten on 200, and we finally persuaded them to declare at lunch on Saturday at a mere 630 for six, Baker still unbeaten for a record 335. As twelfth man, I had a busy day with the drinks tray and two hours of heavy fielding around the boundaries on Saturday morning as Middlesex surged to their unbeatable total. Grace had declared himself unfit to field and retired to the dressing room with his guest from Pakistan. He did not bother to watch the slaughter from the balcony.

So that afternoon Surrey went in again needing 506 in our second innings to make Middlesex bat again, or to stay at the crease for more than six hours to save the innings defeat and by some miracle force a draw. At three o'clock Charlie Belfer drove despairingly inside the line and was comfortably caught behind off the England seamer, Carter, leaving us on a pitiful 33 for four. Persse Grace,

3

whose comments to Pravisar on his team's performance had been insulting and clearly audible to members on the pavilion balconies, and who had sunk three large pink gins while waiting to bat, strode down the steps with a face like thunder, hammered out his guard impatiently and hit the first ball he received from Carter straight on to the upper balcony of the pavilion. It was a typically defiant start to an innings that *Wisden* described later with unaccustomed but justifiable hyperbole as 'the century of the century'.

Having done my best for the supercilious Mr Pravisar, I angled my body to ignore him as far as was possible and settled down to watch the captain doing what he had always done best – imposing his will on the bowlers and tearing an attack to shreds. Within ten minutes the only fielder within 30 yards of the wicket was the wicket-keeper. Grace hit four sixes and four fours in his first 50, which took just fifteen minutes; he was only a minute off Percy Fender's record thirty-five minutes for 100; and when he paused to call for a drink and a new bat he had scored 140 in under eighty minutes, slowing down somewhat but still threatening to surpass Gilbert Jessop's incredible two-hour double century for Gloucestershire at Hove in 1903.

It was thrilling to watch, and even the partisan Middlesex crowd began to applaud every boundary, though up in the Surrey dressing room the enthusiasm was somewhat tempered. For all his public charisma, Grace was not all that popular with his fellow cricketers.

'Lucky sod,' Evans grunted, as a pulled drive narrowly cleared a fielder, scattering the drinkers in the Tavern. 'Anyone else would've dumped it down the bloke's throat.'

'Be fair, Taff,' someone responded. It was Phil Hills, the big fair-haired wicket-keeper. 'The Skip's doing a bloody fine job down there. All right, he's having a bit of luck, but by God we need it just now.'

Smithson sniffed. 'It'll take more than luck,' he said. 'We threw this one away from the first ball.'

'It won't make a blind bit of difference,' agreed Symonds,

4

padded and gloved ready to take his turn when the next wicket went down. 'It's the glory boy bit for the press. Persse can't last. He's as pissed as a fart and batting from memory.' He paused involuntarily to clap a cover-drive which rattled the advertising boards before the two nearest fielders could move. 'But his memory's bloody good. Look at that!' This time a savage hook for six had the spectators in the Mound stand ducking for cover and Grace did not even bother to begin to run as the ball left the bat.

My memory was pretty good too; the batting spectacular taking me back seven years to my thirteenth birthday, when a very similar innings by the same man – at The Oval then – had convinced me that I wanted to become a professional cricketer. My father – Frank North, the bat-maker – had brought me up by train from Sussex as a birthday treat, and we sat baking in the members' stand as Grace hit 150 in 40 overs to carry Surrey single-handedly through to the final of the Benson & Hedges Cup. Even my father, who had known cricket and cricketers all his life, was impressed.

'You see that, Roger,' he said after one particularly scorching drive. 'That's the way a bat should be handled. But that's a Special Mr Grace is using there. I only make them for the best. You'll be doing that one day.' At thirteen, I knew when to say nothing, but going home in the train that evening I dared to interrupt my father's microscopic study of the day's scores in the evening paper. It was not something I did often. Although he was excessively polite and patient with the most tyrannical of his customers, among whom were included some of the greatest cricketers of the day, he was always pretty strict with me when I was younger, and I was completely in awe of him.

'Dad.' I pulled at his sleeve. 'Dad.' I faltered. His cool grey eye over the lip of the newspaper was daunting. The words came out with difficulty. 'I know what I want, now.'

'You'll have to wait until we get home, son. You've eaten all the sandwiches.'

Impatience overcame my diffidence. The future was much more important to a thirteen-year-old than a packet of sandwiches. 'No, Dad, it's not that. I know what I want to *be*. When I grow up. I want to be a cricketer.'

'Hmmm.' He paid me the compliment of taking me seriously. 'It's a very tricky career. No more amateurs these days. You know that we . . . I've always wanted you to come into the firm with me.' It was not a complaint or even a rejection; just a straightforward statement. The quickly amended 'we' was the give-away. He had promised my mother before she died that he would see me safely into manhood, and even he was (almost) prepared to use her memory as a sort of moral blackmail. But his integrity took over, albeit reluctantly. 'All right Rodge. I'll make a bargain with you. You've got the makings of a cricketer, but you've got the makings of a bat-maker too. You stick at school and take your exams and learn the trade in your spare time, and when you're eighteen, if you still want to, I'll get you a trial with the county. Then it'll be up to you, but at least you'll have a trade behind you. In case of injury.'

I knew what he meant. Archie Cornish, the Somerset all-rounder and a loyal user of father's bats, had been forced out of the game before he was thirty with cartilage problems in both knees, and we both knew of others whose careers had ended prematurely. But a thirteen-year-old does not contemplate disaster, and I agreed eagerly with his offer. He held out a hand, shaking mine firmly in exactly the same way in which I had seen him make agreements with fully grown men. There was not a trace of condescension. For my father, a contract was a contract.

We both kept our sides of the bargain, which was why I was now sitting on the players' balcony at Lord's instead of sweating over a spokeshave in the little shed which passed as half of the factory of F. North & Son, Bat-maker, in the Sussex village of Willford. I was wondering what he was doing at that moment, when my attention was jerked back to a change in the rhythm of the happenings out on the pitch. Play had halted for a moment. Grace had left the crease and was making those mystic signs towards the balcony which only cricketers understand. They said: 'Bring me a drink. And a change of gloves. And a new bat. NOW!'

Pravisar spoke again. His voice was high, almost sneering. 'Look sharp there, North. Your master's voice calls.'

'Ay,' said Hills. 'You'd better get a move on. The skipper eats the twelfth man for breakfast.'

But I was already in action, rummaging in the captain's kit for a new pair of batting gloves and his bats. He carried four in his bag, all of which looked new and barely used. I had no idea which one he would want, so I stuck three under my arm.

'Here you are, Roger.' Hills held out a glass of orange and soda. 'I've given it a good snort of gin. We've got to keep his momentum going.'

'Thanks Phil.' I was surprised. Such gestures from the rest of the team were unusual, to say the least. Thus laden, I clattered down the wide steps of the pavilion and trotted across the grass to Grace, who had come half way from the wicket to meet me. He was breathing hard from his exertions and his usually florid face was brick red. He threw down his bat and gloves which were sodden with perspiration.

He brushed aside my congratulations on his innings.

'You took your time.' He seized the glass and drank it down in a couple of gulps. It seemed to hit the back of his throat, and he coughed. A new and unexpected look of respect flitted across his face. 'What the hell did you put in it?'

'Hills said he'd given it a snort of gin, captain – to keep you going.' He preferred 'captain' to the more casual 'skipper' or 'skip'.

'Hmmm. I'll have a word with Hills later.' But he drained the last few drops in the glass and handed it back to me, taking the gloves I proffered in exchange. They had always interested me. Grace had had them made specially. They were of the old-fashioned kind, made of kid leather but with the entire palm cut away. He said they allowed the hands to 'breathe' and for him to keep the 'feel' of the bat. He pulled them on and flexed his fingers, taking the first bat I offered him. He made a short pass in the air with it, tried a drive and handed it back. He did the same with the second bat, but when he took the third he gave it a perfunctory swish and went back to the second bat, which he proceeded to subject to a much more thorough testing. He weighed it in his right hand, tossed it from hand to hand, played a couple of left-handed defensive shots in the air, and nodded.

'That's better.'

I ran back to the pavilion, up the tiny slope and through the gate, where I turned to make sure he had not changed his mind. He was retaking his guard and going through his invariable routine. It was almost like a fetish. Having marked out his block, he turned away from the wicket and forced down the rubber tubing of the handle, using both hands and a considerable amount of strength. Only when he had assured himself that the rubber was as low on the handle as it would go did he turn round and, with a couple more flourishes, took up his stance and awaited the next ball.

The Middlesex opening bowler from Trinidad, Vic Vernon, had been charging up his batteries during the short break in play. He had been treated with scant respect by Grace and was determined to break through the Surrey skipper's defences. Every stride on his run-in bristled with purpose. Any cricketer worth his salt would have bet on a bouncer, but on a wicket as placid as this one even the West Indian's most lethal delivery lost its sting and turned into a fast long hop. Grace met this one with the full face of the bat and, not deigning to hook, pulled the ball viciously for six, clearing the stand and nearly decapitating Old Father

Time. It was a thunderous shot, greeted with even more thunderous applause, and Grace strode a couple of paces up the pitch waving his bat in acknowledgement in his right hand and shaking his left as though the blow had stung him. He took two more paces and then in slow motion sank to his knees and keeled over sideways, like a battleship hit by a torpedo. The applause stopped abruptly as though switched off, and was replaced by a subdued inquiring hubbub.

I dropped everything I was carrying and raced out to the wicket as the Middlesex players crowded round, sensing rather than hearing the sudden shocked silence from the crowd. Grace was unconscious, but breathing with a harsh rattle through his open mouth, and every few seconds a convulsive tremor ran through his body. The colour had gone from his face, which was now a pasty white with greasy beads of sweat clinging to it.

'Is he dying?'

'God knows. It looks like it.'

'What is it? A stroke?'

'Looks more like a heart attack to me.'

'Anyone know artificial respiration?'

'We must get him off the field.'

Mike Marsh, the Middlesex skipper, signalled frantically for a stretcher, while two of the Middlesex players turned Grace onto his back and one began the kiss of life while the other pressed rhythmically down on his chest. Two ambulance men raced out carrying a stretcher and took charge without any fuss. With no apparent effort they lifted Grace's bulky frame onto the stretcher and carried him off at a brisk pace into the pavilion. With nothing better to do, I picked up Grace's discarded bat and stood, aimlessly. Marsh put his hand on my shoulder.

'Come on, son,' he said gently. 'We've got a cricket match to finish.'

I made my way back to the pavilion again. Before I got

there, Symonds was already on his way to the wicket. He paused.

'What was it?'

'No idea. Someone said he thought it was a heart attack.'

'Bad?'

'I don't know. He looked pretty awful.'

'Oh well. Nothing trivial, I hope,' said Symonds lightly and marched on his way to the wicket.

'What the hell was in that drink?' It was the Middlesex player who had tried to perform the kiss of life.

'Gin.'

'I should bloody well think so. He stank like a distillery. No wonder he flaked out.'

'At least I think it was gin. I didn't pour it.'

'You'd better hope you didn't if he buys it.'

I ran through the gate, picked up the gear I had dropped and trailed back up to the dressing room which was in disarray. Grace had been taken straight to the ambulance and off to hospital, so no one knew how ill he was. They pressed me to tell them all I knew about Grace's condition, but I could say no more than that the Captain had collapsed in mid-wicket, and that he had looked, and sounded, gravely ill. Carnock, who combined the roles of manager and coach, had gone with him in the ambulance to the hospital with the press and television trailing on behind. Smithson was reluctantly taking charge, although there was nothing he could do. In any case there was a strong feeling that the rest of the match was a mere formality. With Surrey needing more than two hundred to save the innings defeat and with Grace obviously too ill to take any more part in the game, there was little the lower batsmen could do other than to lose their wickets with some dignity.

Even this was beyond most of them. Symonds was soon back in the pavilion, shamefaced after spooning a gentle catch back to the bowler; Hills at least managed a few lusty whacks before being well caught deep down at third man off a skier; the stock bowler, Muir, saw his middle stump cartwheel and, next ball, Jason touched the ball straight into the hands of first slip. There was a little flurry from the last pair, but a fine piece of fielding at cover stranded Peter Porter in mid-run, and the return hit the top of the stumps with him still a yard out of his ground. Gerry Down was left not out, but missed a well-deserved fifty by one run. By this time most of the crowd had left, while the majority of the members seemed to have ensconced themselves in the Long Bar, whence an increasing well of sound emerged.

'North.' Smithson called across the room. 'You'll take charge of the captain's kit.' He might have added, 'please', but the command was not unreasonable given the circumstances of the Surrey regime in those days. It was Grace's custom to use the twelfth man for all his odd chores, rather like an Army batman. The duties included driving his (sponsored) Mercedes, packing up his gear and acting as a runner to his bookmaker, as well as bowling to him in the nets and losing to him at squash.

I busied myself clearing up the dressing room as best I could – not an easy task as cricketers are not the tidiest of sportsmen – and grabbed my towel, ready for a quick shower before changing into the slacks, blazer and brown Surrey tie that comprised the 'uniform' of the team – provided yearly by the sponsor, one of the big London tailors. I packed my own cricket bag – a cheap tin trunk with my name badly stencilled on the lid – and then Grace's, which was a very different thing. It was a giant of a bag, made of thick but pliable leather with a brass lock and name-plate – PERSSE EVANS GRACE – and it contained comfortably everything the well-dressed cricketer would need. There was a spare set of underclothes; handkerchiefs; three white silk (yes, silk with cashmere and a Jermyn Street address on the label) shirts; three pairs of white flannels, individually tailored, from another Jermyn Street firm; two Surrey cravats and another I did not recognise; two towels and a crocodile vanity case, and spare boots, pads, gloves and protectors for various parts of the anatomy. Bats went into a separate compartment, with a pocket for a small bottle of linseed oil and a rag, neatly encased in a plastic bag. Four well-worn practice balls nestled in one corner and a large, half-empty bottle of gin in another. I added his 'civvies', neatly hanging from two hooks in his favourite corner, checked that I had his key ring and clipped the bag shut. The sight of the silk shirts gave me a sudden thought.

'Has anyone seen Pravisar?'

'Who's he?' asked Symonds.

'The snooty bloke from Pakistan. Captain's pal.'

'The one who bollocked you for saving his life, you mean,' said Phil Hills, who never minced words. 'He left when the skip went down. Bloody good riddance, too. He just stood up and made for the door without a word. Why d'you want to know? Thinking of claiming a reward?'

I grinned. 'For giving him a black eye, you mean? No, it's just that the captain said to look after him. But if he's cleared off, he can look after himself. I couldn't stand the bloke anyway.'

'You're not alone. He's been hanging around the captain for a year or two and none of us can bear him. Persse doesn't like him either, but they've got some sort of business connection. His visits always leave Persse in a filthy mood, which never helps. I'll give you a hand with that bag.'

'Don't bother, thanks. It's finished. But you could give me a lift with it down to the car. It weighs a ton. I'll have to take it back to his place, I suppose.'

'Sure.'

But before we could leave the dressing room, the Lord's attendant stuck his head round the door.

'Mr Smithson. Telephone call for you. It's Mr Carnock.'

'Coming.'

We waited in silence for news of the captain. Through the closed door we could hear Smithson's voice raised in what sounded like astonishment. In a surprisingly short time he was back, grim-faced. The team gathered around him.

'That wasn't Carnock. It was the chairman, from the hospital. Mr Grace died soon after they got there. The doctors couldn't save him. We're all to go straight to The Oval, where the chairman will talk to us. North. You're to take all the captain's gear in his car to The Oval and be sure to lock it when you park it.'

'What shall I do with the keys?'

'Hand them to the secretary. He'll do whatever is necessary.'

'Okay.'

Hills and I each took a handle of the heavy bag and, carrying our own kit in the other hand, barged a way down the stairs and through the eager journalists waiting to pounce. They recognised Hills at once and barred our way.

'What's the latest, Phil?'

'The skipper's dead.'

'We know that. How did he die?'

'Was it natural causes? Was it his heart?'

Hills fended them off with a series of gruff 'we don't know's and, using Grace's bag as a sort of battering-ram, we forced the chattering group back down the staircase and out of the narrow double doors. No one paid any attention to me until a sharp-eyed photographer spotted the name-plate on Grace's cricket bag. Instantly he was down on his knees for a close-up shot, followed by the rest of the rat-pack.

'Who are you? Why are you carrying Grace's kit?'

'I'm only the twelfth man.'

'Ah, Roger North. Right? Bloke who caught the catch on the balcony. You ran out when he collapsed on the field. What was wrong with him?'

'I'm a cricketer, not a doctor.'

'No, but how did he look out there?'

'Bloody awful. He was unconscious and his breathing

sounded funny. We can't tell you any more. Let us through. In any case, we're not allowed to talk to the press.'

A television camera poked its lens roughly through the heads surrounding us.

'ITN here. Mark Lamb. You're the guy who ran out to give the kiss of life, aren't you?'

The clamour rose even higher. I had to shout.

'No I bloody well wasn't! Get out of our way!'

I looked across at Phil, who nodded. We hefted the heavy bag between us and swung it back and forward again as hard as we could. There was a gratifying thump and a yell of pain as it met the cameraman amidships and he tumbled backwards, bringing down his reporter and two others with him in a tangle of cables and forcing a gap in the throng around us. We surged through it ignoring the protests and repeated questions and, trailing press men like a swarm of bees, dashed for Grace's Mercedes. Even after we had managed to throw the three bags in the boot and fight our way into the car, reporters kept pressing round, banging on the roof and shouting questions at the closed windows. The engine started with Mercedes sweetness and I threw the automatic gear lever into reverse, backing slowly but unstoppably through the crowd until I could go into 'drive' and surge down to the Grace Gates and out into St John's Wood Road.

'Thanks, Phil,' I said as soon as we had regained our breath. 'You're better at it than I am.'

'Oh, the press? Don't worry about those blokes. They're only trying to do their job. You'll get used to it. Any road, life should be a bit easier for you now, with that bastard gone.'

His broad northern voice was very bitter. I remembered Grace's face as he lay dying on the shorn turf of the Lord's wicket, and the twitching of his body. I remembered that Phil Hills had laced that last drink that I carried out, and what the Middlesex fielder had said.

'Phil. That orange juice. What did you put in it?'

14

'Gin, of course. Why?'

'How much?'

'Oh, I dunno. A good whack. About a treble, I suppose. Why are you asking?'

'It's just that he didn't look at all natural out there. It wasn't like someone who'd just fainted. Thinking about it now, I reckon he might have been poisoned.'

Hills turned on me angrily.

'What the hell d'you mean? That I poisoned him?'

'No, of course not. I didn't put that very well. But if he did take something that made him ill like that, it had to be in that orange juice. He was okay after lunch.'

'Well, it was all there on the tray on the table. You should know. You put it all there.' He was not mollified. I eased the car another ten yards down Park Lane.

'Yes, but it could have been spiked. By someone else, I mean. Like Pravisar, for example. He looked capable of anything. Or one of the attendants. Or any of the odds and sods who pester us all day long.'

'Ay, or any one of us. But I'd forgotten about Pravisar. I'd take a bet on him, if there was any poisoning done.'

'I didn't like him either. But I only met him today. What do you know about him?'

'Not a lot. Just that he's a millionaire, or something like it. He drives a Rolls Royce, if that's any guide. His family were princes or sultans or something until India went independent and split with Pakistan, but apparently they managed to hang on to most of their cash. He went to university over here. Oxford I think. He began to hang around The Oval about five years ago – he's a friend of the chairman's – and he soon became as thick as thieves with the captain. Some sort of business deal.'

'What has everyone got against the captain?'

'Haven't you noticed? He's a grade A shit.' It was true. The airs and graces Persse Grace assumed as captain of Surrey had been my biggest disillusionment since I had joined the club six months earlier. It was only his occasional extraordinary cricketing ability, demonstrated so well that day, that had made me retain any respect for him at all.

'Has he always been like that?' Hills had been with the team for ten years.

'He was always arrogant, but it's got worse during the last few years. Nobody else knows anything at all about cricket but him – that sort of thing. I reckon he's got delusions because of his name. Sees himself as leading the game into a second Golden Age. Saw, I mean,' he corrected himself. 'But it was his treatment of us, the players, which got us all down. You must have noticed it, even in the short time you've been with us. He bullied everybody, even a senior pro like Smithson, who's as good a player as you'll find outside the Tests, even if he does moan a bit. We've lost three promising fast bowlers and at least two bloody good batsmen in the past three years. Why? Because of Grace's attitude to them. And our results have been going downhill fast. Top four places for how many years? Six, seven, then last year we were thirteenth. And if we go on like this, it's the wooden spoon for Surrey this year. God knows why you decided to come to us. It can't be for the Oval glamour. That went long ago.'

I steered the car through the gates of The Oval, and had to agree that the exterior of the old place could hardly be described as glamorous, despite the swish new Barrington complex and the tarting up of the ancient turnstiles. The exterior walls had been rebuilt, but the few parking spaces looked – and were – totally inadequate for the playing staff, let alone the officials. The narrow concourse was flanked by two mean sets of men's urinals and the fast-food and booze counter. On the left, up a short flight of steps, the main doorway to the pavilion loomed unimpressive and narrow, needing, like everywhere else, a fresh coat of paint. Further along was the great bulk of The Oval itself, settled comfortably in its appointed place like an elderly, shabby but amiable giant who was trying to bring himself up-to-date with pink plastic.

The gateman ushered us to the captain's parking space with a deferential salute to the Merc, if not its driver. We made our way round to the Barrington suite and climbed the concrete stairs to the committee room, which was narrow and long and sparsely furnished, to be greeted by Lord Marcelan, the chairman. Another man sitting with his back to the door and gazing out over the deep green square-patterned grass of The Oval itself, did not stir as we entered. The chairman touched his drooping moustache with a spread thumb and forefinger and held out a bony hand to Hills. His voice was deep and accustomed to authority, not exactly pompous, but straight from Eton and Oxford.

'Good evening. You're the first to arrive. It is very good of you to come so quickly. This is a most unfortunate occasion.' He sounded as though he was accepting full personal responsibility for a minor clerical error in the accounts. 'Hills, isn't it? The wicket-keeper? Good, I thought I recognised you.'

He gave Hills's hand a brief shake, dropped it and turned to me. His clasp was firm but his skin was dry and scaly, like a snake's. Even with the droop of his shoulders matching that of his moustache, I had to look up from my 6ft 2in to meet his eyes.

'And you?' Obviously the twelfth man had not so far come to his notice. But I was mistaken.

'The twelfth man? North, eh? First time I've met you.'

'Yes, sir.' There didn't seem to be anything to add. At the sound of my voice the man at the window swung round, but with the setting sun behind him his face was in deep shadow, though I could see he was wearing an MCC tie.

'You're the man who caught the catch on the balcony, aren't you?' asked the chairman. 'I saw it on television. Well done. I think you've already met my guest.' He gestured vaguely in the direction of the window. 'Prince Suri Jumrat Pravisar, of Qellalabad.'

'Good evening, North,' said the smooth voice before I could recover from my surprise. 'So we meet again.'

'Yes,' I said stupidly. How did you address a Prince? Particularly one to whom you had given a black eye.

Lord Marcelan saved me from embarrassment. 'Prince is a courtesy title these days,' he said. 'It relates to Mr Pravisar's forebears, the Maharajahs of Qellalabad.' Which apparently made it all right for him to be present at a crisis meeting of the Surrey County Cricket team, although the way the rest of the team reacted to his presence as they arrived mirrored my own lack of enthusiasm. The room was nearly full when Smithson drew Lord Marcelan aside and whispered something to him. The old man frowned.

'But he's my guest,' I heard him mutter irritably. Smithson's face set obstinately, but before he could return to the attack Henry Allason, the club secretary who had just come into the room, moved in to smooth over the situation.

'I am sure Mr Pravisar will understand that this is a private meeting concerning the club,' he said blandly and, not giving the chairman a chance to object, turned to shake the Pakistani's hand and move him towards the door, a friendly hand under his elbow. 'Let me introduce you to our librarian,' he said. 'We have some fascinating records here. Some say they rival the archive at Lord's. His Lordship won't be long.'

He ushered Pravisar through the door and down the stairs, still talking. Two minutes later he returned, wearing the satisfied smile of a man who has done a good job.

'He's settled down,' he said. 'There's plenty of material there about Ranji and Duleep. Should keep him quiet for a bit. Chairman, would you like to start?'

Marcelan still seemed slightly put out. 'I don't see why . . .' he muttered. 'Oh, well . . . Gentlemen.' He raised his voice as though addressing a board meeting: 'I know you must all be very distressed by the untimely, er, demise of Persse Grace. We at Surrey will miss him sorely after the services he has rendered to the club over the past, er . . .' he glanced at Allason.

'Twenty-five years,' obliged the secretary promptly. 'He joined Surrey straight from school.'

'. . . twenty-five years. He was a great cricketer and a great captain.'

There was some foot-shuffling and muttering as the obituary droned on for a full five minutes. Eventually His Lordship came to the point of the meeting: 'Er, and I know the committee can bank on you all to carry on as you have in the past, upholding all the great traditions of the Surrey County Cricket Club.'

He stopped, as though waiting for applause which failed to materialise. There was an embarrassed silence. Henry Allason coughed discreetly.

'I think the team would like to know the committee's decision, sir.'

'What? Oh, oh yes. The committee has decided to appoint Mr, er, Smithson as captain for the rest of this season.' There was a subdued round of applause. 'And Mr Carnock will chair the selection committee, with final responsibility for team selection. Thank you, everybody, and, er, good luck for the rest of the season. Now I must see to my guest.'

'The press first, sir, if you don't mind,' said Allason. 'I opened the bar for them.'

'Oh very well. You come with me.' Lord Marcelan walked resignedly to the door, waved a languid hand and disappeared, closely followed by Allason. We crowded round Smithson to congratulate him, in a fairly restrained manner. He was not one to show enthusiasm.

'Thanks, thanks chaps,' he said, waving his hands deprecatingly. 'It's not much of a job, really. Second from bottom in the championship? Well, I suppose we can only go up. All this and Carnock too.'

He had a point. Harry Carnock was a former Lancashire county player who had not made the grade and turned to coaching. He was the epitome of the saying, 'if you can, do; if you can't, coach.' Now, apparently, he was to have the last word in the selection of the team and the authority to override the captain, who would no doubt be in the firing line if we failed to perform up to expectations. It was a position Grace would never have tolerated as captain. His attitude had always been that the committee was answerable to the club captain, not vice versa. And with his personality and reputation, he had ruled Surrey for years. Smithson had a difficult act to follow, and I actually felt a little sorry for him. Competent cricketer though he was, it was doubtful whether he had the drive to fill the large gap left by Grace, particularly with the burden of Carnock hanging like an albatross round his neck.

'Bad luck, Smithie,' said Hills. 'All the kicks and not many ha'pence. Don't worry, we'll do our best for you, not that that's much at the moment. That was a very odd meeting. It didn't feel real.'

'I know what you mean,' added Symonds, the former Cambridge blue. 'The point is, we know the skipper's dead, but how did he die? There's sure to be an inquest. The chairman totally ignored that.'

'Probably drowned in his own bile,' said Jason, the fast bowler who had been the object of much cruel comment from Grace. 'What was in his gin, North?'

'More gin.'

'Grace'd never choke on gin,' said the off-spinner, Porter. 'It was like water to him. But he could still play cricket. I'll say that for him. If you've got to go, what a way to do it.'

Smithson made his decision and issued his first order as captain of Surrey.

'It's time we had a drink,' he said. 'Captain's expenses. Let's go down to the bar.'

He led the way towards the door, but the way was blocked by Allason, holding up a hand. His face was bleak.

20

'I'm sorry, chaps.' His voice was formal. 'You'll have to stick around for a bit. Is everyone still here?' He looked around, mentally counting. 'That seems all right. Now I have to tell you this. I don't think there's anything to worry about, but the police aren't satisfied that Mr Grace died from natural causes, and they've sent a detective inspector from Scotland Yard to ask us a few questions. They're doing the same with the Middlesex team.'

'Does that mean the captain was murdered?' Symonds asked. His voice had an edge, almost of excitement.

'I don't know,' the secretary answered smoothly. 'They're talking about "suspicious circumstances", whatever that may mean. Apparently the doctors are having difficulty in establishing the cause of death. Anyway, they're not happy, and Detective Inspector Light is down in my office now and wants to see each of you in turn.' He turned to Smithson. 'You'd better go first, Don.'

'That's one way of getting out of paying his dues, any road.' Hills's comment was meant to be heard, and Smithson heard it.

'Don't worry, Phil. Your beer's safe.' He turned to Allason. 'We were just going down to the bar. Can you get some beer and sandwiches sent up for the lads? It could be a long evening.'

'Yes, I'll do that. It's not a good idea to go down to the bar, anyway. The Surrey Tavern's packed full of press and television people and we've had to post a couple of coppers on the stairs to prevent them taking over the entire Oval. Which reminds me; the county rule on no talking to the press applies more strongly than ever in these circumstances. Be polite, but firm. No losing your temper. We've already had two complaints of assault by cricket bag, and we don't want any more. Swearing at the camera doesn't help either, North. These days it merely ensures that you'll be on the news, as you were this evening. I'll go and see about your beer and sandwiches. Lagers all round?'

Without waiting for anyone to dissent, he had gone, closely followed by Smithson, who looked none too happy about being the guinea pig for Scotland Yard. Hills and I grinned at each other. As far as we were concerned the 'assault by cricket bag' had been the only enjoyable part of the whole day's incidents, the secretary's strictures notwithstanding. All the players settled down round the long table to drink the secretary's lager and eat his sandwiches, which arrived on two big silver salvers which had seen better days, but it was only about five minutes before Smithson put his head round the door to say, 'Next, please. He wants to see you first, Gerry,' he said to Down. 'You were batting when Grace collapsed. And after that, you, North. You took the drink out to him. After North, it doesn't matter what order you go in.'

Down shrugged and wandered out without saying anything, hands in pockets. He had been born in London, but had inherited the coal-black countenance and phlegmatic nature of his Guyanese parents. 'One of nature's stonewallers,' Symonds, the most articulate among us, called him. 'Except when he's got a bat in his hand.' Scotland Yard were not likely to glean much information from him.

'What did he ask you, Don?' said Hills. 'Did you get any idea of the way they're thinking?'

'Not a clue,' said Smithson, coming into the room. 'He was very close. He said they didn't know how Persse died, but I don't believe him. He didn't seem all that bright to me. He knows as much about cricket as I know about netball. He just wanted to know routine things – how long I'd been with the club, how well I knew Persse, what I thought of him. That sort of thing. No sweat. When the inspector's finished with you, you can go.'

He changed the subject. 'I've had a word with Carnock. We've got nothing on now until the county game against Lancashire on Wednesday. We want everybody in the nets at ten on Monday. We'll have a game in the middle in the afternoon, and we'll put the team up on the notice board immediately after that. We'll travel to Blackpool on Tuesday, leaving here not later than ten. It's a long drive. I'm off now. I want to get away without being caught by the press. You'd better try to do the same. Remember what the secretary said. Ciao.'

He waved goodnight and left. Jason turned to me and laughed, lifting the corner of one lip.

'Right in the frame again, young North, eh? Been on telly again?'

He dug a sharp finger painfully in my ribs. He was as tall as I was, but bulkier, and he had the heavy features of the Cockney bully that he was. He had made it plain that he did not like me from the day I joined the club, a feeling I naturally reciprocated, in spades.

'Lay off the lad, Jay,' said Hills mildly. 'He's done nowt to harm you.'

'He'd better bloody well not, either. Otherwise he'll get done.' There was a current of viciousness in the word 'done' that made several players look up. No one said anything, and I slowly unclenched my fists and let out my breath. Brawling in the pavilion with a senior professional would certainly put a swift end to the twelfth man's career.

I stared back at him until his eyes fell. I said as calmly as I could: 'What are you worried about, Jason?'

Whatever was eating him, for some reason he decided not to press the matter any further just then.

'You watch it,' he said, and turned away. I determined to grow eyes in the back of my head and to avoid dark streets at night. I wondered what I had done to inspire such obvious dislike. It was not pleasant, but there was no getting away from Jason, or any one else for that matter, in the day-by-day confines of a county cricket dressing room. I determined to have it out with him some time, but now was not the moment.

Down wandered back through the door, hands still in pockets, and gave me a cheerful wink.

'Now is de turn of de twelfth man,' he said in the

Caribbean accent he often affected. 'Now off you go, young Roger, and no delay, mind. And don't you be giving de policeman no black eye, man. Give you a game of squash and a beer after? I'll go down and book the court,' he added in his normal south London accent.

'Okay. Good.' I grinned at him. I liked Down. He and Hills had done the most to make me feel welcome in the Surrey side. And a good workout on the squash court was just what I needed after three days of comparative inactivity as twelfth man. Down's was the sort of companionship I had met all too rarely since choosing my career.

I found the man from Scotland Yard lounging in a swivel chair behind the secretary's desk, a small notebook open in front of him. As I entered the room he swung round from contemplating The Oval through the window on his right.

'You're North? The twelfth man? Good.' He thrust a hand across the desk. 'Detective Inspector Light, New Scotland Yard. Please sit down and relax. Just a few routine questions. We have to ask them when anyone dies in suspicious circumstances.'

'What suspicious circumstances?'

'I was hoping you'd tell me, Mr North.'

'I don't know anything.'

'People always say that. You'll be surprised how much you actually do know. Tell me what happened. In your own words.'

'The captain signalled for a new bat, a change of gloves and a drink. As twelfth man it was my job to take them out, so I did. I took out three bats and a pair of gloves from his bag. And a glass of, er, orange juice. He had a drink, then tried the three bats and picked the middle one. Then he finished the orange and went back to the crease. I ran off and turned to watch at the pavilion gate. The captain hit the first ball for six and then collapsed a couple of paces up the wicket. I ran back to see if I could help him, but the Middlesex boys were already doing everything they

24

could, and their skipper had sent for the ambulance men and a stretcher. So I went back to the dressing room with the stuff.'

'Did Grace say anything to you at the wicket?'

'He asked me if I'd mixed the orange juice.'

'Why would he do that?'

'Because it had been strongly dosed up with gin.'

'Did you do that?'

'No.'

'Who did?'

'Hills, the wicket-keeper. He said it would keep the captain going.'

'Is that usual?'

'I don't know. I don't think so.'

'But Grace didn't object?'

'No. He liked it. He finished it up. He'd had a few before he went out to bat in the first place.'

'Why did he do that?'

'He was very angry at the way we were playing. Middlesex were making us look like kids. He told Mr Pravisar so in the dressing room while he was waiting to go in to bat.'

'Mr who?'

'Pravisar. I think he's from Pakistan. A prince or something.'

'What was he doing in the dressing room?'

'He's a friend of the captain.'

'Could this Mr Pravisar have doctored the gin, or the orange juice, while he was there?'

'No, I don't think so. Not while I was looking after him, anyway – after the skipper went in to bat.'

'Why should you look after him?'

'I'm twelfth man. Part of the job.'

'Not a part you relish, then?'

I shrugged. 'Not much. You have to go through it.'

'What else do you have to do? As twelfth man, I mean.'

I reeled off a list of the duties of the Surrey twelfth man, as dictated by Grace. 'Take the drinks out, of course; field if anyone is hurt; bowl to the batsmen in the nets whenever required; bat to the bowlers ditto; give them fielding practice ditto; act as bookie's runner to the captain, and team; clean the captain's car for away matches and act as his chauffeur; see his cricket gear is kept spotless; drink with the sponsors during county match lunch breaks.'

'In fact,' said Light, 'You're everyone's skivvy, and the boss's batman. Not much of a job for a young man like you.'

'I don't mind most of it,' I said. 'You've got to go through it, like I said. It's a sort of apprenticeship.'

'I suppose it means that you're in the frame if anyone's hurt. Like an understudy in a play.'

'Not necessarily. Once a game's started, all the twelfth man is allowed to do is to field in the place of anyone who's sick or injured. He can't bowl or bat or keep wicket, and if he's a specialist slip fielder, for instance, he's not allowed to do that.'

'So Grace's death doesn't mean you'll take his place in the team?'

'Not necessarily. There are seventeen of us in the first team squad. I'm an all-rounder, so I might be lucky. Or they could choose a specialist batsman, which he was.'

'Oh.' He sounded disappointed. 'So *you* had no reason to spike the captain's drink. What did you think of him?'

'He was a great cricketer. Look at what he did today.'

'As a captain? As a man?'

'I've only been here a few months. You'd better ask the others.'

'I want *your* opinion.'

I hesitated. Light took that as an opinion.

'So you didn't like him. Why not?'

'I didn't say that. He . . . he wasn't what I expected. He . . . he wasn't always fair. With his criticism. And he always had to be right. About cricket. About everything.'

26

'You mean he was a bully.'

'Yes, to everybody. But it was worse than that. He seemed to enjoy putting people down.'

'A bit of a sadist?'

I nodded. I wasn't quite sure what the word meant, but it sounded right.

'What did the rest of the team think of him?'

'You'd better ask them.'

'I'm asking you.'

'Well, he wasn't popular, if that's what you mean.' But I refused to be drawn any further, and he let me go. On the way out, I remembered about the captain's Mercedes, so I asked Angie, the girl in the secretary's outer office, where Mr Allason was.

'He's somewhere round the ground, Roger, with that nasty little man.'

'Pravisar?'

'Yes, that's him. Mr Allason's giving him a tour of The Oval. He says he wants to put money into the club, for old time's sake. He really gives me the creeps.'

I had no desire to run into the objectionable Mr Pravisar again.

'Thanks Angie. Will you tell Mr Allason that I've still got the captain's car and all his gear. I'll put it in the garage at the flat overnight and bring it in tomorrow. Tell him not to worry. I won't go joy-riding.'

'I'll tell him. Good night, Roger. Oh, by the way, you look good on telly. That was a great catch.' She was more enthusiastic than usual.

'Don't tell me. I can still feel the bruise. 'Night.'

I blew her a kiss, fetched my squash racket and kit from my locker in the dressing room, started the car, waved goodnight to the gateman and drove slowly round to the squash club, only half a mile or so away just off Borough Road. I parked it on a single yellow line in the side road outside the club. It was after 6.30 and the car was safe from the depredations of traffic wardens. I inserted the key in the lock and heard the satisfying click of the central locking system.

'I'll have the keys.'

Two large men had materialised, one on either side of me. The one who spoke looked vaguely familiar, but I could not place him. He had a heavy, swarthy face and the build of a prize-fighter gone to seed. He was holding out a hand, while in the other was a vicious-looking cosh. The other man appeared to be unarmed, but moved in close and took my left arm in a muscular grip. I closed my fist over the keys.

'Let me go, and say please.'

Without warning, the first man swung his cosh at my groin. Hampered though I was by the second man's grip, I managed instinctively to half-twist and bring my knee up, taking the force of the blow on my thigh. I swung my right fist round at the man holding me, raking the keys across his face. He let go of my arm and staggered back with blood spurting from his nose and mouth. I tried to turn, but my right thigh was 'dead-legged' and, numbed by the blow, collapsed under me, bringing me to my knees suddenly, making the man with the cosh miss with his second shot. I felt rather than heard the cosh whistle past my head and then wrapped my arms round his knees and jerked his legs from under him. The back of his head hit the wing of the Mercedes on the way down, which rather broke the force of its collision with the ground, but the blow was enough to stun him.

I picked up the cosh and dragged myself to my feet, breathing heavily and bearing my weight on my left leg while rubbing hard at my right thigh. The second assail-ant was running unsteadily down the street, his hands to his face, leaving a small trail of blood on the road behind him. The first appeared to be out cold, so I limped heavily across to the squash club and rang the bell. A metallic voice asked for my name and an electronic buzz announced that the security locks had been opened for me. Thankfully I limped into its sanctuary and found Down in the changing room. He was already in shorts and a singlet.

'There you are. You took your time, didn't you? Good God, mate, what's wrong? What's happened?'

I dropped the cosh on the table. I found that I was trembling, and panting as though I had been running. I had difficulty in getting the words out.

'I'll be all right. Only a dead leg. Two men . . . attacked me. Outside. God knows why. They wanted to steal the skipper's car.'

'Two men? Where are they?'

'One ran away. The other's knocked out. Down by the car. Give us a hand, and we'll get him in here and turn him over to the police.'

'I'll do it.'

Down left the locker room at a run. Very quickly, he was back.

'No go, Rodge. No one there. Are you sure there were two, man? You're not hallucinating?'

2

I hurried out to the car as quickly as my bruised thigh would allow. Gerry Down was quite right; the Mercedes stood apparently unmolested, and there was no sign of any assailant. A close look at the road revealed a few drops of blood making a faint trail down the road, but I'm no bloodhound, and there didn't seem much point in pursuit.

'That's that, I suppose.'

'What d'you mean, Rodge?'

'There's no point in calling the police. No evidence.'

'You've got the cosh. And that.' He pointed to my thigh. 'That's evidence.'

I didn't think it was enough, painful though it was. But thinking about it brought the realisation that something had to be done, and fast. Luckily, Jock Swift, the manager of the squash club, was an old friend of Surrey cricket and a qualified physiotherapist accustomed to coping with sundry physical injuries to his playing members.

'Ach,' he said, examining the purpling bruise with careful fingers. 'How d'ye come by this? It's no a pretty sight'.

'Gerry hit me with his racket,' I said quickly before Down could reply. 'It was my fault. I got in the way. Can you do anything about it, Jock? I've got nets tomorrow. I don't want to turn up a cripple.'

Swift looked sceptical, but was used to the demands of

sportsmen. 'We'll see,' he said. 'I can help, but you'll have to run through the worst of it yourself on the treadmill.'

He brought out an instrument resembling a flat-iron, but with a base of close-set plastic pimples. 'Ultrasound,' he said briefly. He plugged it in and applied it gently but firmly to my bruised thigh. As he turned up the power a high-pitched whine filled the treatment room and rose still higher until it passed out of the range of the human ear. Minute warm pins-and-needles flooded my quadriceps, which almost immediately began to lose its numbness. After a couple of minutes he switched off the gadget.

'That's enough modern rubbish,' he said, tipping a generous amount of creamy pungent liquid from an unmarked bottle into the palm of his hand.

'Embrocation?' I asked, wincing as he slapped the liquid onto the bruise and began to work it into the flesh with strong fingers.

'Horse liniment,' he said, massaging away mercilessly. The skin was burning under his hands. 'I've got a mate at the brewery stables. It'll feel pretty warm. You shouldn't use it if the skin's broken at all.'

After a few minutes of the treatment he stood back.

'Now,' he said. 'It's up to you.'

He took me through some brief exercises, bending and stretching and working on the exercise bicycle. The dead leg was better but the muscle was still sore and stiff. Then he made me run on the treadmill, which I found utterly boring. I was never a jogger.

'Can't I play squash instead?' I pleaded with him after five minutes. He must have been bored, too, as he switched the thing off.

'Aye, it's probably the best ye can do,' he said. 'Ye're young. You'll be okay. But don't forget to loosen up properly before ye bowl in the morning. And ye owe me a couple of lagers.'

'More than that,' I said. 'What do I owe you?'

He grinned. 'A couple of quid for the court and the

lagers for the liniment,' he said. 'And one day ye can pay me back for keeping my mouth shut. I don't think the county would appreciate their promising young bowler scrapping in the street. I saw you from the office window. I'd recognise them again, if you need me. But I wouldn't tangle with them again, if I were you.'

'Thanks. But don't worry, I'll steer clear of them,' I said fervently. And meant it.

Gerry Down was a good squash player, and let me down lightly in the first game. But I'm nothing if not competitive and, forgetting my damaged leg as I warmed up, took him to set-all in the second before losing 10-8.

'Jock's right,' he said as we leant against the cool wall, sweating profusely and panting. 'You'll be all right in the morning. But I still think you should go to the cops.'

The exercise seemed to have cleared my brain. I could not see why or how, but I was convinced that the attack was not a simple attempt at robbery; somehow it was connected with the death of Persse Grace. I said as much to Down while we were showering.

'Man, now you *are* hallucinatin',' he said scornfully.

'Look. No one in his right mind would want to steal Persse's car. It's the only Merc in the world that's painted cream and brown and covered all over with his name and Surrey County Cricket Club in six-inch letters. Even our cops would spot it in a couple of minutes.'

'Nuttin in that, man. They drive it straight into a garage or a lock-up and respray it in ten minutes. You know that. Happens every day.'

'I suppose so. But there was something about the man with the cosh. I thought I recognised him; but I can't place where I've seen him.'

'Well then tell the police.'

'They'd just laugh at me. They've got better things to do than worry about some crazy ideas in the head of some young cricketer.'

'Okay, let's forget about it, Rodge. Come and have

32

a beer. At least we got our game in. You owe me, I think.'

'For letting you win, you mean?'

Down swung a friendly punch at my head and then we sank a couple of unreasonably expensive pints of anaemic lager at the club bar, discussing the situation at Surrey after the death of Grace. Down thought I stood a good chance of a permanent place in the first XI. I was more sceptical, but said I didn't want to continue indefinitely as twelfth man. Talking to Detective Inspector Light had crystallised my thoughts. I decided I'd rather play second team cricket than spend the summer acting as dogsbody to the first team squad. If it didn't work out I'd chuck it all in at the end of my contract in September and go back to the little factory in Sussex to join my father. He was nearing sixty and could do with the help. At least making cricket bats was a man's work.

We collected our squash gear and parted at the door. Down would not accept my offer of a lift, saying he wanted to walk off the beer, so I drove home to Dulwich alone. Thanks to Dad's cricketing contacts, I had been lucky enough to find a pleasant two-roomed flat at the top of a semi-detached Victorian house belonging to Emma Marchbanks, the widow of a former Surrey cricketer who had died in his fifties. They had bought the house and its acre of land with a pools windfall in the days when £10,000 was a great deal of money. When Charlie Marchbanks had died of a heart-attack Mrs Marchbanks had split the house into flats for renting out, and lived quite happily for nearly thirty years on the proceeds.

Now seventy-two, she was still a formidable woman who, fortunately for me, still had a soft spot for cricketers. For years she had resisted the pleadings of relatives and rejected the blandishments of estate agents trying to persuade her that she should sell the house for a king's ransom and buy sheltered accommodation in Bognor or Bournemouth. She had no intention of going into 'one of those places'. She could, and always would, look after herself.

At some stage she had built on a sturdy two-car garage at the side of the house with an electrically-operated door and a security system that could have guarded Fort Knox. One half of it was occupied by her bright scarlet Triumph Roadster, which she had preserved, spotless and gleaming, since her husband had bought it for her from the proceeds of his county 'benefit' years before. Mrs Marchbanks was almost a tourist attraction around Crystal Palace as she drove – always with the hood retracted, unless it was raining – to Croydon on her weekly shopping expedition. The other half of the garage housed my battered MGB, nearly as old as the Roadster but in nowhere near as good condition.

That night I moved the MGB out and parked it at the roadside, wondering what the insurance company would give me if it was stolen, and ran the big Mercedes in beside the tiny Triumph. The Merc looked out of its class, for all its modern gadgets. I locked up the garage and moved through the big old-fashioned kitchen to the hall. Mrs Marchbanks kept a constant eye on all her tenants by not providing us with separate entrances. She retained the ground floor, and we all had to pass by her door. I knocked at the sitting-room door and found her, as usual, reading a paperback novel and simultaneously watching the news on television. A bottle of Johnny Walker Black Label stood on a silver tray beside her chair, with an ice bucket and chunky Waterford crystal glasses.

'Hello,' I said quietly, not wishing to disturb her concentration, but she waved me silently to a chair. Without taking her eyes from the screen, she used silver tongs to place two cubes of ice into a squat glass and poured a deliberate measure of whisky over them, making them crackle. She held out the glass, which I could hardly refuse, so I sat there sipping the strong spirit until Bill Giles finished the weather forecast. Mrs Marchbanks switched off the set and laid down her book.

'Now Roger,' she said. 'Tell me what happened.' She loved a good mystery.

'You've just seen it all on the screen, Mrs M,' I said. 'It seemed pretty complete to me. I haven't got much to add.'

'Yes you have,' she said comfortably. 'They whisk through it so fast. What do the police mean by 'suspicious circumstances'? Was it murder? It wouldn't surprise me. I always said that if Grace had been an officer in the army, he'd have been shot by his own troops. Too arrogant by half. What was in that drink you took out to him?' She shot the question at me.

'Gin and orange. More gin than orange. Phil Hills mixed it. It seems that that's what Persse always liked to have in the middle of a big innings.'

Mrs Marchbanks sniffed. 'That's what they used to say about Denis and Bill. I never believed a word of it.'

'I don't know about Compton and Edrich; but didn't Andy Sandham like a snort at a century?'

She sniffed again dismissively and changed the subject. 'Before my time. What did the police ask you?'

'About the gin. And who disliked Persse.'

'What did you say?'

'I think I gave them the impression that it would be harder to find someone who actually liked him.'

'Including your friend Hills?'

'Phil thinks Grace was a bastard. Excuse the language, Mrs M. So do most of the team. But they wouldn't have poisoned him. If any of them had wanted to murder him they'd have belted him over the head with a cricket bat in a fit of rage. I wouldn't have blamed them, sometimes. Actually, Phil wouldn't hurt a fly. I've seen him catch one in his hands and put it out of the window rather than swat it.'

'And you?'

'Same as the rest. But I'd have swatted that fly.'

Mrs Marchbanks did not press the matter. Instead: 'Do you know where Persse Grace got his money?'

I had no idea. Grace had exuded affluence. I had always assumed that his money came from a rich family. For the past few months I had placed most of his bets and anyone who could gamble in fifty-pound notes, as he did, had to have cash to burn. The old lady's eyes were bright in her face. 'You'd better ask your father,' she said, rendering me speechless for a moment. She twinkled at my astonishment. 'Just ask him,' she said, and once again changed the subject like an inquisitor.

'What was all that driving in and out of the garage just before you came in?' She didn't miss a thing.

I explained about Grace's car.

Mrs Marchbanks rounded on me. 'That was a stupid thing to do, Roger. That will make the police suspect you more than ever, even if they didn't already. Didn't you *think*? Oh dear, what can one expect from a silly young cricketer?' She sighed theatrically.

'Come off it, Mrs M. You've been reading too many of those whodunnits. Why should the police suspect me of anything?'

'Well, if they didn't they will now,' she said. 'Why didn't you wait until Mr Allason was free to take the responsibility? They'll think you're trying to hide something.'

I suddenly recalled the attack and attempted robbery. She saw my face change.

'What is it? what have you remembered?' she asked sharply.

'Nothing, Mrs M.' I had no wish to alarm the old girl any further, but her suspicions were aroused and there was nothing I could do to evade her questions.

'Very well,' she said, when she had wormed the whole story from me. '*Now* shall we telephone the police?'

'Mrs Marchbanks speaking ... Yes, that's right ...

Mr North? Yes, he's here. One moment.' She held out the instrument, covering the mouthpiece with her free hand. 'It's for you. Detective Inspector Light. I told you so. Be careful.'

I took the telephone.

'North here.'

He wasted no time.

'Light. Why did you take Mr Grace's car from The Oval?'

I explained carefully, trying to sound casual. I did not fancy the role of suspect.

'You have it there?'

'Yes. It's locked away in Mrs Marchbanks's garage. It's perfectly safe.'

'It had better be. Keep it that way. And don't try to move it. I'm coming down now with a warrant to collect it. I'll be there in under half an hour. Don't leave the house. You've some questions to answer.' There was a pause. 'That's an order.'

I choked back 'Keep your hair on,' and said merely, 'I'll be here.'

'Do.'

I replaced the telephone.

'How soon will he be here?' Mrs Marchbanks stood up.

'Half an hour, he said.'

'Come with me,' she said. It was another order. She led the way to the garage and switched on the central light.

'We're going to have a look at his cricket bag,' said the old lady. I gaped at her.

'What for?'

'To see what we can find before the police do. Open the car, Roger.'

'We can't do that. The cops will be furious. That's tampering with the evidence,' I protested. Mrs Marchbanks was adamant.

'Not if you're careful. Don't fuss, Roger. We haven't much time.'

37

Reluctantly, I unlocked the boot of the Mercedes and heaved Grace's heavy bag onto the concrete floor.

'Now take the things out carefully, one by one, and put them on top of the car. And stop muttering at me.' I did as I was bid, and emptied the bag until the garage resembled a car boot sale. The old lady peered closely at each article – without touching it, I was glad to see.

She echoed my thought. 'It's all right if your fingerprints are there,' she said. 'But mine would be a complication.' She was particularly interested in the half-empty gin bottle, asking me to unscrew the top while she sniffed at the contents.

'Well, that *smells* like gin,' she said dubiously, and turned her attention to the five North Special cricket bats laid out in a row on the roof of the car.

'Which one was he using?'

I pointed to the battered weapon Grace had used to such good effect on the Middlesex bowlers. It was peppered with reddish marks, undulations and minute cracks where it had struck the ball often and powerfully to all parts of the field. Most of them were concentrated towards the 'meat' – the centre of the face about six inches from the bottom – where every batsman would like to position his shots.

'No. The one he took from you.'

That was more difficult to tell. The remaining four bats were identical in appearance. They had each been 'played in' – used in practice a few times before the real thing – so there was no distinctive marking. Although I was a pretty good judge of a bat, thanks to my father's training, I hadn't done more than to grab three of them from his bag and take them out to the wicket. I picked them up one by one and examined them closely, running my hand up the smooth creamy blades, feeling for rather than seeing the slightest indentation on each surface.

'I can't tell.'

'Try the weight of them. Do hurry up, Roger. They'll be here soon.'

I had no desire for the police to catch me prying into Grace's kit. I hefted each blade as Grace had done, tapping a block gently on the concrete and playing a couple of mock drives. They were all beautifully balanced. As I bent my wrists the 'pick-up' flowed smoothly along each blade and I marvelled, not for the first time, at the supreme art of the bat-maker. Three of the bats, including the one used for the bulk of the innings, I judged would have sat on the scales within a quarter of an ounce of 2lb 7oz. Although the weight felt the same, there was something about the fourth which made me pause and flourish it once more.

'What is it, Roger?'

'I don't know. It feels the same, but it picks up differently.' I held the bat towards her and Mrs Marchbanks examined it minutely, even sniffing the blade and the handle.

'I can't see anything different. It's just a cricket bat. What d'you think is wrong with it?'

'I don't know.' It was just one of a number of things I didn't know that day.

'Never mind. Put it all back in the bag just as it was. Except that bat you're holding. Carefully now . . . you'd better put it up with your stuff in your room. We haven't got time to look at it now. What the police don't know won't harm them.'

I demurred, strongly.

'Why on earth should we do that, Mrs M? And what if they search my room? They're sure to find it. They'll think I pinched it.'

'Don't be daft, boy. It hasn't got his name on it, has it?' She pronounced the word 'daft' in the Yorkshire manner, the short 'a' incongruous among the long south London vowels. 'You're a cricketer, aren't you? Four bats in Mr Grace's bag is quite enough for any policeman. And there's every reason for you to have one of your dad's in your room.'

Even more reluctantly I bundled the gear back into the

cricket bag, humped it into the boot of the Mercedes and ran upstairs to shove Grace's bat into the pile of sporting equipment in the old-fashioned wardrobe. It looked quite at home among the pads and gloves. I heard the front door ring and made for the stairs to answer it. But Mrs Marchbanks had beaten me to it. She was already at the front door as I stepped into the hall and saw her unfasten the double safety lock. As she turned the handle the door was thrust violently from the outside, slamming her sideways into the wall and choking off her indignant scream as three large men burst through the doorway. Two of them were pointing sawn-off shotguns and they all wore scarves over their lower faces.

'Get your effing hands up!'

I raised my hands, thinking as I did so that I had had too many orders that day. My hand brushed against the hat-and-coat-stand which stood by the wall at the foot of the stairs. It was one of those Victorian curved-wood constructions once favoured by tea-rooms and it was laden with raincoats and a thick old khaki greatcoat which Mrs Marchbanks used for gardening.

'Where's the effing car?' The man without a gun spoke again. Even muffled by his scarf, his voice sounded ominously like that of the man outside the squash court. The gun-barrels twitched at me encouragingly.

'In the garage.'

'Keys.' He gestured impatiently. The barrels twitched again. The keys were in my trouser pocket. Mrs Marchbanks had slid down the wall and was crouching on one knee, her face in her hands, her shoulders shaking. I prayed she would stay there.

'Upstairs in my room. But they won't do you much good. The police are due to arrive here any minute.' I raised my voice. 'And look at her.'

Mrs Marchbanks fainted, slipping noisily to the floor, out of the immediate line of fire. Three pairs of eyes swivelled towards her and I seized the hat-stand, swinging it in front of me parallel with the floor so the coats hung down, and charged blindly down the hallway. Both guns exploded with shattering reports in the confined hallway, but the loose flapping coats absorbed most of the shot and I felt only two stings on the cheek as the curved horns of the hat-stand and my momentum swept the men stumbling backwards out of the front door and crashing down the six steps to land with a thud at the feet of Detective Inspector Light and a uniformed constable.

I leant panting on the hat-stand and watched with interest as, with commendably speedy reactions and professional expertise, the two policemen tackled the men with guns and soon had them handcuffed and lying face down on the front path. The third man twisted out of reach and sped away out of the garden and across into the dusk of the Dulwich College grounds opposite. Light stood up with his foot on the neck of his captive and the constable used his radio to call for reinforcements.

'Thanks,' I said. 'You might have come a couple of minutes earlier. Come inside. I want to see if my landlady's hurt. I think she's only fainted.'

Light told the constable to send for an ambulance as well.

'Don't worry. I can look after her. She won't go into hospital. She's very independent.'

'It's not for her,' said Light. He led me into the hall, clambering over the coats and the hat-stand, and pointed to the large oval mirror on the wall. 'Take a look at yourself while I see to the lady.' He bent over Mrs Marchbanks.

Two shotgun pellets had creased along my right cheek leaving a double furrow from which blood had flowed freely down my face and chin, soaking my track suit. I was indeed a gory sight. I had hardly felt a thing at the time but with realisation came the soreness. I touched my face tenderly as Mrs Marchbanks stirred, opened her eyes slowly and looked up in bewilderment at Light stooping solicitously over her.

'What happened? Who are you? What are you doing

here?' Her voice gained quickly in strength and indignation as her recollection grew. She saw me over Light's shoulder. 'Roger! You're hurt!' Thrusting aside Light's hands she got to her feet with surprising agility.

'Don't worry about me, Mrs M,' I said. 'I'm okay. It's only a couple of scratches. This is Detective Inspector Light and that's his constable, down with the bodies outside on the path. The third man got away.' I pointed through the open door.

'But what happened? And why are the coats all over the floor?'

Light picked up the hat-stand and set it on its feet. As he handled the old greatcoat there was a pattering as twelve-bore shot fell to the tiled floor. He held up the coat to the light. Two ragged holes showed where the khaki cloth had taken the full force of the blast and shot had lodged in the back and in the material of the raincoats. As he spoke Light folded the clothes carefully. His voice, still deliberately official, nevertheless seemed to have lost its suspicious edge.

'We'll take these for evidence. As I see it, Mrs March-banks, this lad of yours is a lucky young fool who probably deserves a medal. When he went for these men with the hat-stand, only the fact that the coats were flapping loose saved him from being killed, or at least pretty well-ventilated. And if we hadn't arrived at that precise moment, that's exactly what would have happened to him anyway.'

'But I don't understand. Why should we be held up? And with guns, too?'

'That's what we have to find out, Mrs Marchbanks. It could have been simple armed robbery. I want to ask you—' He was interrupted by the arrival of a squad car, a Black Maria and an ambulance, their sirens wailing into silence as they pulled up in the road outside. Light promptly took charge, issuing sharp orders. In a couple of minutes the captives were bundled off in the van to Dulwich police station, Mrs Marchbanks had been given a cup of hot, sweet tea and my cheek had been washed and examined, pronounced clear of lead shot and dressed with two large pieces of sticking plaster. Four policemen were despatched on a fruitless search for the leader of the attackers.

Light sat with us in Mrs Marchbanks's living room and continued speaking as if there had been no interruption. 'I was going to ask you if they gave you any clue as to what they were after?'

'They were after Grace's car,' I said. 'The leader wanted the keys.'

'Did he say "Grace's car?"'

'No. But I'm sure they, or rather he, had tried once before.'

'When? What do you mean?'

I told him of the earlier abortive attack outside Jock's squash club and that I thought I had recognised the same voice behind the scarf. I showed him the bruise on my thigh and brought out the cosh.

'Why didn't you report this before?'

'There didn't seem much point at the time. I didn't want to make a fuss. I thought it was just a botched attempt to nick the car, and I didn't think there were any witnesses to the actual attack. Jock did see it though. I felt a bit guilty about borrowing the car anyway, without laying it open to being hijacked.'

'You do realise, don't you, that failing to report a felony could be tantamount to aiding and abetting. We've now got two charges of attempted murder, or at least GBH. But what's it all about? What the hell is the attraction of that car?'

'I don't have a clue,' I said truthfully. 'You could ask the guys you've arrested.'

'They won't know what day of the week it is,' said Light scornfully. 'And if they did, they'd be too scared to talk. They're just rent-a-thugs. We need the boss and he'll be in Timbuctoo by now. Oh, well, not to worry.

Let's give Mrs Marchbanks another cup of tea and find out what we're looking for.'

For once Mrs Marchbanks did not demur, but permitted herself to be steered into a chair in the warm kitchen while Light put the big kettle on the Aga and bustled about finding mugs, teabags, milk and sugar. Witnessing such domesticity in the policeman somewhat revised my opinion of him, but the professional coolness and efficiency were back in force as he searched the Mercedes in the garage. He worked methodically through from front to rear, beginning with the glove compartment and ending with the boot, lifting the seat cushions and carpeting and punching the plush leather-work of the upholstery to reveal any hidden objects. He emptied the cricket bag methodically as I had done earlier, but displayed no interest in the cricketing gear and the bats beyond a cursory flourish. The only object he found of real interest was a small cricket scorebook of the old-fashioned kind – the sort an enthusiastic schoolboy might take along to the county ground to record the deeds of his favourite players. It had been partly filled in with an appropriately amateurish lack of consistency.

'Does it mean anything to you?'

Light passed the book over. I scanned the first few pages quickly. The entries were written with a ballpoint pen in a small, neat hand and they seemed to be very rough and incomplete details of minor but multi-racial matches played some time in the intermediate past. In cricketing terms they made no sense. The first match appeared to be between England and Pakistan, but no date was given and I had heard of none of the players. The scores were not complete; one batsman had nothing beside his name which also appeared in the bowling columns, with nothing beside it either. There were some totals, which sometimes tallied and mostly didn't; and nor did the bowling figures. I handed the book back to Light.

'No idea. They could be the scores of cricket matches,

but they don't make sense. They're the sort of thing I did when I was ten, but worse.'

'How do you mean, worse?'

'Well, any schoolboy knows how to keep a batsman's score going and run a bowler's figures through an innings. Whoever did this lot didn't. Some of the totals add up, but the details don't match. Besides, I've never heard of any of the players.'

'None of them?'

'No.'

'Not even this one?' His finger jabbed at number six on the 'Pakistan' side – P.R.A. Visar. He had top score.

'Never heard of him.'

Light looked at me sideways.

'Take another look.'

I spelled it out slowly. 'PRAVISAR. Oh, I see. Like a crossword clue. Pravisar. That's odd.'

'Very. Do you know if he's a cricketer? Or has been?'

'He didn't mention it at Lord's today. But it's the first time I've met him. He certainly knows the game, from the remarks he was making. And he is, er, was a friend of the captain's. The chairman called him Prince of somewhere. Qellalabad, I think.'

'Well, it looks as though he can bat, too. His name's not among the bowlers. It should be easy to check him out. Can you recognise any others?

I could not. The 'Pakistan' side consisted of fairly typical Asian names, with an Akhtar, a couple of Singhs and a Khan, none of them familiar. The 'England' team also comprised a number of players I'd never heard of, though in a nondescript list the name of C.E.S. Presager stood out, both for its individuality and for its unusually high score – 165 out of a total of 222.

'Sorry, Inspector, I can't help you. They're all complete strangers, except for Pravisar, and I've told you all I know about him.'

'Not to worry.' He turned his attention to the gin bottle.

He wrapped a handkerchief round it and unscrewed the top, sniffing at the contents.

'Did Grace always carry a bottle in his bag?'

'Yes.'

'And this was the bottle Hills used to top up the orange juice you took out to the wicket?'

'Yes, I think so. It was on the tray.'

'Why do you only think so?'

'Well, there wasn't another bottle in the dressing room, as far as I know. No one else drinks gin during a match. We all knew it was there, but I didn't actually see Phil do it. He just told me what he'd done.'

'Hmmm. Otherwise there was only orange juice, some mineral water and a jug of iced tap water on the table.'

'That's right.'

'They were all cleared away by the Lord's staff?'

'I suppose so.'

'Still, we must check.' He swung round to face me. 'Look here Mr North,' he said forcefully. 'For God's sake don't do any more bloody silly things like appropriating a car that could be evidence in a murder inquiry. Don't take on thugs with guns – leave that to us. And don't withhold information. Any more of that and I'll have you inside before your feet touch the ground.'

'No, Mr Light,' I said meekly, thinking of the bat I'd hidden upstairs. I was relieved that Light had neither searched my bedroom nor questioned Mrs Marchbanks; but realised he would probably get around to that when the shock had worn off. If he was unaware of her background there was no reason for him to suspect that she might have some knowledge, or even insight, which might help his inquiry. I didn't want to enlighten him. I had a strong urge to talk to my father first. I needed his advice.

'There's one other thing,' said Light. 'In my job you get a certain feel about cases. This one smells, and I don't like the attention you're getting either. Make sure to look both ways when you cross the road – don't smile, I'm serious – and keep your door locked at night.'

'Why would anyone want to harm me? I don't know anything. I'm only a cricketer.'

'Look, son. One attack may be bad luck, two may be coincidence, but the third could be fatal. Maybe you don't know what you know. Or what they think you know. You watch yourself, and call me immediately if anything happens to make you suspicious. Or if you remember anything you think might be useful.'

He fished out a business card and scribbled on the back. 'That's my number at the Yard. The other's my private number. Ring at any time. Any time at all.'

'Thanks.'

'We'll be in touch.' He accepted a plastic carrier bag in which to place the gin bottle and the little scorebook, relieved me of the car keys and got behind the wheel of the Mercedes. He touched a button and the electric window slid down without a sound.

'You know, I'd give my eye teeth for that little beauty.' He indicated the Roadster. 'You'd have to pay me to drive this monster.'

I helped him back out onto the road and thankfully watched the tail lights disappear in the direction of London. I wondered why he had let his guard down. It didn't seem very professional. Suddenly I felt very tired; my bruised leg was throbbing and my cheek was beginning to smart. I said good night to Mrs Marchbanks, who was nodding in her sitting-room in front of the television set again as though nothing had happened, ran myself a hot bath and luxuriated in it for ten minutes before the water cooled off. Before I dropped into bed I took a last look at Grace's bat to make sure it was still there and lay down expecting sleep to claim me instantaneously. But perversely, sleep would not come. Independent of my will my mind replayed the day's events, slowly, jerkily, like a disjointed series of old movie clips. Again I saw the ball sailing through air straight at us on the balcony, heard my yell of warning and felt the ball smack into my palm. I saw myself hurrying to the wicket laden with bats, gloves and a glass of gin and orange for Grace, watched him change his batting glove and select his bat.

I sat up in bed. In my mind's eye I watched him thrust his weight down on the rubber grip of the handle as he always did until he made sure it was forced down to the blade; saw him take guard; stand relaxed except for the tapping of the toe of the bat against the block-hole; saw the arrogant pull for six; the totter up the wicket; the collapse. *That* was what I had forgotten: the idiosyncratic obsession with the grip.

Wide awake now, I switched on the reading lamp beside my bed and fetched Grace's bat from the cupboard. I examined it all over, minutely. There was nothing unusual to be seen. Using both hands, I rolled the rubber grip up and over the top of the handle, leaving it indecently exposed in its underclothing of closely-bound black twine. Without a lathe or a spindle of any sort it was a tedious job to unwind the thread to examine the handle itself, but I persevered, winding the twine round a pencil into a neat ball. Now the handle was completely naked, stripped down to its essentials: sections of cane glued fast together round a central sandwich of a sprung steel strip encased in orange rubber. I could see nothing amiss.

I tiptoed downstairs as quietly as I could. Mrs March-banks, who had gone to bed, was the proud possessor of the compact edition of the *Oxford English Dictionary*, packed in its own stiff cardboard casing with a large magnifying glass in a separate drawer. Back in my room, I used the glass to cover every inch of the handle and after a few minutes, half-way down the handle I found a hole the size of a pin-head drilled into the tightly-packed cane. It was what I had been dreading, but without the proper tools there was nothing more I could do to investigate further. I set my alarm for four-thirty and tried to sleep.

This time exhaustion did take over, and when the alarm woke me I had to drag myself from the depths to shower and shave. At a quarter to five on a beautiful misty morning there was only the occasional milkman or early bus out on the roads, so I cleared south London's maze in twenty minutes and well before six o'clock braked for the double S-bend which heralded the entrance to the village of Willford, eased along the main street between the Norman church and the fifteenth century Royal Oak, and turned into the lane which led to F. North & Son, Bat-maker.

The house in which I had been born and brought up was unpretentious enough. My grandfather, a carpenter, the first Frank North, had used his gratuity at the end of the Second World War to buy a pair of farm cottages of indeterminate age with a couple of acres of willow wetland around them. My father, then in his early teens, had helped him strip off the roof and key in fresh oak joists to lift the gable ends by five feet and steepen the pitch of the roof. They built in dormer windows on both sides to give width and light to four bedrooms and a bathroom and used the original beams throughout to make a home fit for Alexandra, my grandmother, to live in. That took some doing; I had never known my grandmother, but village legend had it that she had 'married beneath her'. When the house was complete, old Frank cut down the willows and laid concrete foundations, on which he built a 30ft square workshop. He split the willow into clefts, stood them out to mature for six months and then started making cricket bats. Alexandra, to the villagers' surprise, ran the business side with arrogant efficiency and within a very few years the cricket world began to beat a path to their door. By then old Frank, and after him young Frank, my father, had resisted any temptation to expand beyond their capacity. Both, in their turn, had turned down lucrative takeover offers from the 'big five' manufacturers, and the house with its original workshop still stood exactly as I had known it all my life, tucked in among the willow trees alongside a muddy stream, with tall stacks of clefts drying in two open sheds.

Although it was not yet six o'clock, my father was already up. I spotted him through the kitchen window as I went round to the back door. He was pottering with the kettle and the big brown teapot, and I was surprised to see that he had already set out two of the blue and cream Denby ware mugs he and my mother had used all their married life. He greeted me at the door, a small and upright figure, thinner than when I had last seen him at the beginning of April and more drawn, but looking very fit. His handshake was as muscular as ever and his welcome as warm.

'Good to see you, Rodge. I heard the car arrive and thought you'd like a cup. Tea or coffee?'

'Tea please, Dad. They don't make it like you do any more.'

'Ah, that was your mother's doing. She couldn't abide teabags.'

The tea was hot and strong and full of flavour, the sort one can still get at a wayside 'greasy spoon caff', but is but a distant memory at the fast food establishments which litter today's English highways. At that hour of the morning it put fresh life into me. We talked about the sensational events of the previous day at Lord's. My father had been busy making bats during the day but had watched the television news coverage. He did not seem concerned by Grace's death; he seemed indifferent, which was not like him and which puzzled me. He had known the Surrey captain for many years, and until fairly recently had had a business connection with him. He had never said why it had been broken off, but he still supplied Grace with free bats.

'Dad, there's something odd going on. I've come down because I want your help. Will you look at a bat for me? It's one of yours.'

'Is there something wrong with it?'

'You'll see when you look at it. I think it's the bat Persse was using when he died. Some blokes attacked me twice yesterday. I think they were trying to get that bat.'

'Have you told the police?'

'They know all about the attacks. They don't know about the bat.'

'Why not?'

'It's one of yours, and if there's anything wrong with it I . . . I wanted you to know first.'

He gave me his direct look.

'You've probably been a bloody fool. The police won't thank you for withholding evidence, if it *is* evidence. At any rate, let's find out.'

I brought in the bat and the grip from the car. He took it, weighed it in his hands and then sniffed at the bare handle. He turned it over and studied the FNS logo stamped into the face and SPECIAL across the splice. He ran his hands and eye swiftly over the handle. His face was set in stone.

'Your instinct is correct. There are a number of things wrong with this bat. In the first place it's a forgery. It's a good one, but I didn't make it. I'm surprised you didn't spot that.'

'I thought there was something odd about the pick-up, but I couldn't make out what it was. But how can you prove you didn't make it? It looks pretty authentic to me.'

'Come with me. I'll show you.'

He unlocked the workshop and led the way inside. He placed the bat in a padded, V-shaped vice and turned the screw until it was held firm. He beckoned me over to look at the handle.

'Smell it,' he said.

I applied my nose to the handle. Beneath the clean odour of the sandpapered cane I could detect a synthetic tang. I wrinkled my nose.

'That's not our glue.'

He nodded. 'Now try that.' He pointed to a filthy old

51

saucepan sitting on a gas-ring on his work-bench, a grubby stick emerging from the coagulated brown mass inside. His glue-pot: during the day a bubbling, stinking brew of liquid bone. I knew it well from hundreds of hours working within close range of its pungent fumes. I waved my hand under my nose at a respectful distance.

'They're quite different.'

'That's right. That one' – he waved a deprecating hand at the bat – 'is glued up with epoxy resin, which I never use. Can't stand it. None of the modern adhesives will do the work of my muck, filthy though it is. But that's not all. Reach me down a bit of that cane.'

The open rafters of the workshop served as useful storage space for any number of items, among them the constantly replenished supply of bamboo from which my father made up the handles of his bats. Except for the rubber grips, every bat was made by hand, with the minimum of mechanical aid. I reached up and pulled out an off-cut from an eight foot cane. My father clamped it in the horizontal lathe and held a piece of glass-paper to its end. Then he compared it with the bat handle. The handle was much darker than the cane.

'That bit's part of my regular supply. Do you remember where it comes from?'

'Sarawak.'

'Correct. I never order from anywhere else.'

'And the bat handle?'

'I'm not sure. It could be Sierra Leone. But under a microscope you'd see that the grain of the fibres is very different.'

'Why has the bat got our logo on it, then?'

He smiled mirthlessly. 'Has it?' he said and produced the ancient branding iron used to imprint FNS on all our bats. Placed over the logo on the bat in the vice, it was obviously no fit. The branding iron was about a quarter of an inch too small all round.

'Now let's get down to the real business. You say the handle has been interfered with?'

'Yes, that's why I've brought it to you. But I used a magnifying glass. You saw it with the naked eye.'

He smiled again, but there was a sadness in his face. Almost under his breath he said: 'But I knew what to look for.'

Before I could comment, he took a hammer and chisel and began to dissect the handle, cane by cane, with delicate probing taps. Suddenly, it split lengthwise away from the centre spring. He placed the broken piece on the bench, face up. There, mitred expertly into the cane at an oblique angle, was a tiny spring-loaded hypodermic syringe, its needle pointing upwards and outwards.

He showed me how it would work. Downward pressure, such as one would use to force down the rubber grip, would 'cock' the plunger, forcing the needle into but not through the rubber. But then a sharp blow, such as the ball hitting the bat, would 'fire' the needle, striking into the palm of the batsman's hand. With his cutaway gloves, Grace would have been totally vulnerable.

'Don't touch a thing.' Despite its sharpness, his voice was tired, resigned even. He said: 'Whatever and whoever killed Grace, there will certainly be traces left in that thing. Are you going to telephone the police, or am I?'

There were many questions still to be asked, but the look on his face stopped me. I fished Light's card out of my pocket and dialled his home number.

3

Detective Inspector Light was none too pleased to be woken by the telephone at quarter to seven in the morning. He took a minute or two to pick up the receiver and his voice was thick with sleep.

'Light.'

'It's me, Mr Light. Roger North. I . . . I think we've found out how Mr Grace was killed.'

'What? . . . What the hell do you think you're talking about at this hour of the morning. We? Who's we?'

'My father . . . er . . . he's taken Grace's bat apart. There's a syringe with a needle built into the handle.'

'How the devil? . . . Oh, save it. I'm coming down straightaway. Don't touch it. Don't touch anything. You've done enough damage already. Where are you, exactly?'

I told him.

'I'll be there within the hour. With my boss, Detective Chief Superintendent Ashcroft. He's in charge of the case, and I don't think he'll be any too pleased with you, young man. Concealing evidence is a criminal offence.'

'We're not concealing it. We're revealing it.'

But he had hung up. I replaced the telephone gently in its cradle and glanced along the short hallway into the kitchen. My father had put the dismembered bat away in a cupboard to await the police and was busying himself with the teapot again, trying to give the appearance of being wholly at ease. He poured milk with an over-steady hand, found teaspoons and put out the sugar bowl. He pulled a chair to the kitchen table and sat down clumsily. He was usually neat in all his movements. I sat down opposite him.

'What's the matter, Dad?'

'Nothing.'

'You can't fool me. Tell me. There's an hour before the police get here. Plenty of time.'

He stirred his tea unnecessarily. He didn't take sugar. As he lifted the mug to his lips a drop of tea fell onto the front of his cardigan. He brushed it off irritably. His eyes shifted from mine. For the first time in my life I felt as though I was the adult, he the erring child. I didn't like the role reversal.

'Is it to do with Persse Grace?'

He said calmly enough, 'You're not going to be satisfied until I tell you the whole story, are you? I don't blame you.'

I said sharply: 'You don't mean *you* killed him? *You* fixed up that needle in the bat handle? YOU? I'll never believe it.'

He smiled, or at least creased his lips. 'As the police might say, you wouldn't, would you? Thanks Rodge. But you must listen to what I say and form your own judgement.'

'Try me. I'll never believe you could do anything like that. Never in a million years.'

'That might not be what the police believe, given the circumstances.'

'What circumstances?'

'Well, in the first place I'm one of the few people in this country who'd know how to doctor a bat like that, or could have made it in the first place.'

'I still don't believe it.' As forcefully as I could utter it, the denial sounded like unconvincing repetition even to my ears. 'Nor will the police.'

'There's also a motive. They like motives.' He pulled

from his shirt pocket a much creased letter and passed it across the table. It was from a London firm of solicitors and was dated five days earlier.

Dear Mr North,

Further to our previous correspondence, we are instructed to inform you that our clients have concluded regretfully that they can no longer carry the increasing burden of sustaining an uneconomic enterprise. We have to inform you that unless the monies owing to our clients are repaid, in full, within one month of the date of this letter, we are instructed to institute legal proceedings against you and your estate to recover the amount in full, with interest due and costs. As at this date, the amount owing, with interest, is £283,567.50. As an alternative our clients are prepared to accept the freehold property owned by F. North & Son at Willow Lane, Willford in the County of East Sussex, including house, factory, all equipment and stock in full and final settlement of the debt and will undertake to employ you, Frank North, as maker of cricket bats for a period to be agreed and at a salary to be negotiated; and to rent the domestic premises to you at a fee also to be negotiated. In the event of satisfactory agreement to the above offer within one calendar month of the date of this letter, our client will undertake not to institute proceedings for the recovery of this sum. We look forward to your early reply.

Yours sincerely,

A.P. Harrison
pp Harrison, Powell and Harrison, Fleet Court, London EC4 2QT.

I read the letter again.
'That's blackmail. It can't be legal.'
'I'm afraid it is, Rodge. Legal blackmail. I've been to old Warrender in Lewes and his advice is that I haven't a legal leg to stand on.'
'But the house and the land are worth double that

at today's prices, and double again for the business. And where does Grace come into all this? Is he "our client"?'

He nodded.

'And how the hell do you come to owe him a quarter of a million?'

'It's a long story, Rodge. You were nine when my Nancy died and you probably never knew how low I was. She left such a . . . hole . . .' He stopped.

I said more gently, 'She left a hole for me too.'

'I had never realised how much she had done and how difficult it would be without her. Mother – your gran – had taught her everything. Without her I couldn't keep the books straight and keep the work going at the same time. I made cricket bats. That was the easy part. Nancy ordered the willow, negotiated with the salesmen, dealt with the sponsorship and the cricketers and the bank. She ran the business and brought you up at the same time. I managed for five years somehow before I began to get letters from the bank. Then the taxman called to check the VAT. My returns weren't satisfactory. He was kind and sorted me out, but not before he'd worked out that I owed him eight thousand pounds. He took my cheque when he left. That meant I had to cut my order from Silver's of Essex by half, which they didn't like, and negotiate an overdraft for the first time in my life. Then we had that fire which destroyed most of the stock. The insurance money only replaced half of it. And then Persse Grace walked in and ordered 60 bats if I could deliver within a month. It was the biggest single order I'd ever received, but Persse advanced the cash for the clefts and there was a time penalty clause which I failed to meet by a couple of days. That cost another five hundred.'

'I remember; when I was fourteen. I helped you rough-cutting and glueing the handles, and wound them too. It was during the school holidays. You gave me my first pay packet.' Until then, I had often felt left out after my mother died, and this was the first time my father had ever asked for, and accepted, my help. I had bought my first real cricket ball, a Reader, with the money.

He went on: 'Grace was a big name in cricket. Captain of Surrey, always in the press. He was very impressive and very positive. Clever, too. He didn't take me out for lunch, but we went to the Royal Oak for a couple of pints. I suppose I felt flattered. I told him all about my problems with the bank and the VAT man, and the difficulty of managing on my own. He made me an offer, there and then: £50,000 and no strings. Just a sleeping partnership. It was manna from heaven. If Nancy had been alive she wouldn't have fallen for it. But I did. I could pay off my debts, order more stock, have the house decorated, pay for your schooling. So we shook hands on it and later we signed a few papers which Grace said formalised things, and that was that.'

'When did you learn that your sleeping partner was a tiger in your bed?'

'Not at first. For the first year, Grace was as good as his word. No interference. Just a couple of favours for friends. A bat here, a set of stumps there. All good for public relations, he said. I sent some gear overseas. He seemed to have contacts all over the world. I had one or two nice letters of appreciation, and when the touring teams came over, Grace would bring three or four of them down and present them with bats. It was all good for business.

'I remember that too. The County Gazette did a write-up. When the Indians came.'

'No, that was the Pakistanis. It was soon after that that things began to slip again. Grace had fixed up two more nice little orders – one in Yorkshire, the other in Durham I think – but for one reason or another I couldn't get the clefts. It just seemed like bad luck at the time. A lorry caught fire on the M25 and then Morgan's went out of business in Suffolk. I could only get second grade timber as a replacement. Next the shippers lost a year's supply of cane and the insurers refused to pay out. Nothing seemed to go right. I got behind with my payments on the loan and Grace was most helpful again. He said they could "roll over", which meant that the interest could be added to the capital.'

'At compound interest, of course. And the bank rate was going up.'

'Oh, yes. But there was nothing else I could do at the time. Then Grace came down last autumn with another proposition . . .'

I broke in. 'He wasn't very original. The same ploy, only a bigger one, I suppose.'

'Much bigger. A friend of his in Pakistan wanted a thousand bats quickly – within a month or two – and because of the rush was willing to pay the full retail price for them, £80 each. I said it was impossible – the best part of a year's work for me, and I had all my regular orders to fulfil. I told him I couldn't do it in the time. I hadn't got the grade A clefts, in any case. Grace wouldn't take no for an answer. I hadn't seen that side of him before. He got very nasty. He said I could take on a couple of young carpenters he knew to help, and I could use any old rubbish I could lay my hands on for the bats, so long as they had my stamp on them. The profit would be trebled and the Pakistanis wouldn't mind. They'd never know the difference. I told him what he could do with his order.'

He paused, his face set.

'We had a huge row. I told him to get out of the factory. I thought he was going to hit me, he looked so angry. But he caught hold of his temper and what he said was even worse. Unless I agreed to carry out the order, he would bankrupt me and put me out of business. And he threatened you. He said he'd make sure that you'd never have a career in cricket. I tell you, Roger, I was holding a chisel at the time, and I had to hold myself back from, well, killing him.'

'Why didn't you tell me any of this?'

'You'd just been taken on by Surrey, and I didn't want your career to be ruined at the very start. If I'd told you,

you'd have gone for Grace, and God knows what he'd have done.'

'I *would* have killed him. So you took the order?'

My father flushed.

'There was nothing else I could do. Grace sent down his men from London. They weren't bat-makers but they could handle tools, more or less, and we churned out the bats before Christmas. I didn't make much out of it anyway, by the time I'd bought the willow – I wouldn't send out rubbish with my name on it – and paid off Grace's men, who didn't come cheap. There wasn't enough even to meet the interest payments, let alone reduce the debt.'

'I can't believe you turned out anything second-rate, Dad. Did you have any complaints from the customer?'

'None at all. But then I never knew who the customer was. It couldn't have been one of the regular Pakistani sports goods firms. I know them well and they're no fools.'

'Surely you knew where you were sending them?'

'Not even that. Grace had it all fixed up. A couple of men in a plain van called every fortnight to pick up a batch and I never saw where they were going. I didn't much care, to tell the truth.'

'Didn't they talk to you?'

'Not much. I was glad. They were a rough lot. They weren't particularly careful with the bats, either. When I told them to go easy, to stop chucking them into the back of the van, they told me to eff off. Said it was no business of mine what happened to the bats after I'd made them. I didn't want to have anything to do with them.'

'Was one of them big and heavy, with a swarthy complexion and black curly hair?'

'Yes, that sounds like the boss. Why? Surely you don't know him?'

'Possibly. I met a guy last night who took too much interest in Grace's car.' I changed the subject. 'Let's get some breakfast. Anger makes me hungry.'

Breakfast at the North household traditionally meant

60

eggs in the plural, bacon, mushrooms, tomatoes, and whatever else one could find in the larder. I had inherited my father's habit of stoking up early, often eating nothing more until supper time. It was one of the things which set me a bit apart from the rest of the Surrey team, who judged opposing counties by the quality of the lunches they provided rather than their cricket and in consequence were likely to approach an afternoon session at Lord's, say, where there was always a generous helping of roast and two veg, with something close to lethargy.

This morning I chucked a few rashers into the pan and, against his protests, made my father sit down while I hash-fried a couple of eggs with some potatoes I found on a saucer in the fridge. He looked rotten, but ate with concentration and by the time he had washed a generous plateful down with more strong tea some colour had returned to his cheeks. Suddenly he leaned forward across the table over his folded arms, his knuckles showing white as his fingers dug deep into his biceps.

'There's more,' he said.

'I thought there might be. Mrs M said you'd be able to tell me where Grace got his money from. I always thought it was inherited.'

'Trust Emma,' he said. 'She knows more about cricket than any dozen cricketers, and more about many cricketers than they know themselves.'

'She seemed to think there was something fishy about Grace's finances. I know he's spent a hell of a lot of money on the geegees. I've spent as much time as bookie's runner over the past few months as I have playing cricket, and he never backed a horse for less than fifty pounds. He lost as much as he won, if not more.'

'I don't know a great deal more. Persse was certainly born with a silver spoon – silver-plate, anyway. His father left him a small fortune made from import and export between the two wars, and he married money. There was some scandal about his wife's death; she committed suicide, I think. But a couple of months ago I had a telephone call from Arthur Preedie in Wakefield. You remember him, Roger; the big dark chap I taught to make bats. A good craftsman, but very ambitious. He went up north to start a factory for a couple of entrepreneurs but they let him down. So Arthur took a chance and opened up on his own with little more than a work-bench in the corner of a garage. He did well, too. He had a bit of luck when that Yorkshire opener, Broadribb, scored a century with a Preedie bat in his first Test match. It put Arthur on the map.'

I was growing restless with this leisurely exposition, but my father would not be hurried.

'At any rate, a couple of months ago, Arthur rang me up. He's always kept in touch from time to time since he went north, but he's never asked for help or advice, and I've never offered any. I'd heard in the trade that he'd been going through a lean patch, but I had troubles of my own to worry about. He was in a right state, I can tell you. He wanted to know what connection I had with Grace. No, he didn't just want. He demanded to know. I told him Grace had put a bit of money into the firm, but I didn't say anything more. I remember his exact words. "Then you're for the chop, too, Frank. The bastard's just foreclosed on me. And he's got his hooks into three or four more of us." It shook me, I can tell you.'

That telephone call had stirred my father into some sort of action. He began inquiring round the trade and discovered that over a period of three or four years Grace had gained control of several small independents like F. North & Son. As well as Preedie in Wakefield, Alan Smith in Chester, Butterfield in Colchester, and Hampton in the West Country had all succumbed to the Grace treatment. With all these, he had gained effective control of a sufficient number of independent bat-makers to rival any one of the 'big five' in size, and Alan Smith had told father that he thought Grace had been buying his way into one of them

62

as well, although he didn't know which one. In every case he had followed the same pattern, forcing the genuine craftsmen into near bankruptcy and then making them prostitute their skills to fulfil large sub-standard export orders to Pakistan, India, Australia and South Africa. Some had even gone to Argentina and the United States. In every case the name of the importer had been hidden from the manufacturer, each transaction being handled by Grace's own firm, World Bats, which placed the orders, organised their collection piecemeal, and paid, always in cash.

'Always? Never a cheque?'

'Never. He didn't pay for an order in the normal way. The men who collected the bats just handed over an envelope containing the cash for that week's delivery, in new fifty-pound notes. It became quite a joke with old Strachan at Lloyds when I paid them into the account. He always asked me what black market I was dealing in, or if I was pressing banknotes instead of cricket bats. But it made keeping the books a nightmare, dealing with all that cash.' He shrugged his shoulders grimly. 'Which is another reason why I can't dispute the lawyer's version of my accounts with Grace. I've got no evidence.'

'Let me think.' I glanced around the kitchen, looking for inspiration which failed to materialise, then out into the yard. 'There must be some way . . . Good God, who's that? It looks like a girl.'

He followed my eyes. What was undoubtedly a girl had swung off a bicycle, which she leant against a stack of clefts. She went straight to the factory door, shoved it open with the familiarity of one who knew her way about, and went inside.

'That? Oh, that's Sally.' He looked even more embarrassed. 'That's something else I haven't told you about. My new apprentice, Sally Lang. Persse's stepdaughter. She was part of the bargain over you. Grace took you on to become a professional cricketer; I took Sally to teach her how to make a cricket bat.'

'Whose idea was it? His, hers or yours?'

'Well, hers really. I'm surprised you don't remember her. Grace brought her down last summer to look around. He said she had just left school and wanted to know how a cricket bat was made. She sat on a stool for two hours and watched me without saying a word. I didn't mind. I preferred her to keep quiet. She thanked me when they left and that was that, as far as I was concerned. The next day Grace telephoned and asked me to take her on as an apprentice. She had been the rounds of the small bat-makers, and wanted to come to me. I couldn't believe my ears. This isn't women's work. But you can – could – never say no to Grace. You do this for me, he said, and I'll take on *your* son. The inference was that if I refused, he would block your chances with Surrey. That was the way he did business.'

'He probably sent her down here to spy on you.'

'That did occur to me. But in fact, Sally was the only real favour Grace ever did me. She's learned fast and she's a good worker. And I like her. Very much. Whatever her stepfather has done.'

'Hmmph.' I wasn't feeling very gracious. 'Her father died yesterday. Why is she still down here? You'd think she'd want to be in London. What about her mother?'

'There's no mother. You remember, she committed suicide. Sally came to see me last night, after the news, and told me there was no love lost between her and Grace. In fact, she said in so many words that she hated his guts. She wouldn't be mourning, she said, because that would be hypocritical. She didn't say much, but I gather she has always blamed Grace for her mother's suicide, and has never forgiven him.'

'A likely tale, I don't think. I'm going to have a word with her.'

Ignoring his protests, I strode out of the house in some dudgeon and across to the little factory. I had to pass the workshop window and I paused to peer through the dusty pane. Looking in from the bright sunlight I could only just make out the blurred outline of a figure moving rhythmically in the comparative gloom. I opened the door quietly and was greeted by a wave of Mozart coming from a pocket-sized radio on the work-bench. Sally Lang was working over a half-made blade with a spokeshave, moving to and fro along the willow with the art of the born bat-maker, her eyes intent on her task. She hadn't noticed my entrance. I could hear the hiss of the knife, now silken, now coarser, as it caressed along and against the grain of the willow. Slowly the blade's shape emerged, the bulge tapering gently towards the splice, and the spokeshave's leisurely stroke changed to a shorter, sharper hiss as the girl worked the downward curve to the toe. All I could see of her from the doorway was the top of her head with straight, close-cropped curls that matched the ash-white of the willow she was working, and slim brown arms emerging from a man's red, checked working-shirt and blue denim overalls. She removed the blade from the vice and weighed it in her hand.

'Damn,' she said quietly to herself. 'Two four and a half. Still heavy.'

'Excuse me,' I said, taking the bat from her hand and weighing it in mine. 'Two five. Too light.'

I was subjected to an ice-blue glare.

'Two four and a half. And you obviously haven't heard of Betty McGrath, captain of the England women's team. She plays with a 2lb 3oz bat. What can I do for you?'

'Nothing. I'm Roger North, Frank's son.'

'So? I'm Sally Lang. Persse Grace was my stepfather.'

'So you can finish what you're doing and pack your bags.'

The glare intensified. Blue lasers looked me up and down. A pink spot appeared on each cheekbone. She stood up to her full height, which brought her to about the level of my chin. Her voice was as keen as the spokeshave's blade.

'I take orders from the organ grinder, not his monkey.'

'From now on I'm giving the orders. We don't want a

spy working here. In any case, shouldn't you be in London? Your stepfather died yesterday.' I didn't feel charitable.

'What I do is none of your business.' She was still cold as ice. 'I have no interest in my stepfather's death, nor in who killed him. Someone was bound to, one of these days.'

It seemed that Grace's stepdaughter had as little love for him as most of the rest of the people who knew him. The knowledge made her no more acceptable to me, but she was right. It was none of my business. But from the way she had worked on that bat, she might even have had the skill to rig up the hypodermic syringe in the handle of the bat that killed Grace. Would she be capable of that? She looked tough enough at that moment.

'How do you know your father was killed? He might have had a heart attack. No one knows how he died yet. Officially.'

'He wasn't my father. He was my stepfather. And he was a bastard. Of course he was murdered. I wish I'd done it myself. And it's still none of your business.' Her voice was still cool, but the two pink spots had reappeared.

'What happens to Frank North & Son is my business. Frank is my father, and Persse Grace was doing his best to ruin him. So Grace's death is my business too, because the police think I had something to do with it. I can just see the picture. It's too easy. Persse forced my father to take you on, using me as a lever. Fine, you play at making cricket bats, report back to Daddy from time to time that Frank North is going broke. Meanwhile doing your best to help him on the way.'

'If you think that, you're an even bigger cretin than you look. It might be more difficult for you to sack me than you think. And if you can think at all, you might consider that, as my stepfather's only remaining relative and his sole legatee, it's very likely that I shall inherit his estate which, if you're right, includes F. North & Son, this factory and that house.'

I felt the muscles of my face contract in harmony

with the clenching of my fists. Only the fact that she was a woman prevented me from lashing out at her. She must have seen it in my face, for she stepped back, cannoning into the handle of the vice, which swung her body round and forced a gasp of pain from her. Ignoring it, I stepped forward, seized her left wrist in my right hand and wrapped her arm round my body, swinging her off her feet. I carried her under my arm like a recalcitrant child across the yard to dump her unceremoniously on the concrete beside her bicycle. I felt better.

'You know where the gate is. Don't bother to shut it on your way out,' I said. 'We're waiting for the police to arrive.'

Sally Lang said nothing, rather to my surprise. Nor did she cry, or launch into a tirade. She picked herself off the concrete and dusted off her knees and the seat of her overalls. She was obviously unhurt. Then she found the big chopping-block on which we split the clefts and perched on it, crossing her legs and crossing her arms over them.

'There's a big boy, then,' she said in the tones one might use to a favourite dog. 'Does he feel better then?'

In spite of myself, I laughed.

'Yes, he does,' I admitted. 'I apologise. I shouldn't have lost my temper. But you must admit you provoked me. Is it true?'

'About my inheriting? Probably. I don't know. I'm not very interested in my stepfather's affairs. I've had as little as possible to do with him since my mother died. I'm sorry, too, for what I said, but you did jump to conclusions. Your father's one of the kindest people I've ever met, and I wouldn't lift a finger to harm him. I only came here to learn how to make cricket bats and I'm still learning. I'm happier here than I've been since mummy died. I wouldn't have known about his problems but a letter came by special messenger which seemed to upset him very much. He spent the rest of the day sitting

67

at his bench, hardly working at all. I pestered him to tell me what was the matter and eventually he just passed the letter to me to read. I think he'd forgotten who I was. It was a lawyer's letter, a filthy, blackmailing one.'

'I know, I read it this morning. But it doesn't mention Persse Grace by name. Just an anonymous client.'

'I knew the way my stepfather worked and I'd seen what he'd done before to other bat-makers. I put two and two together and made Frank admit who the client was. He didn't want to tell me at first.'

'Naturally. Seeing who you are.'

She chose to ignore the thrust.

'I drove up to London to see Persse, to try to persuade him to let up on Frank. He said I was soft like my mother. So I threatened him – I can't tell you how, but I threatened him – and he said it wasn't up to him, he was only doing what he'd been ordered to. I hated him. I could have killed him myself then.'

She looked quite capable of it and not in the least bit soft.

'I'm sorry,' I said again. 'You can't have had a very good time.'

She shrugged. 'It's no business of yours,' she said toughly. But before I could reply an unmarked black Rover swung into the yard and pulled up smoothly outside the door. Detective Inspector Light climbed nimbly out of the driver's seat, while the front passenger door opened to allow a large figure in crumpled tweeds to emerge much more deliberately. He seemed familiar though I'd never met him. Light introduced me to Detective Chief Superintendent William Ashcroft and threw an inquiring glance at the girl.

'I'm Sally Lang, Persse Grace's stepdaughter. I work here,' she said directly. 'I've met you,' she said to Ashcroft. 'In the Long Bar at The Oval.'

'Yes, indeed,' he replied. His pleasant smile did not reach his eyes which, I saw suddenly, were of the same slate grey as Light's – policeman's eyes, watchful, suspicious and penetrating. 'We had a pessimistic discussion on the prospects of Surrey gaining one of the major prizes. I'm afraid we were both right.'

I wondered if he was going to ask Persse Grace's step-daughter what she was doing in the depths of East Sussex while her father was lying on a mortuary slab in north London, but he merely gazed round at the stacks of clefts and sniffed appreciatively.

'It must be more than thirty years since I was last here,' he said. 'Your father made me the first bat I ever bought that didn't come off a shelf. I gather he has something of almost equal importance to show us.'

'He's inside. Come with me.' I led the way into the kitchen where my father was still sitting quietly at the table, his hands clasped in front of him. He rose to his feet as we entered. To my surprise, Ashcroft moved forward and shook him by the hand. It didn't seem to be the action of a policeman about to arrest a suspect. But then he hadn't heard the story yet.

'Ashcroft, Scotland Yard,' he said. 'You won't remember me, Mr North, but I used to buy bats from you.' I saw Light looking sideways at him in some astonishment. You could see he wasn't used to seeing a Detective Chief Superintendent addressing a witness – a potential suspect – in the tones of a suppliant. My father looked confused, too. But his memory was as sharp as ever.

'Ashcroft, Kent Seconds. Back in Denness's day, I think. You had a good run in the Seconds for a year or so but didn't quite make it into the county side. I heard that you'd become a policeman.'

'And made the First Eleven,' murmured Light. Ashcroft threw him a withering glance and answered my father.

'Yes, Mr North, that's unfortunately why we're here. This talkative young man with me is Detective Inspector Light, who is shortly to hand over to me the proceeds of a small wager we had on the strength of your memory. He has already met your son. I gather you have something to show us which you believe explains the death of Persse

Grace . . .' There was an audible gasp from Sally at my side and she gripped my arm tightly . . . 'And you, young man,' he swung round on me '. . . have an apology to make to Light here, unless you wish to be charged with concealing evidence. The more abject the apology the better.'

'I'm sorry,' I said to them both. 'Really. I had no idea the bat was important. I couldn't sleep last night. I kept turning over and over in my head what happened at Lord's and the way Grace had handled the bat at the wicket stuck in my mind. I felt there was something wrong about it but I didn't want to make myself appear a fool so I tried to find out what it was. Then I got scared of messing it about and so I brought it down to father. He took the handle apart and we found a tiny syringe. That's when I telephoned Mr Light. I didn't intend to conceal anything. I'll get the bat for you.'

They were sitting around the kitchen table when I returned with the bat, the dismembered pieces of its handle carefully wrapped in polythene and the little syringe nestling in its niche. Ashcroft examined it minutely through his spectacles from every angle and beckoned Light to do the same. Neither touched anything, which reminded me that our fingerprints had probably obliterated any chance of finding real clues, except possibly on the syringe itself. Sally Lang stared silently across the table at the bat, the blood drained from her face and the translucent skin stretched tight across her cheekbones. She looked like a Valkyrie riding into battle.

'Hmmm.' It was a long contemplative sound. Ashcroft took off his glasses and scratched his head. His face was as rumpled as his tweed suit and gave just as little away. He looked at me.

'There was a strong suspicion that Persse Grace was murdered,' he said formally. 'This,' indicating the bat, 'turns that suspicion into assumption. In any murder investigation the police have to answer three basic questions: who did it, how it was done and why it was done. In other

70

words: murderer, means, motive. This would appear to be strong circumstantial evidence as to the cause of death. It will have to be confirmed by our forensic department and may turn out to be nothing more than an elaborate red herring, but, assuming that appearances are proved correct, we have the means. That being so, we may be closer to discovering the man, or woman, responsible.'

He turned to my father.

'Frank,' he said directly. 'Could you fix up something like that?'

My father looked down at his hands and flexed his fingers. 'I could,' he said. 'But that's not to say I did.'

Ashcroft's gaze did not move from father's face. 'Any skilled carpenter might have done it, but it would take a skilled bat-maker with knowledge of the batsman to set it at exactly the right angle for the device to work?'

My father nodded.

'Could your son have made it?'

'No. His work isn't accurate enough.' A slap in the face for me, but in the circumstances, welcome.

'Or Miss Lang?'

'She hasn't the expertise yet. She will have.'

'But you have both the accuracy and the expertise, Mr North?' Not 'Frank' this time.

My father's eyes looked strained. I longed to step in to protect him, but sensed that to interrupt would only make matters worse.

'*Did* you make it, Mr North?'

'No.' Firmly. 'I did not make that bat.'

'Not that one. But have you made a similar one before?'

My father nodded miserably. The words were dragged out of him, one by one.

'Yes.' I could not watch his face.

'When?'

'A few years ago.'

'For whom?'

'Persse Grace.'

71

'Why did you do that?'

'It was an order. He said it was a joke. He thought of the idea to teach someone a lesson. He said this man was always borrowing his bat without asking for it and wanted to catch him red-handed. I filled the syringe with red ink.'

Ashcroft pointed to the dismembered bat on the table. 'How can you be sure that this isn't the same bat that you made?'

'This isn't one of ours. It's a copy. The logo doesn't fit and the cane in the handle is wrong. The one I made is three or four years old and the willow will be darker. This is a new bat, made within the last month or two.'

'Hmmm.' Ashcroft seemed satisfied. 'You can prove that, of course. Have you seen the original one since Grace took it?'

'No.'

'Did he give you any idea whom he was trying to catch out?'

'No, he didn't. Though I don't think it was an overseas player. He said when I delivered it to him, "Good, I'll catch that bastard now." He was like that.'

'It wasn't Pravisar?'

'No. Why should it be? He wasn't a player.'

'What was your opinion of Grace?'

My father smiled. He looked weary.

'I hated his guts. There's no point in denying it. He was going to bankrupt me and steal my business. You'll find out, anyway. You might as well know now, Mr Ashcroft.'

He passed over the solicitor's letter. Ashcroft and Light read it together in silence.

'I see. "Our client" was Grace. Do you dispute that you owed him the money?'

'I knew I owed him a lot. It had been building up for some time. The total seems very high, but I have no proof.'

He retold the story he'd told me earlier, leaving out nothing. Ashcroft sat massive and silent during the recital, nodding occasionally. When it was finished he said:

'Grace's death doesn't alter the fact of the debt, but it may change your position. It would depend on his heirs and executors of his will. Miss Lang, do you know if your stepfather made a will?'

'When he tried ...' She stopped and started again. 'When he was boasting one day he told me that I would inherit a great deal when he died. But that was a few years ago, when I was still at school, and I've never thought about it since. I've kept out of his way as much as possible. We don't – didn't – get on very well. Correction. We didn't get on at all. The last time I saw him was six months ago when he got me this job with Frank. I think he was trying to get me out of London and away from his business dealings, which were always dubious. I was only too glad to go. I've never wanted any of his money. I've got my own. My mother left it for me in trust before she ... she ... committed suicide.'

Ashcroft avoided embarrassing her further. He merely said: 'Thank you. The solicitors should know. It's Sunday, but see if you can raise them, Amber.'

Light rose obediently. I showed him the extension in the tiny room that served as my father's study and left him trying to prove his identity to the telephonist at New Scotland Yard. 'Ring me back here when you've got the number,' he said. Back in the kitchen Ashcroft was waiting for me.

'What did you know about the difficulties your father's in?'

'Until this morning, nothing.'

'What would you have done had you known?'

I paused.

'Well, I could have helped him a bit with cash. My mother left me twenty thousand when she died. I've hardly touched it, and it should be worth a bit more by now, what with the interest, and inflation, and whatnot. It doesn't worry me. I can get by.'

'What did you think of Grace?'

'The same as most other people. I didn't like him. But he was a bloody good cricketer. If I'd known what he'd been doing to my father I'd have knocked the shit . . . sorry, beaten the hell out of him.'

'I can understand your feelings. Did you know about the joke bat?'

I shook my head. My father broke in.

'I never told a soul about that. I was ashamed of it.'

The telephone rang, sharply, and there was a 'ting' as Light picked up the extension. In a moment he put his head round the door.

'Message for you, Roger, from your landlady. She's had a call from the Surrey coach. You're wanted for a special net at half past ten. Captain's orders. Okay?'

I looked at my watch. It was just before nine. I would have to move fast.

'Chief Superintendent, are you going to arrest me? Or Dad? If not, have you any more questions? I have to go now. I'm due in the nets in just over an hour and it's a long way to go.'

'As I said earlier, we have no proof yet that a murder has been committed, so there is no cause to arrest anyone. Mr Light regards you as trustworthy, if headstrong, so I see no reason to detain you. Off you go, and break a leg!'

I blinked at him. 'What d'you mean.'

'I'm told you have every chance of playing for the first eleven against Lancashire on Wednesday. "Break a leg" is an old theatrical expression meaning "Good luck". Perhaps it's not so suitable for a cricketer.'

'Thanks, er, sir,' I said, recalling where I had seen the large crumpled figure before that summer – in the committee room at The Oval talking to Allason. It did no harm to butter up a friend of the secretary and, for a policeman, he seemed a decent sort. Just then there was another 'ting' as Light hung up his telephone.

'Not much help,' he said, coming into the kitchen. 'They're basically debt collectors and aren't into will and probate. They've no idea who handled Grace's personal affairs or if he made a will. They've only acted for his World Bats company for a few months and they didn't deal with Grace. Their contact was the chairman, a Mr Pravisar, from Pakistan. That explains the friendship with Grace.'

'Do you know where Grace banked,' he asked Sally.

'Coutts, I think,' she said. 'He was a snob, too.' She turned to me. 'Are you going to London? Do you mind giving me a lift?'

'I'm only going as far as The Oval. Will that be okay? I won't have the time to drop you off anywhere else.' It didn't sound too gracious, but she took no offence.

'Thanks. I won't take you out of your way. I'll get the tube or a cab from there. I'll just get my things.' Surprisingly, she went across and kissed my father on the cheek. 'Don't worry, Frank. It'll all work out.'

'I hope so,' he said gloomily. I said my farewells and Light followed me out to the car.

'I've got one more question for you,' he said. 'Why did you take that bat from Grace's bag?'

'I can't really say,' I said. I didn't wish to implicate Mrs Marchbanks. 'I just wanted to see if I could spot the one Grace had been using. I picked this one, by instinct I suppose, and took it back to my room to have a good look at it. Then those blokes with the guns came and I didn't think about it until all that was over and I was back in bed. I began to look at it, but thought I'd bring it down to Dad. He's the real expert. I never meant to conceal it. It was just one of those things.'

Light grimaced. 'It's just as well for you that Old Bill in there is a cricketer. I'll leave it for now. Off you go. And don't, repeat don't, go biting off more than you can chew. You've been lucky twice. There's always a third time.'

'Thanks. I'll be careful.'

Sally threw a hold-all into the back of the car and

settled herself into the passenger seat with the minimum of fuss. The MGB gave out its familiar growl as I pulled the starter button and blipped the accelerator. Sally shivered, although the sun was already high and warm in a clear sky, and I felt guilty about my boorish behaviour earlier. After all, Grace's death, however much she disliked him, must have shocked her. I tried to speak gently.

'Why did you dislike your stepfather so much?'

'You knew him. You worked for him. You played cricket with him.'

'Yes, but he was your . . .'

'Stepfather.' The ice was back in her voice. I glanced across at a face to match. 'He killed my mother. The coroner said it was misadventure, that she had taken an overdose of sleeping pills probably by mistake when she was depressed. He said what a tragedy it was for the popular cricketer and captain of Surrey. But I knew he had driven her to it. I was fourteen at the time. I went for him at the funeral. I was trying to push him into the grave with her. They stopped me, of course, and it was hushed up so nothing was reported. Then he took me home and ripped down my knickers and thrashed me. I didn't mind that; I hated him so much and it was a good reason to hate him more. But it got him worked up and he held me down and assaulted me. Sexually, I mean. He was stinking of gin and his hands were everywhere, but I was strong for my age and got away by kicking him between the legs as hard as I could. It really hurt him. He fell onto the floor and lay there holding himself and writhing about, calling me a bitch and a whore, "like your mother". I was scared, but got the big poker from the fireplace and held it in both hands and said I'd kill him if he ever came near me again. I meant it, too, and he knew it.'

'Did he ever try anything again?'

'No. I didn't give him the opportunity. Luckily, he was away a lot with the cricket, and I was at boarding school during term time, and I usually managed to spend most of the holidays with one friend or another. I persuaded the PE teacher to set up a judo class. I wanted it to be karate, but the school wouldn't allow it. Not suitable for young ladies. Then there was Bettsie – Mrs Betts, our housekeeper. She looked after me when I was at home in Blackheath; a sort of surrogate mother. My stepfather tried to bully her just as he bullied everybody, but she was too tough for him. They were always rowing furiously, and he tried to sack her at least once a month, but she refused to go. She'd promised mummy that she'd look after me, and mummy had left money in trust for my education as well as for me. I think Bettsie knew too much. She scared him. In any case, he didn't need to sack her because she was killed. I don't know why I'm telling you all this.'

'It's my sympathetic nature. How was she killed?'

'It was a hit-and-run accident outside our house. They never found out who did it. That was last year, when I was eighteen. Mummy's education money had run out and I don't get my inheritance until I'm twenty-one. I refused to be dependent on my stepfather. I hadn't got any qualifications and school had given me up as an academic failure. The only things I was any good at were woodwork and judo. I remembered how Bettsie had handled Persse, so I went to him and told him that I wanted to make cricket bats, and that unless he found me a job I would go to the tabloids and tell them about his nice little habits at home. Twenty things you ought to know about Persse Grace, captain of Surrey.'

'How did he take that?'

'Badly. He went to hit me, but I caught him in a wrist-lock and told him I'd break his fingers one by one and invited him to try again. So then I went the rounds of the bat-makers and found Frank and Persse fixed it up. I don't know how.'

'As a *quid pro quo*. He swapped you for me.'

'I got the best of the bargain. You got Persse. How did you find him?'

'Much the same as everyone else, I reckon. But he was a bloody marvellous cricketer, for all that. I'll never forget his last innings. It's a crime he never played for England.'

'Are you going to be as good as he was?'

'No chance. I can bowl a bit, bat a bit and field a bit – a good twelfth man. I'll be lucky to make a regular first team place. Are you going to be as good a bat-maker as Frank?'

'Yes, I am.'

'Christ! No you bloody don't!' It was not a reply to her sacrilegious remark, but a reaction to a black Jaguar which, in defiance of all the laws of the road, had forced its way past the MGB on the narrow A22 and cut in viciously across my bumper. I braked hard and swerved to avoid a collision, slammed the gear lever into second and trod hard on the accelerator. The power surge made the tyres screech on the tarmac as the little car leapt forward. A right-hand bend gave me a glimpse of fifty yards of clear road ahead and, taking a chance, I swung the wheel over and swept the MGB past the Jaguar with my foot flat down to the floor. As I did so, the Jag accelerated too, trying to force me into a head-on collision with a petrol tanker lumbering up in the oncoming lane.

'Hold tight!' I yelled at Sally, but the shout was drowned by the howling engines and the sudden huge blast of the tanker's horn and a ripping crash as I squeezed the MGB into a rapidly decreasing gap amid a cacophony of noise. Then we were through and still alive, minus both wing mirrors and a great deal of paint. The Jaguar was still crowding us, but behind the tanker was a long line of traffic, and I made sure its driver had no opportunity to repeat his manoeuvre. The A22 between Lewes and East Grinstead is no place for a stock-car race, twisting its old-fashioned way through high hedges and farm land, interspersed with stretches of dense coppices and woodland.

'Do you always drive like that?' The girl spoke conversationally, as if she genuinely wanted to know.

'Only when I think I'm going to be killed.' I tried to make my voice as cool as hers and hoped she did not notice the sweat from my palms on the steering wheel ... 'I think he's going to try again. Fasten your safety belt. We're about to enter an area of turbulence. Keep an eye on him, will you? I'm going to take a slight diversion.'

I failed to tell her that I thought I had recognised the driver of the Jaguar as the man who had attacked me the night before. Nor did I tell her how I planned to accomplish my objective. We were approaching a stretch I knew well. A mile or so ahead of us, one of the farmers with land just off the A22 raised three acres of willows which F. North & Son culled in rotation every year. These were reached by tracks winding through the woodlands of hazel, ash and oak. Judging the distance as best I could, I dropped the MGB's speed to forty to give myself space ahead, then put my foot down, hard. The space between the two cars expanded and began to contract like elastic as the Jaguar's driver reacted a little slowly to the manoeuvre. He was only twenty-five yards behind me and coming up fast when I whipped the gear down into second and sent it in a four-wheel drift into the bramble-covered gap between two trees. Protesting, the MGB bucked and snaked wildly as I fought to keep her upright and bring her under control again. Thirty yards into the wood I brought her bumping to a halt in a cloud of dust, but more or less in one piece, and in the centre of the rough, narrow track. Sally Lang was twisted round in the passenger seat peering through the narrow rear window, but she was still held fast by her seat-belt.

'I think your friend in the Jaguar hit an oak tree,' she said.

I wound down the window. Amazingly, the mechanism was still intact. The noise of the traffic interspersed with faint shouts filtered through the foliage. I pressed the starter and the engine growled obediently into life. They knew how to make them in those days.

'Let's get on,' I said. 'Someone will come looking to

see if we are all right.' I let in the clutch and drove cautiously through the wood. No one followed us. The low-slung MGB wasn't built for cross-country work, but by avoiding the deeper ruts and more obvious tree-stumps, we made reasonable, if uncomfortable progress and after fifteen minutes' driving I pulled out onto the A22 again, half a mile from where we had left it so abruptly. The south-bound queue of traffic had halted, but the north-bound lane was clear.

'I don't think we'll be bothered again this morning,' I said, turning the car onto an empty road. 'That must be quite a hold-up. We should be able to make up a good bit of time. They say driving in France is like this.'

'Roger,' said Sally Lang. It was the first time she had called me anything but 'you' or 'cretin'. 'Roger, can a member of the public watch the Surrey team in the nets?'

'I don't see why not. Nets aren't all that exciting as a spectator sport. Why? Are you interested?'

'Not much. But if I'm going to make your cricket bats, I want to see if it's worth doing.'

'Fair enough,' I said. 'But you're going to have to answer a couple of questions first.'

'That depends on what they are.'

'First, if you're so hot at judo, why did you let me pick you up like that?'

'Because I wasn't frightened of you; and you obviously wanted to let off steam – by showing how macho you were. Next?'

'How are you so cool? Most girls would be screaming to be let out of the car after what I've put you through in the last five minutes. But you don't even ask questions.'

'It's the same answer, really. I've always had a high panic level. I just go cold. It doesn't help the driver if the passenger goes off her head in a crisis. Especially when the driver is trying to go through a space that wouldn't take a bicycle. But I haven't asked any questions because I've been trying to get my stomach back.'

80

I grinned at her.

'Thank goodness for that. So have I. I was beginning to think you were Superwoman.'

'What the hell's going on? That's what I want to know. Who hates you enough to want to kill you? Or at least put you in hospital?'

'I wish I knew. But that's the third time in the last twelve hours that someone's had a go at me. God knows why, but it's something to do with Persse's death.'

I sketched in the events of the previous evening.

'Did you get a look at the maniac driving the Jag?' I asked.

'Not properly. It all happened so fast. But I think he had black hair and a beard – or stubble.'

'So did the guy who first attacked me last night. But that doesn't mean a thing. By the way, I apologise for those wrong conclusions I jumped to.'

'Yes, you did. But so did I. Where did you learn to drive a car like that?'

'Rallying. And I've been to Brands Hatch most weekends until the cricket season started. Formula three stuff.'

'With this crate?'

'No fear. She's much too valuable. A friend of dad's lets me drive his Porsche.'

'I hope you don't treat it like that.' She pointed to the battered wings. 'I've been thinking, I wouldn't let you drive my Mini.'

I made no comment. In fact, the MGB had been developing steering drag to the near side over the past few miles, and I pulled over into a lay-by to inspect the damage. All four tyres seemed firm, but a glance under the front end revealed that the front wheels were badly out of line. There was nothing I could do but curse and limp along a couple of miles to the next garage where, even though it was Sunday, a red-headed cockney mechanic had the car up on a ramp in a minute. A moment later he emerged to announce cheerfully that the steering rods had gone and the suspension had twisted, but there was nothing he could not fix, given three days, the spare parts, which were a bit of a pain these days, and five hundred quid.

'But I've got to be in London in half an hour,' I said. 'Is there nothing you can do?'

He looked at me closely.

'I know you,' he said. 'I saw you yesterday on the box. You were the bloke on the telly. Bloody good catch, that. Shocking thing about Grace, though. Great player. Should have played for England. Stupid bloody selectors. Where are you going? The Oval? Tell you what, you leave that wreck here for a few days and I'll lend you one of the bangers in the front there. No skin off my nose. The boss is away. Just sign the insurance form. That's it – the Alfa. Goes like a bomb. I'll put your stuff in the boot. Here are the keys. Think nothing of it . . . fix me a ticket for the Oval test. Keep smiling. Ciao.'

He waved us off in a three-year-old Alfa Romeo saloon worth three times as much as the MGB and twice as fast and by ten forty we pulled through The Oval's cast-iron gates under the inquisitive gaze of Archie the gateman.

4

Perhaps the presence of Sally, a lone figure sitting in The Oval's sea of plastic seating (she chose the blue rather than the peach-pink), made me try that bit too hard, or perhaps the residual stiffness in my upper right leg inhibited my bowling action. Whatever the reason, I scarcely covered myself with glory during that Sunday morning session in the nets. I am not one of those cricketers like Geoffrey Boycott, who never felt complete unless he had enjoyed an hour's batting in the nets, preferably two. To me, there's something distinctly claustrophobic about batting surrounded on three sides by black nylon netting, with a bloke on either side cracking apparently effortless shots to all points of the compass and distracting your attention by sneaking a ball under the netting onto your pitch at the precise moment that a fast bowler is hurling one down on a length. Bowling is even worse. I like to run a full twelve paces in before delivery to settle my rhythm, and unless there is a particularly observant coach to clear a path for me through the trundlers and part-time spinners, my run-up bears a strong resemblance to an army obstacle course. That morning, apart from being bowled three times by one of the 'rabbits' and not hitting the stumps once myself, I was even hit on my bruised leg by a smart drive from Smithson as I was bending to field a mis-hit pull from the next net. My temper was not improved by a bellow of 'Keep your eye on the ball, North' from Carnock.

However, I acquitted myself with rather more distinction on the slip-catch cradle, which I always enjoy. This is literally a cradle made of curved slats of chestnut on a cast-iron frame onto which you throw a ball in such a manner that it skids off at varying pace in varying directions, giving the catcher plenty of practice in taking the ball at unexpected speeds and angles. There's another version, a sprung net, which you can use by yourself, but it's not so much fun. I got something of my own back on Gerry Down for the previous night's thrashing at squash, stinging his hands a couple of times and forcing him to drop five catches to my two. One finishes a ten-minute session on the cradle with warmly throbbing fingers and palms and much sharpened reactions, ready for a run round the outfield and then high catching practice. As twelfth man, I was relegated to hitting the ball to the rest of the team standing round me in a circle for close catching and then doing the same over long-distance to the outfielders, who returned it in desultory fashion to Phil Hills the wicket-keeper, standing over a solitary stump beside me. After ten minutes or so of this tedium, Smithson, the new skipper, called me back into the nets. He was padded and gloved, and had gathered all the practice balls together in a little clump around my run-up mark.

'I want you to bowl me an over or two, Roger,' he said. 'The coach got the impression you weren't all that happy this morning. As well as being late for the net.'

'Sorry about that, Skip. I had car trouble on the way back from Sussex. I went down to talk things over with my father.'

'And came up with Persse's problem, I see.' He nodded in the direction of Sally's solitary figure. 'I heard she was making cricket bats. Any good?'

'At bat-making,' I answered carefully. You never know in a cricket team what such a remark might be referring

84

to. 'Anything else, I wouldn't know,' I added a trifle stiffly.

'Keep your hair on,' said Smithson. 'I'm not prying. I want you to bowl a couple of overs flat out. I've just had my knock and I've got my eye in. The wicket's okay. There's twelve to win and two wickets to fall.'

I understood this was some sort of test, and marked out my run carefully, thinking of nothing but the batsman. Smithson was one of the old school of Lancastrian openers; one of the best; solid, experienced and dependable and the least likely batsman to take a risk or make a mistake. An accumulator of runs rather than a striker of the ball. As an opening batsman he was the despair of many a fast bowler; the faster they banged it in the more dead the bat he offered. When he was accused of making his runs through the slips he would defuse argument by stolidly agreeing that the edges of his bat were his best friends. 'Ah hold t'bat slack,' he would say, 'and t'ball doesn't carry for a catch, nine times out o' ten.' He was tough; the last man I would want to bowl to in a net. He had a weakness or two, however, which a clever bowler could try to exploit. Once pushed onto the back foot, he had the habit of retreating further and further across the line of the ball until his back foot came perilously close to treading on the stumps and a fast, accurate yorker could creep under his guard. And he could sometimes be tempted into driving with the bat well away from his pads, leaving a late in-swinger or fast off-cutter to nip in through the gap between bat and pad.

I gave him a couple of slow half-volleys as looseners, both of which he dispatched gently and easily in the general direction of the on-side field, and then switched on the power to try to intimidate him with a fast bouncer, which he hooked very hard to square leg. The next ball was my fastest and best so far, pitching a trifle short and rearing straight for Smithson's throat. He covered up fast, lifting his bat in front of his face, the ball snicking the outside edge and flying off on a downward path toward the territory of the slips. I stifled an appeal and the skipper looked up the pitch at me, a slight grin on his face.

'More like four off the edge, young Roger,' he said, and I trudged back to my mark promising him the fastest yorker in the business. In my eagerness, I let the ball fly a fraction of a second early, and the intended yorker became a near lethal full-toss. Smithson, already back on his stumps, had no room to manoeuvre his bat, and made a hapless stab at the ball as it whistled through, taking the top of the middle stump on its way. I beat him all ends up with the next two balls and, as a final bonus, had all three stumps out of the ground with my final ball.

'That's enough.' Smithson strolled out of the net, taking off his gloves. He did not seem at all perturbed by being bowled by a mere stripling. 'You'll play on Wednesday if you can do that again in t'middle tomorrow.'

'Thanks, Skip.' Treading on air, I showered quickly and, ignoring the suggestive speculations of my team-mates, ran off to pick up Sally. I had in mind lunch along the river and, depending on progress, an afternoon and evening spent putting the more attainable suggestions of my colleagues into effect. Sally was nowhere to be seen. I toured The Oval in increasing frustration, even checking the ladies' lavatories. Sally had disappeared. My disappointment turned to annoyance and then to anger when I found that the car had gone too. I remembered her saying: 'Leave me the keys. I want to get some things out of the boot to freshen up.' I had tossed her the keys and run for the dressing-room. I asked Archie if he had seen her leave.

'Yes, Mr North,' Archie said cheerfully. 'Saw them go myself, I did. The young lady with a dark chap. She was driving. I don't think she wanted to go. They was arguing and she looked really angry. I couldn't help but notice. No, I couldn't hear what they was saying. They had the windows up.'

'What did he look like, this dark chap?'

'Couldn't say, sir. They all looks alike to me. Well

dressed, though. He had an MCC tie on. Been stood up, have you sir?'

'You could say so, Archie.'

I was more angry than worried. I checked back in the pavilion to see if Sally had left any sort of message, and then went to find Phil Hills, or Gerry Down or someone to have a drink with. After all, I reasoned, we hadn't made a definite arrangement to spend the afternoon together. It had just seemed implicit from the way in which we had been talking. Perhaps something had come up suddenly over her stepfather's death; his will, his business, anything. Sally Lang owed me nothing but common courtesy and, after the way I had treated her down at Willford, perhaps not even that.

'Where's the luscious blonde?' said Down as he ordered pints in the lounge bar of the Surrey Tavern. 'I thought you were well in there, man.'

'So did I. But she's disappeared with a bloody black man. And taken my car. A black man wearing an MCC tie. Do you know anyone like that? . . . I don't . . . Wait a minute, though . . . I wonder.'

'Something rung a bell?' asked Hills.

'Ye-es, I think so. I'm going to find a telephone directory.'

There had been someone like that at Lord's the previous day. Pravisar. And he was supposed to be a partner of Grace. Could Sally have gone away with him? If so, why? And without leaving a message. She hadn't mentioned Pravisar during our talk in the car. It was all very mysterious, but the telephone directory was of no help. There was no Pravisar listed in London, nor P.R.A. Visar, nor any other variation on the theme. I tried Directory Inquiries, with no further luck. There was nothing more I could do, except curse female caprice. Which I did, heartily. I rang home at Willford, to see if my father had any ideas, but there was no reply. I rang the village pub, but he wasn't there, and hadn't been seen that morning either. I returned to the bar, where my companions were sympathetic but not helpful.

'No luck?' Down inquired. 'I'd go to the police, man. After all, she's nicked your car.'

'It's not even my car, which makes it worse,' I agreed. 'But I'm certain there must be an explanation. I can't go to the cops.'

'Perhaps she's been kidnapped,' suggested Hills, half seriously.

'Thanks very much,' I said sarcastically, but the thought nagged at me. So much out of the ordinary had happened in the last twenty-four hours that I was beginning to believe anything was possible. 'Surely that couldn't happen? At The Oval? In broad daylight?'

'Well, you can't see old Archie stopping a kidnapper, can you? He has trouble enough with a ten-year-old gate-crasher.'

I sighed. It was true. It was also true that I was growing very angry at being stood up, so between fear and bad temper I wasn't very good company that lunch-time. I made an excuse and left Hills and Down to their second pint and to straighten my thoughts set out to walk back to Mrs Marchbanks's house in Dulwich. An hour and a quarter later, with a clearer head but none the wiser, I was seated in the big kitchen drinking an ice-cold lager and being fussed over by Mrs Marchbanks, who wanted to know every detail of what had happened over the previous twenty-four hours. I didn't tell her about Sally's defection to a Pakistani millionaire; I didn't want to worry her unnecessarily. She professed to being shocked and horrified by the discovery of the syringe in the handle of Grace's bat, but was obviously revelling in playing a part, however peripheral, in the current sensation. She was also bursting with righteous indignation.

'Look at that,' she cried, brandishing a copy of the *Sunday Scream*, one of the more sensational of the tabloids. 'It's disgusting. Raking up all that old muck. It ought not to be allowed. That Ted Symonds. Who'd ever have thought it of him? He doesn't need the money. I'm going out in the car. It's a lovely day for a drive. I'll be back to get you some tea. You stay here and read that.'

She pointed to an article under the name of 'Celebrated Cricketer Edward Symonds, Cambridge University and Surrey, as told to Rick Wright'. Above it was the headline, in two-inch lettering: **DIS-GRACE**! It was sub-titled:

EXCLUSIVE! THE SENSATIONAL DETAILS OF THE DOUBLE LIFE OF PERSSE GRACE, A SPORTING HERO TO MILLIONS BUT A B****** TO THOSE WHO KNEW HIM WELL.

I whistled. If Symonds had really spilled the beans, if he knew which beans to spill, the *Sunday Scream* really did have a sensational scoop. One of the newshounds haunting the Surrey Tavern must have offered him a queen's ransom, for the Surrey committee would be down on him in a flash. Not that Symonds needed the money, as Mrs M said; he was as close to being a true amateur as was possible nowadays. His father was the millionaire head of a company producing international soft porn magazines, he lived in his own flat in the family mansion in Hampstead, and it was common knowledge that he donated his salary back to Surrey. He sponsored himself, as it were, to play first-class cricket, so he was in an invulnerable position. I wondered why he had lent his name to the article. I began to read.

Persse Grace, the captain of Surrey who died mysteriously at Lord's yesterday in the midst of a sensational innings, was a hero to millions of cricket fans throughout the land. But to his Surrey team-mates and to many on the inside, he was known as a bully and feared as a sadist. On his day a brilliant batsman, his career was never crowned by the reward he really craved; an England cap. His few friends thought that the selectors held a

89

grudge against him, but those in the know say that it was felt that he was not a fit and proper man to represent his country. All the members of the team knew that he could not be trusted with a wife, a girlfriend or a sister.

And Grace was a gambler; a compulsive gambler who was suspected of 'throwing' important matches in order to win large sums from the bookmakers. His critics point to last year's NatWest Trophy final, when Surrey were 3-1 on. Grace was batting when Smithson (57) and Hills (12) were run out through 'misunderstandings' between the batsmen, and Grace himself (whose powers were demonstrated so devastatingly at Lord's yesterday before his mysterious collapse and death) gave up a 'dolly' catch when he had scored only 9. Subsequent rumours of a betting scam were never confirmed, but Scotland Yard Fraud Squad began an inquiry which twelve months later is still unfinished.

I was one of several junior members of the team who took bulky sealed envelopes from Grace to different bookmakers in the days before that final. We all knew that Grace never laid less than fifty pounds on a horse, but those envelopes contained much more than fifty pounds.

I have seen him manipulate the bowling until it seemed he was trying to hand a match to the other team. Against Yorkshire, again last year, he kept the seamers going for hours on a hot day with a hard pitch breaking up and ideal for spin, but Porter our off-spinner only had three overs at the end of the day when Yorkshire were on 350 for 3.

If anyone criticised him or tried to make a suggestion, Grace would bawl him out publicly. On three occasions I have been made to field at deep fine leg at both ends of the field and, having run over two hundred yards between the overs to get to my position, been bullied for not being in the right place. Even so, it wasn't as bad for me as it was for some of the other players. I am fortunate in having an income outside cricket, so I have not been dependent for my living on keeping in Grace's good books.

Several of my fellow cricketers, all of them first-class players, including Phil Hills, probably the best

wicket-keeper in county cricket, have been dropped
from the team and their wages docked for arguing
with the captain, or at least disagreeing with him
and being unwise enough to say so out loud. Little
Harry Carnock, the coach, went in fear of his job if
not his life, every day. Grace would never have dared
to bully me like that. I would have left the club and
taken a million pounds' worth of sponsorship with me.
And even Surrey's miserable committee wouldn't have
worn that, even though Grace treated all of them, from
the chairman down, as though they were a pack of
lap-dogs. In the same way they will take no action
against me for writing this article, although I have
broken all the rules by doing so. My reason is simply
this: you cannot libel a dead man, and I want to
set the record straight publicly about a man whose
demise, however spectacular, leaves the world a better
place.

Even leaving out the journalistic hype, it was a major
piece of character assassination. But what Symonds wrote,
or had written for him, held more than a grain of truth.
When Grace's decisions as captain had on occasions suc-
ceeded brilliantly, he was praised as a genius; but at other
times when they had been disastrous, they had been written
off as idiosyncratic. Symonds's strictures corresponded with
the dressing-room opinion. As Hills had said on more than
one occasion: 'The man's bloody mad.' But the mutterings
about 'fixing' games had never been more than that – just
mutterings.

I threw down the paper and dialled my home number in
Willford. There was still no answer, and I began to worry.
The events of the last two days had made me suspicious of
anything out of the ordinary. Perhaps dad had been taken
ill, or injured himself in the workshop. I dialled again, in
case my fingers had slipped the first time. The ringing tone
pealed away in my ear. No reply. I dialled the operator
and asked her to check the line. All in order, she said. I
felt dull and aimlessly incompetent, with no idea what I

should do next. I put the phone down, then on impulse picked it up again and dialled the number Light had given me at Scotland Yard.

'Ashcroft.'

The unexpected voice threw me.

'Oh, er, I thought I'd be speaking to Inspector Light.' I pulled myself together. 'Sorry, it's Roger North. I'm ringing because I'm worried that something might have happened to my father.'

I told him what had happened on the journey up to London that morning. Ashcroft listened to my story without interrupting me.

'You may think I'm worrying without reason, Mr Ashcroft.'

'Not a bit. I'll have the local man go round right away and check. I'll call you back and let you know what he says. Was there anything else?'

'It sounds a bit stupid, but I've lost Miss Lang. Sally. She came to The Oval to watch the nets and we were going to have lunch. When I went to collect her, she'd gone. With a black man in an MCC tie. And taken my car. The gateman told me.'

'Your MG? What's the number?'

'No, the MG was bent a bit in the chase. It's a hire-car we borrowed from a garage. A red Alfa. I'm afraid I don't know the number.'

'A black man in an MCC tie being driven by a girl in a red Alfa shouldn't be too difficult to spot. Leave it with me. We'll call you back when we have any news.'

Without being pompous, he sounded efficient and re-assuring. I felt better. At least he hadn't told me not to worry. So I could worry with official blessing, and did. After half an hour he had not rung back and I had tired of worrying and decided that action was better than sitting in the flat trying to watch a dull Sunday league match on television. My little black address book contained, among those of a number of other girls, the telephone number of the redhead in the Surrey secretary's office. I was lucky. Angie was at home, and bored.

'Of course I'll help. It's exciting, isn't it? Persse's daughter abducted! Have you told the police?'

'Yes, I have, but I can't sit still and do nothing. Can you meet me at The Oval in half an hour? I want to find a telephone number?'

'Is that all you want, Roger?' She sounded disappointed.

'It's an ex-directory number. It might be on the membership list. And it may be under a different name.'

'Who is it?'

'I'll tell you when I see you.'

The thought of solving a little mystery was enough.

'I'm not doing anything else this afternoon. I'll meet you outside the gate in half an hour. Security will let us in. I've got my keys.'

'See you there.'

I was lucky to find a taxi quickly, but even so Angie was there waiting for me. I recognised the green eyes, but the rest of the image was transformed from the severely suited, bespectacled secretary who protected Allason, the secretary, from the weekday crush of members and the public with ruthless efficiency. This Angie had a figure, a very good figure obviously unencumbered by a bra – under a diaphanous cream blouse, and cut-away shorts which could have been applied with a paintbrush. The auburn hair, freed from its usual constraining bun, floated down to her bare shoulders. The security man at the gate could not take his eyes off her. I didn't blame him. Angie was fully aware of the effect she was having.

'Thank you,' she said prettily to him as he opened the iron gate for us. 'We'll only be about twenty minutes in the office, I think.'

'Yes, miss,' he said, shutting the gate behind us. I was sure I heard him add 'Lucky sod' under his breath and I could feel his eyes on us, or rather on Angie's behind, as we made our way up the short flight of steps to the main door. I saw what he meant.

'Why are you so quiet?' she asked me maliciously as she unlocked the double doors leading into the office. 'Cat got your tongue?'

'Not exactly,' I said. 'I can't think how to put it.'

'We'll see about that later,' said Angie briskly, switching on an Amstrad word-processor on her desk. She touched a few keys. 'Who are we looking for?'

'Pravisar.' I spelt it out. 'PRAVISAR.'

'Is he the kidnapper?'

'It looks that way. But Sally might have gone with him of her own accord.'

'Instead of you? You mean she had a better offer.' Angie's fingers paused from their expert caressing of the keys. She glanced up at me. Her eyes seemed very green. 'I can't see why.' Her voice changed. 'Here he is.'

I moved round the desk to look over her shoulder at the green lists on the screen. The little flashing cursor was on 'Pravisar, Suri; Bat World, Flamenco St, 63A, London W1. Telephone (bus): 071 837 4231.*'

'What's the star for?'

'It's a cross-reference to a special file Mr Grace kept for himself. Only he knew the password. We can't get into it on the computer. Even Mr Allason can't.'

'Someone must be able to.'

'Only the chief accountant, Mr Thorogood. He's got the key to control the system.'

'Where does he hang out?'

She flicked the keys again. Mr Arthur Thorogood lived on the edge of Hampstead Heath in Tanza Road. I dialled his number. There were three rings and a click, and a metallic voice said: 'Mr and Mrs Thorogood are unable to answer the telephone at the moment. They will return shortly, and if you leave a message will attend to your request on their return. Please speak after the tone. Thank you.'

I said: 'Mr Thorogood, this is urgent. I am Roger North, the Surrey twelfth man. Would you please contact me at The Oval or at Willford, East Sussex, 0294 78 444 as soon as possible. Or through Mrs Marchbanks at 520 9624. It is about the death of Mr Grace. I repeat, this is urgent. Thank you very much.'

'I'm impressed,' said Angie. 'I like men who are decisive. Are you going to phone Mr Pravisar now?'

'No, I'm not. I want to take him by surprise, if I can. A phone call will let him know I'm coming.'

'Good. Then you've got time to be decisive as well as sounding it.' She leaned back in her chair, stretching her body luxuriously. Her nipples stood out taut against her flimsy blouse. She passed the tip of her tongue across her bottom lip, slowly. 'You were saying you didn't know how to put it. Have you made up your mind?'

She pressed her head back against my stomach as I stood behind her chair, rubbing her hair from side to side. I still did not speak.

'Mmmm,' she said. 'Strong and silent too. Particularly strong, I can feel.'

I stepped back, with a considerable effort. Although the invitation was obvious, I had more important things on my mind. Angie swung the swivel chair round, bringing her bare knees up to her breasts and clasping her arms round her legs. She was sexy – and persistent. She looked up at me sideways.

'Mr Allason's always talking about having people on the carpet,' she said, wriggling her bottom on the leather seat. 'I'd like to tell him I've had you on the carpet. Come on. I won't eat you. Or maybe I will,' she added reflectively.

'Angie, my love,' I said, 'last week you could have had me for breakfast, dinner and tea. Maybe next week, too. But not just now. Thanks, and all that. But no thanks.'

She pouted. 'Pity. It was worth a try. But that's your lot. I never ask twice.'

'I'm sure you don't,' I said. 'I'm flattered you asked once.'

Angie switched off the computer and covered it tenderly. On the way out she smiled sexily at the security man who smirked knowingly as he locked the gate behind us.

'That didn't take long, did it?' Angie told him. 'We were only just over twenty minutes, weren't we? Thank you very much.'

'And thank *you* very much for nothing,' she said, pressing my arm as we walked to the Underground station. 'You know what I wanted.'

I grinned at her. 'You could have fooled me. Do you always seduce your men like that?'

'Only when they're young and beautiful.' She squeezed my arm harder still. 'Damn you. I do want you. Now!'

She stopped dead on the pavement, halting me in my tracks. She reached up both arms and pulled my face down to hers, clamping her lips on mine and thrusting her tongue deep into my mouth. I held her close to keep my balance, and felt her body pressing its length against mine. Suddenly she shuddered, going limp, and let me go. She was panting. Her hair was damp and little drops of perspiration collected on her forehead. She smiled at me, a little crookedly.

'I've never come in the street before,' she said. 'It's all your fault.'

There was nothing I could say to that, so I called a taxi, hustled her away from the mercifully few passers-by and bundled her into it.

'I'm sorry, Angie. Really.' I gave the driver her address. 'Thanks again. Anything I can do, just ask.'

She held the door open to stop the cab driving off. 'You're not very romantic, are you? Where are you off to?'

'Soho.'

'Flamenco Street?'

'Yes. I must find Pravisar.'

Angie leaned forward in her seat.

'Be careful,' she said. 'I don't like Mr Pravisar. Nor does Mr Allason. I think he's afraid of him.'

'Don't worry. I'll look after myself.'

'I'm not so sure,' said Angie, smiling to herself but still looking worried. 'She must be something special, this Sally. 'Bye.' She blew me a kiss as the cab moved away.

I found myself flushing as I searched for a pay phone to dial home again. There was still no reply. Scotland Yard told me that Chief Superintendent Ashcroft and Detective Inspector Light were out of the building. The lack of news seemed to add urgency to the need to find Pravisar. I made my way to the West End by underground, my temper not helped by a hot and sticky journey with one of those incomprehensible Northern Line delays with the train stationary for ten minutes under the Thames.

Soho was coming to its normal sleazy evening life, but Flamenco Street was empty except for a mangy cat which disappeared into an anonymous hole at the sound of my footsteps. It was one of those grim, tiny cul-de-sacs tucked in between Dean Street and Wardour Street, and number 63 was a graffiti-scrawled door in a blackened brick wall with no windows. It had an old-fashioned Yale lock and a small brass plate announcing WORLD BATS in tastefully-etched one inch capital letters above an intercom grille. I pressed the small button. There was a pause, then a click, and the grille issued its metallic message: 'Who is calling?'

'Roger North. I'm looking for Mr Pravisar. Is he there?'

There was no reply, but a short buzz signalled that the door had been electronically unbarred. I pushed it open, and was confronted by a narrow carpeted flight of stairs. World Bats appeared to be behind a smart modern door on the first floor on which I knocked. Once again the door was opened electronically and closed behind me as I entered. Pravisar was seated behind a large, empty desk in a chair that would have graced 'Mastermind'. He did not get up, but waved me to a slightly smaller version.

'Sit down, Mr North. To what do I owe the honour of this visit?' The slight emphasis on 'honour' managed to convey sarcasm, contempt and irritation. I decided that my initial impression at Lord's had been correct.

'Where's Miss Lang?'

'My dear fellow, how on earth would I know? Who is this Miss Lang? I've never heard of her.'

'Sally Lang. Persse Grace's stepdaughter.'

'Oh, *that* Miss Lang. Yes, of course I know her. But why should I know where she is?'

'Because you took her away from The Oval at lunchtime today in my car. She was going to have lunch with me.'

'On the contrary. We had made an appointment to meet at The Oval and lunch together. At the Savoy, where I am staying. It was a business matter.'

'I don't believe it. She was waiting for me. I had driven her up from Sussex. She wouldn't have done that.'

Pravisar stood up. He was as tall as me, but willowy as a snake. He had a wide, thin mouth with a twist to the upper lip, high cheekbones and brown eyes so dark as to be almost coal-black.

'Miss Lang is not your property,' he said. 'There is no point in demonstrating your jealousy. She is only a girl, after all.'

'What the hell do you mean by that?'

'I think you English say that there are many more fish in the sea. For her as well as for you. If Miss Sally Lang prefers to lunch with me that is her choice. I would advise you not to interfere. There may be extremely unpleasant consequences.'

'For me? Or Miss Lang?'

'As I said, you would be well advised to mind your own business.'

I looked at him. He was quite calm, unemotional even. But his voice had assumed an undertone of menace which there was no mistaking. I would get no further here. But two could play at his game.

'No,' I said. 'I won't mind my own business. I'll be seeing you again, Mr Pravisar. Or is it Mr P.R.A. Visar?

98

Or Mr P. Ravisar? Whichever it is, will you tell him that the next time he sends his friends to see me, they are liable to find themselves talking to the police. Good evening.'

I turned and left, feeling his eyes on my back as I went through the door, shutting it behind me with a tingling sensation between my shoulder-blades. There was no one on the stairs, and Flamenco Street appeared as deserted as when I arrived, but I had a keen sense of being observed as I strode purposefully out into Wardour Street. The first public telephone box I found had been vandalised, its wires ripped out and hanging forlornly from the wall, the second refused to accept my 10p coin, spitting it straight through into the reject slot, and the third was jammed solid. Life was too short to protest to British Telecom, so I went into a nearby pub and ordered a pint of beer. The bar was empty and the pay phone was at the end of the bar fixed to a wall. It accepted my 10p without a murmur. I dialled home and listened to the ringing tone, leaning against the wall and watching the door. There was no reply after twenty rings so I hung up again and tried the Scotland Yard number. A polite voice informed me that Detective Chief Superintendent Ashcroft had left a message to say that he had had no luck and would contact me in the morning. So much for police efficiency, I thought. What do I do next?

The answer, it turned out, was not left up to me. As I returned the receiver to its resting place for a second time, three large men came swiftly through the door.

'There he is,' said the man in the lead loudly and with spurious *bonhomie*. 'Roger, my old lad. We've been looking for you all day. Four pints please, squire,' he shouted to the barman. 'On our friend here. It's his round.'

I was hemmed in, surrounded by large muscular bodies. There was no one else in the pub to help me, and no room to move, even if I had felt I had a chance to escape. The barman pulled four pints of bitter and set them on the counter. The best thing to do seemed to be to play along with the charade. I felt in my back trouser pocket and came up with my last ten pound note.

'One for yourself,' I told the barman. At least he might remember me later. He grunted, rang up the total on the till and put the change in a glass behind him. As he turned round, the men on either side of me kicked me simultaneously behind both knees so my legs collapsed. As I went down the man in front punched me hard in the pit of the stomach and head-butted me as my body doubled forward. As my world turned full circle, through the pain and the shooting stars in my head I felt my arms grabbed to support me and heard a voice say: 'He's a bit pissed. Keep the change, mate. He'll never notice. We'll take him home. C'mon, Roger. The car's outside.'

I tried to speak but could not get my breath, and my tongue seemed to fill my mouth so that all that came out was an unintelligible wheezing. My newly-found 'friends' hustled me through the door and thrust me into the rear of a car where I slumped limp, hurt and helpless between two of them. The third, whom they called Dixie and who seemed to be the leader, got behind the wheel and drove off. I sat still, trying to control my whirling senses and to see where I was being taken, calculating that the quieter I kept the less I would get hurt. I was wrong again. My friend on the right produced a short piece of lead piping and hit me scientifically behind the right ear. My head exploded in a flash of pain and when I woke up the world was pitch black and I was lying on a hard cement floor with my face buried in wood shavings. My wrists were taped behind my back and my ankles were taped together. I could bend and straighten my legs, but that was all. My head ached like hell and when I tried to move it a shaft of pain shot from my neck and seemed to envelope my whole body.

With considerable muscular and mental effort I worked my eyebrows up and down. The pain soon stopped that, but not before I discovered that my eyes had been taped across too. That explained the darkness. My nose twitched, and I realised that the smell was familiar. I sniffed again. Willow shavings and cattle-hoof glue. I was taped up on the floor of a bat-making factory. I calculated that against all reason, it must be our own shop, in which case I knew the layout like the palm of my hand. I had no idea what I was doing there trussed like a chicken. The blow on the back of my neck seemed to have wiped out my memory, but it was slowly beginning to work. Painfully. Cautiously, using my legs to propel myself along and my feet as sensors, I worked my way round the floor.

It did seem like our own work-room. This was the main bench, with the specially-shaped vices for holding bats. At the further end my feet identified the cast-iron stand of the bat press cemented into the floor. Behind my head, in the centre of the room, there ought to have been the small sawing-bench. I pushed myself backwards carefully, but nearly passed out again when the sore part of my head struck the metal stand. When it cleared, I rolled over onto my stomach and, using the bench as a lever, raised myself slowly and with exquisite agony to my knees. Immediately I felt better able to breathe. Behind my back I felt the hard timber of a workbench. By a sort of hula-hoop movement, I sidled along it until my hands touched the handle of the vice and grasped it. I pulled myself upright and leant against it, searching with my taped hands as far back and along the bench as I could reach. My fingers touched a round wooden handle. I picked it up, and worked my grip along it until my fingers felt the cold steel angles of the blade. A chisel. I had no wish to risk committing suicide by cutting my wrists to pieces with its razor-sharp blade, but I had no alternative. I managed to reverse the chisel so that its handle lay between my fingers and the blade pointed upwards between my wrists. Slowly, with infinite care, I worked my fingers down the handle, pushing the blade upwards through the narrow space between my taped wrists. The cutting edge reached the tape and instantly began to slice into it. Forcing my wrists apart to increase the tension, I made my fingers press against the chisel. I felt the tape begin to give, and increased the pressure. There was a burning sensation in my left wrist and I felt blood running down between my hands but I ignored it and pressed on. The tape gave suddenly and the chisel fell onto the bench with a clatter as I brought my hands round with some difficulty and tore the tape from my mouth and eyes.

My instinct had been correct. I was standing in the Willford workshop, my ankles still taped together and blood from the cut on my left wrist already congealing. I used a piece of the tape as a temporary repair job and quickly freed my ankles. My head was no better, but I ignored the throbbing ache as best I could and tried to take stock of my situation. Slowly my memory began to come back and I recalled being thrust into the car. How long ago was that? I looked at my left wrist, but my watch had gone. The chisel cut crossed where the strap had been. Indeed, there was my watch, the strap slashed, on the workbench where it had fallen in my efforts to free myself. It was still functioning and told me that it was five o'clock. The cool light indicated morning. What had I been doing? My aching brain reluctantly returned the answer; looking for Sally. Sally who? Oh yes, Persse's stepdaughter. And my father. Father? Real fear overrode my lassitude. With increasing haste I searched the workshop. There was no sign of him. I ran into the house, not noticing that the doors to both the workshop and the kitchen were unlocked, and moved swiftly through the rooms, calling him. Nothing. There were a couple of plates and a cup and saucer soaking in the kitchen sink. It was his habit to rinse crockery off before putting it in the dishwasher, and it looked as though he had just finished a meal. Apart from that, the house was undisturbed, and my concern grew as I searched fruitlessly through each room in turn.

I went to the telephone. As I lifted the receiver a folded piece of paper fell onto the desk. I picked it up and unfolded it to find one line of type: *If you telephone the police you will never see either of them again.* It was unsigned. Very slowly, I returned the telephone to its cradle and sat down to try to figure out what to do next. As I looked at it, my mind blank with worry, it produced an answer. It rang.

'Pravisar here. I gather you have managed to free yourself. You got my note? Good. I trust you have not contacted the police?'

The arrogance in his voice flicked my worry into anger. 'If you've hurt either of them, I'll . . .'

'I don't think so, North. They will not be harmed if you do exactly as I say. First, you will destroy that note and tell the police nothing. Second, you will instruct your agents to arrange to export container shipments of five hundred cricket bats to each of the addresses I shall give you in Trinidad, California, the Netherlands, South Africa and Australia. And third, you will continue to play cricket for Surrey, if selected, to the best of your ability. Is that clear?'

'What if I refuse?'

'Then you will receive your father's right ear in the post tomorrow morning. If you continue to act stubbornly, you will receive a piece of Miss Lang's anatomy. Shall we say a nipple? I am sure you would welcome that.'

When I could find words to reply, they were totally inadequate. 'You're a bastard,' I said.

'Maybe. But if you do as I say, neither Mr North nor Miss Lang will be harmed. You have my word on that.'

'But all this doesn't make sense. It's crazy. There's no way we can export 2,500 cricket bats at once. We'd have a job to find twenty-five within a month.'

'That need not concern you. I will arrange delivery to the shippers. Telephone me when you have made the necessary arrangements. Here is the number.'

He read out a London number, different from that in the Surrey office files. He made me read it back.

103

I said: 'I don't know what you're trying to do, but you're not going to get anywhere. The police are already looking for you. And Miss Lang. Since yesterday afternoon.'

'If they find me,' he said. 'It will be your father's funeral.' And hung up.

I sat and looked at the telephone some more, but it still offered no inspiration. Then I picked it up and dialled Dulwich. At least there was one person I could talk to, though what a motherly widow of a former cricketer could do in these circumstances, I had no idea. There was no reply.

Sick with renewed fear, I dialled again and listened to the ringing tone. I was getting used to it, but it did nothing for my state of mind. My father's keys were still on the hook in the kitchen where he always left them, so I took them and got the red Scirocco out of the garage and drove back to London, my foot flat down all the way until I met the morning traffic through Croydon. Even so, I must have broken most traffic laws and several speed records around Crystal Palace before pulling up with a squeal of brakes outside Mrs Marchbanks's house in Dulwich. Her scarlet Roadster was standing on the little drive in front of the garage and Mrs M herself was sitting at the kitchen table enjoying a cup of coffee. Its fragrance hit me as I burst into the room. She gave a little scream.

'Good heavens, Roger. How you startled me. What's the matter? Are you all right? You look white. Have a cup of coffee.'

'Where've you been?' I demanded. 'I couldn't get you. I've been trying to phone.'

'Oh, it was such a beautiful morning that I couldn't resist going for a little drive. Before the traffic, you know,' she said complacently, pouring out coffee as she spoke. 'Now settle down, Roger, and tell me exactly what's on your mind. There's nothing like getting things off your chest. Are you in trouble with Surrey?'

'I'm in trouble all right,' I said grimly. 'But not with Surrey.'

'It's something to do with Persse's death, isn't it?' Mrs Marchbanks said shrewdly.

'I don't really know but, well, yes, I think so. Can I tell you? I've got to talk to someone, if only to sort myself out.'

'You'd better start at the beginning. I'll get on with some breakfast while you're talking,' she said, tossing a large rasher of bacon expertly into a pan, where it began to sizzle and spit invitingly. I told her everything, from my father's confession that he had doctored the bat onwards. Mrs Marchbanks placed a hot plate in front of me and there was a pause while I negotiated a breakfast fit for a king, provided he wasn't on a diet, while my landlady sipped a large mug of coffee and listened as I finished my story slightly incoherently through large mouthfuls of toast.

'So you see why I can't go back to the police.'

Mrs Marchbanks sniffed.

'I don't think you have any alternative. This is blackmail. You *must* tell the police everything. They're the people to deal with it. They'll know what to do.'

'But why should they believe me? It all sounds so far-fetched.'

Mrs Marchbanks put down her coffee firmly and fixed me with what could only be described as a glare.

'Are you in the habit of lying to the police, Roger? Or to anybody?'

'No-o. I suppose not.'

'Then why should you start now? You know whatsis-name, Inspector Light, and he likes you. You'll have to tell him everything sooner or later, and if it's to be any help it'd better be sooner. Ring them now.'

For all her comfortable appearance, when Mrs March-banks spoke in those tones she intended to be obeyed. Meekly I picked up the phone and dialled Scotland Yard.

But before the switchboard answered I replaced the receiver. I knew only too well that Pravisar would not hesitate to carry out his threat. I had a bruised body, an aching head and a slashed wrist to prove it.

'I'm sorry, Mrs M,' I said. 'I can't do it. There's too much at risk.' A thought struck me. 'And please, don't you go calling them either.'

'All right, Roger. I promise. But you will be careful, won't you? This Pravisar sounds a very dangerous man indeed. He'd be better behind bars. What are you going to do?'

I wished I knew. I was worried sick with fear and anger. My only plan of action was inaction; to play along with Pravisar's demands and try to discover where Sally and my father were being held. I changed into shorts and a T-shirt and told Mrs Marchbanks that I was going for a run. I have often found that physical action helps and that a few laps round the Dulwich College playing fields does wonders for clearing the brain. Half-way round my first lap I had sorted out one clue; by the end of the third I had had another and had decided on my next step. I ran home, showered and shaved and headed for The Oval. I wanted to be there before the rest of the players.

I was lucky. The dressing room and showers were empty. I chose a locker where I could watch the door and changed into whites before the first man arrived. It was Jeff Jason, the surly all-rounder with whom I shared a strong mutual dislike. He dropped his cricket bag with a crash when he saw me.

'What are you doing here, sonny boy?' he sneered. 'Sucking up to the skipper again, I suppose?'

'Not this time, Fleece,' I said mildly. It was a nickname the erudite Symonds had given him and it had stuck. 'I wanted to talk to you. Have you got a brother?'

'What if I have?'

106

'I'd like you to give him a message from me,' I said. I stood up and idly took a bat from my bag, twirling it in my fingers. 'Just tell him to leave me alone if he values his health. And his liberty.'

'I don't know what you mean,' he said sullenly. 'Are you threatening my brother?'

He stood up belligerently to defend the Jason family honour, so I hit him firmly below the belt with the toe of the bat. Jason collapsed onto a locker clutching himself, his face a study in pain and rage.

'You little f. . .'

I interrupted him by pointing the bat at his nose.

'Don't say it. I'm bigger than you are.'

He said it anyway, and lunged forward to grab the bat. Instead of pulling it away, I jabbed it forward far enough to meet his oncoming nose with some force and send him back into a sitting position with blood spurting between his fingers.

He cowered as I moved closer to him. I did not have much time. The other players would be arriving at any moment. I spoke slowly.

'Tell him that I want to talk to him. Alone. Tonight.'

'Why should I?'

I motioned with the bat. Jason flinched.

'Tell him if he doesn't talk to me he'll have to talk to the police.'

'Where?'

'Tell him where we met before. The first time. He'll know.'

'Bob won't meet you. Bastard.' The last word was muttered under his breath. I chose not to notice.

'Tell him. He'll come. And alone. Understand?'

He nodded, looking at me through his fingers. I threw him a towel and told him to clean himself up before the rest of the team arrived. Possibly understandably, he went to the washroom with a bad grace and I made another mental resolve to watch my back in daylight as well as

107

in the dark. Jason had the air of one who would bear a grudge for a very long time.

My first egg was laid. I would have to wait to see if it would hatch.

5

In spite of the stiffness caused by my bruising and the growing concern for Sally and my father, 'practice in the middle' went pretty well that morning. I have often noticed that a distraction – a slight muscle strain, for example – can relax you on the field of play itself, removing some of the tension which causes you to try too hard and having a similar calming effect to the mild beta-blockers used by top musicians before a performance. I revelled in the release of physical energy in the open air and thoroughly enjoyed a stint of eight overs. I found my rhythm on my first run-up and felt my arm go over high and straight and with that little extra 'zip' which injects life into the blandest of pitches. I felt in control of myself and the batsmen, and they sensed it. I obtained greatest satisfaction by hitting Jason just above his 'box' first ball and having him caught behind the wicket by Hills two overs later. After the session Smithson told me: 'Okay, Roger. You're in against Lancashire. Open at one end and bat number nine. Well done, lad. What's up with your arm?'

He indicated the substantial piece of sticking plaster on my left wrist.

'Nothing. Just a scratch with a chisel on the bench.'

'Off you go to the physio and have it dressed.'

'Okay Skip. But it's not giving me any trouble. I don't want to bother her.'

Jayne Osborne was a physiotherapist whose treatment made short work of most of the various aches and sprains a fit cricketer sustains through the long hot summers, and it suited the county to save the expense of a doctor and regard her as expert in everything affecting the human body from pneumonia to acne. Short of major surgery, there was little Jayne did not undertake to cure with common sense, an elastic bandage and an aspirin, and she affected deafness to the inevitable coarse suggestions both from cricketers and crowds. However, the Surrey players regarded her warily, for once on the treatment couch they were at her mercy, and she was physically very strong. She was also inquisitive and I did not want to face a series of penetrating questions about the origin of my various aches and pains. Cricketers are not supposed to indulge in brawling, particularly during the playing season. So I avoided the physiotherapy room and made instead for the secretary's office. Inexperienced fool that I was, after the previous day's encounter I felt I might receive gentler and more personal attention from Angie.

'The Secretary's not seeing anyone today,' she told me briskly. She wore a high-necked blouse with a cravat under a mannishly-cut jacket, and her hair was screwed severely into a bun. 'And players shouldn't wear boots in the pavilion.'

'I just wanted to see if there were any messages and if you were free for lunch,' I said, disregarding her manner.

'The answer is no.' Her eyes had changed colour, like her manner. They were more grey than green today.

'No messages? Or no lunch?'

'Lunch. I don't go out with cricketers.'

That wasn't the impression I had received the previous day, but her manner was so definite that I felt it wiser not to pursue the matter. I began to realise that rejection to Angie was a mortal insult.

'But there was a message?'

'Three. You seem to be popular this morning.' Her tone

suggested that she could not see why. 'Detective Inspector Light would like you to call him at Scotland Yard. He said your car has been found. Miss Lang left a number for you to call her. And your father rang to say would you call him at home as soon as possible. It seems you were making a great deal of fuss about nothing yesterday.'

So that was it. She didn't believe me. Through some strange process of reasoning Angie had persuaded herself that I had invented the whole story. To seduce her? Hardly; she had been the leader of the office dance the previous day. I felt the bruise at the base of my neck behind my ear and decided against showing it to her.

'Can I use the phone?'

'Not in the office. There's a pay phone outside the dressing room for the use of the players.'

I dug in my pocket and found a pound coin.

'Have you got 10p?' But Angie was not to be softened.

'Sorry. Try in the shop,' she said brusquely, turning back to her keyboard. 'I haven't got time for gossip. I'm busy.'

I looked at her unresponsive back. My head was still spinning, but her news gave even the most pointed snub a roseate hue. I suppressed a mild desire to run a finger down her attractive spine and headed for the dressing-room telephone.

Angie's messages had been correct. My father was at home, and worried why I hadn't been in touch with him before. He seemed to have lost a whole day or more; he remembered my departure with Sally on the Sunday morning and talking to the Scotland Yard men, but very little after that. Monday was a complete blank and he had woken up that morning in his bed with a headache. He had not realised it was Tuesday until he looked at the cricket reports in his newspaper.

'Father, has Pravisar been in touch with you?'

'N-no, I don't think so. It's funny, but I can't remember anything at all about yesterday. There was something . . .

a man came into the workshop in the morning early and everything's a blur after that until I woke up this morning. I must have had a turn. Heart or something. I don't feel too good today. I'll have to go for a check-up.'

'Do that, Dad. Go to the doc. This morning. I expect you're right.' It was good advice anyway, and I didn't want to tell him that he'd been got out of the way so that Pravisar could teach me a lesson: to do what I was told.

'He made me a proposition,' I told him. 'He wants to use us to export a hell of a lot of bats we haven't got.'

'Hmm. To act as his agents, do you mean?'

'Something like that.'

'I don't like the sound of it, Roger. You'd better come down and we'll talk about it. You haven't committed us, I hope.'

'I'm afraid I had to. I'll tell you about it tonight on the blower. Haven't got time now. I'm off to Liverpool. I'm in the team against Lancashire.'

The enthusiasm came back instantly to my father's voice.

'Good lad. Batting or bowling?'

'Bowling, mainly. I'll be opening. I'll be batting eight or nine, probably.'

'I won't wish you good luck, lad. If you do your best you'll be fine.'

'Thanks, Dad. I'll call you tonight.'

Sally was at home, in Blackheath, and indignant that she had heard nothing from me since before lunch on Sunday.

'I thought we were going to have lunch together, and you said something about going out for the afternoon. You left me sitting there, so I . . .' Her voice trailed off.

'So you what?'

'I . . .' she stopped again.

'I looked for you everywhere, I was worried. You went out to lunch with Pravisar,' I said.

'I did?' She sounded genuinely surprised.

'He said you did. At the Savoy. He said it was a business lunch. You had an appointment with him.'

'I . . . I can't remember.'

'Lunch at the Savoy isn't something you forget easily. Even with a creep like Pravisar.'

'Look,' she said, and her voice held a sort of desperate earnestness. 'I can't remember, honestly. I . . . I seem to have lost a couple of days. I do remember Suri coming up to me at The Oval. After that it's all a bit of a blur until I woke up this morning. I've been expecting to hear from you all day. I've still got your car. The one you hired.'

For the time being, I let her use of Pravisar's first name pass. She sounded sincere enough, but the loss of memory seemed too much of a coincidence with what my father had said. Could Sally be making excuses? I wanted to believe her, but something was happening that I did not like or understand.

'Stay right there,' I said. 'I'm coming over to collect it. I need it. I'm driving up to Liverpool tonight.'

'Oh.' She sounded a bit flat. 'Liverpool? Why?'

'I'm playing cricket for Surrey against Lancashire tomorrow. At Aigburth. It's my job. Or don't you remember that?'

To my astonishment, there was a muffled sob over the telephone.

'Don't get cross with me. I can't help it.'

'And don't go all "little girl" on me.'

I put the telephone down with a bang, but underneath my spurt of irritation I was seriously worried. The whole conversation seemed so out of character for the self-possessed, business-like girl who had enjoyed the thrill of the chase at 80mph only two days before.

In the cab on the way to Blackheath I tried to make sense out of a situation which was fast getting out of hand. It seemed that Pravisar wanted to establish some sort of hold over me, although I could not understand why. He seemed to have everything he wanted – a firm place in the bat-making industry, money and influence. I had none of these things. Why should he set the bully boys onto me? I had done nothing to incur his wrath, except save him from injury at Lord's. What had happened to Sally and my father? Had he drugged them somehow? Again, why? And what, if anything, did this all have to do with the death of Grace? Nothing made sense.

Sally wasn't much help, either. She handed me the keys of the Alfa with a dismissive air and fended off my questions about what had happened on Sunday. I tried the oblique approach.

'I didn't know you knew Pravisar.'

'Why should you? Suri was a friend of my stepfather's. A business friend. What's it got to do with you?'

'You might have told me you were going to have lunch with him.'

'But I wasn't. I told you. Suri found me at The Oval when I was waiting for you. I think he said something about you being called away. By the captain, or secretary. After that, I don't remember what happened.'

'The man at the gate said you drove off with Pravisar in the Alfa. You were driving.'

'I suppose I must have been. Suri doesn't drive.'

'Why do you call him Suri? Do you like him?'

'No, not really. He's a very interesting man. He's been everywhere. He can speak seven languages. But I think he's creepy.'

'Do you remember what you talked about at the Savoy?'

'You keep saying we had lunch at the Savoy. I don't remember that at all, I keep telling you,' she said crossly.

'Where did you have lunch, then?'

'I don't know.'

'And you don't remember driving back here?'

'No.'

'And you woke up in bed this morning?'

'Yes.'

114

'Dressed, or undressed?'

She flushed. 'Don't be personal.'

'No,' I said gently. 'But if you don't remember how you got home, or going to bed, who took your clothes off?'

'I must have undressed myself,' she said. 'In any case, it's no business of yours. Do you want some tea before you go?'

'Don't worry, I won't trouble you,' I said with some bitterness. 'I know when I'm not wanted.'

Unaccountably, she began to cry. It was so unlike her that my annoyance evaporated in anxiety. I moved across the room to her chair and put my arms around her. For a moment she relaxed against me and then stiffened and pulled away.

'Don't, Roger, I can't. Suri . . .'

'Suri what?' I stopped myself shaking her. 'What has he done? Tell me.'

'Nothing. It . . . it's none of your business. Leave me alone.'

I could get nothing more out of her, except that she had no idea what business Pravisar was engaged upon, and that she was going down to Willford to carry on learning to make cricket bats. After the extraordinary events of the weekend, I wasn't too sure how safe that was, but at least my father and Sally would be able to keep an eye on each other.

'Take care,' I said, and meant it in more ways than one.

It was time to drive to the squash club. It was a few minutes to seven so I parked the Alfa on the single yellow line and waited for the man I knew as Bob Jason. I wondered if I had been foolish in asking to meet him. To my surprise at exactly seven o'clock a burly figure appeared alone around the corner, hands in jacket pockets. It was the man who had tried to hijack Grace's Mercedes and who had driven the black Jaguar. He had a large bruise on his forehead and his face was decorated with several pieces of sticking-plaster. I surmised that he had gone through the windscreen. He looked pretty tough. I wondered if he had found another cosh. I got out and stood with my back to the car, trying to appear completely at ease. I did not want to appear a sitting duck.

'What d'yer want with me?' He spoke in a rough, defensive voice.

'Get in the car and you'll find out,' I said as harshly as I could. 'I'm not going to hurt you.' I hoped he had similar intentions towards me. But I calculated that while I kept the car on the move, he wouldn't be foolish enough to attack me again.

'Where we goin'?' he asked as I let in the clutch.

'Nowhere in particular. Just for a drive.' I headed down the A2.

'What d'yer want?' he asked again, belligerently.

'Information.'

'That costs,' he said, keeping his eyes on me. I eased a ten pound note from my inside jacket pocket.

'That's for the ride. There's more for the information.'

He snatched at the tenner.

'Who's paying you?'

'Dunno 'is name. 'E's black. Posh-spoken.'

'Is he called Pravisar?'

'He might be.'

'What did he want you to do?'

'Just nick the gear in the boot and rough you up a bit.'

'Did he say why?'

'Nah. Except there was something 'e wanted.'

'What about Dulwich?'

'That's all.'

I fished out another ten pound note and repeated the question.

'You were a bit tougher than we expected. We wasn't going to hurt you. Much. 'E was particular about the old woman, too. Not to 'urt 'er.'

'Where do you meet him?'

116

'Anywhere. Mostly pubs, different ones. In Soho.'

'Have you worked for him before?'

He hesitated. Another tenner changed hands.

'Done a bit of van driving. Pickin' up cricket bats and so on.'

'And a bit of Jaguar driving on the side?'

He scowled. 'We was only going to put you off the road. 'E was getting mad with you. You got lucky, this time.'

'Where did you pick up the bats?'

'Willford, in Sussex, for one. Couple of places in Essex. One near Hitchin. One up in Yorkshire. Liverpool.'

'Write down the addresses. There's a biro and a notebook in the glove box.'

He did so, laboriously. It cost me another tenner to discover where Jason delivered the cricket bats he had collected. There was a place called Fairbridge Farm near Witham, in Essex, he said, where a modern barn had been turned into a warehouse. Several hundred bats were stacked there; maybe a couple of thousand, but there was room for many more. There was a work-bench with a lathe and other tools. He thought there were two more teams picking up bats for Pravisar.

'Do you know what he's going to do with all those bats?'

'Export them I suppose.'

There was nothing more I could get out of him, although I suspected he was not half as dumb as he seemed. Although his brother Jeff was a cricketer, Bob professed to know nothing about the game. He had worked at Smithfield and Billingsgate and 'in the motor trade' until Jeff had introduced him to Pravisar a couple of years ago. He seemed frightened of Pravisar, although I could not discover why. He knew nothing of Persse Grace except that he had 'died on the telly'. But he was in no doubt about my future, or lack of one.

"E'll get you. 'E always does. You'd better watch out,' was all he would say. I pulled up in Brixton High Street.

'You've had forty quid from me today. Let me know when he's coming to get me, as you put it, and you can double it,' I said. 'If you don't, you'll be dealing with Detective Inspector Light of Scotland Yard.'

Eighty pounds seemed reasonable insurance for advance warning of another attack. Thinking of the way Grace died I shivered inside. When it came to violence Pravisar seemed to have a wide range of options. I did not really think that Jason would do what he was told. In fact, I was certain that he would report the whole interview to Pravisar, which was partly my intention. I had to find out what lay behind all this, and one way seemed to be to provoke Pravisar into showing his hand. There was always a chance, too, that a man of Jason's moral calibre would see the opportunity to play both ends against the middle and make a two-way profit. I thrust the piece of paper he had given me with the addresses into my blazer pocket, dropped my dubious new ally off and headed north for the M1, trying to concentrate solely on the driving and to put the problems of Pravisar from my mind.

It was a good drive and the Alpha ran like a dream, but it still took four hours before I checked in to the plastic luxury of the Apollyon. There was a note from Hills, my room-mate, saying they would be in the bar if I wasn't too late. At a quarter to midnight, the bar was fairly full, mainly with under-dressed and over-made-up girls and Liverpool's version of Hooray Henrys, but I could see no sign of the Surrey team, so I ordered a pint of orange juice and a plate of sandwiches, found a space at a table in the corner and sat down to relax.

'Bit late, aren't you, son? I saw you come in. I was waiting for you.'

It was Harry Carnock, the coach, pint glass in hand and eager for a chat. He sat down and, without asking, stuffed one of my sandwiches into his mouth. I realised why the rest of the team had gone to bed. He was a gingery, colourless man, with eyebrows so light that he appeared not

118

to have any, and very pale, slightly protuberant eyes.

'I was held up on the motorway.' I did not want to discuss anything with Carnock, but he pressed on.

'Jason said you were meeting his brother.'

'Yes,' I said, shortly.

'They're a rough bunch, Roger,' said Carnock, frowning seriously into his glass. 'You don't want to get mixed up with them.'

'How do you know that, Harry?'

'You'd be surprised what I know,' he said. 'Let me give you a bit of advice, lad.'

'What's that?'

'If you want to get on in this world, you've got to know your place,' he said enigmatically. 'And do what you're told.'

The whole team knew that it was a dictum that Carnock had followed meticulously all his life. It had not endeared him to them as a man or as a coach. The unproven, probably unfair suspicion was that Grace had employed him because he had no mind of his own, and would act as an informer in the ranks. I wondered what he was getting at.

'How's Frank?' he asked, raising those invisible eyebrows. For a moment I wondered what he was talking about.

'Frank? Oh, Frank,' I said stupidly. 'Father's okay. Busy. I didn't know you knew him.'

'Known him for years,' said Carnock. 'I wouldn't want anything to happen to him. Better get a good night's sleep. 'Night.'

He emptied his glass purposefully, set it on the table with an air of finality, and strode off, leaving me looking at his retreating back. I shrugged. I must be getting paranoid – Carnock was just one of the less pleasant facets of a cricketer's life.

Without looking back, he passed through the swing doors to the bar. I made to follow him, but found my way blocked by two girls wielding autograph books and ballpoint pens. They both spoke in broad Liverpudlian. The dark-haired girl went into bat first.

'We follow the cricket. We know who you are. Sign there,' she ordered, thrusting a pen into my hand. I scribbled quickly and gave it back to her.

'Sorry, I'm in a hurry.' I brushed between them.

'In a hurry to go to bed?' said the blonde. 'Can we come with you?'

'Not tonight, Josephine.'

As I pushed through the door, I heard one of them say: 'Cheeky bugger. How did he know my name?'

Carnock had gone, and the indicator on the lift registered the eighth floor. Going back to finish my drink and the few sandwiches Harry Carnock had left me meant being accosted again, so I abandoned them to the groupies and made my way slowly to the room I was sharing with Hills. He'd taken the bed nearest the window and, as I expected, he was already fast asleep, breathing rhythmically and (mercifully) quietly. At least, I thought as I unpacked my case and brushed my teeth, he doesn't have the smoker's snore. On a previous trip as twelfth man I had been kept awake for hours by the regular foghorn trumpeting of Gerry Down, but this night I slept like a log through to seven in the morning, when I was awakened by the sound of Hills in the shower. I telephoned home, where my father reported that all was well. Sally Lang had returned the previous evening and was staying in the spare room and was, he said with some satisfaction, cooking bacon and eggs at that moment. He had decided to comply with Pravisar's scheme for exporting cricket bats, not because of my fears, but because he had persuaded himself that Frank North & Son would make a very good profit for no risk and no outlay. He had told Strangs, our shipping agents, to get busy on the paperwork. I could hear the basic doubt in his voice: 'They said that everything should be ready by the end of the week, providing there are no complications.'

120

'Complications? Why should there be? Providing Pravi-sar's got the bats. And he says he has.' I hoped I sounded convincing. I think we were trying to hide the truth from ourselves and from each other.

'Oh, well.' He sounded as though he was still having second thoughts, so to cheer him up I told him about Josephine the night before, but that only provoked another worry about the company he thought I was keeping.

'Don't fuss, Dad. I'm a big boy now, remember? In any case, I'm rooming with Phil Hills. He'll keep me under control. Do you want to have a word with him?' He knew Phil, and liked him. I handed over the phone, and they exchanged a few pleasantries. Hills said goodbye, put down the instrument and said:

'Keep your left elbow up when you're batting and your left shoulder high when you're bowling. Them's your instructions. That's all.'

'Thanks. He won't wish me good luck; it's bad luck, he says. That's all the advice he's ever given me.'

'That's all you'll ever need, with your action and your eye. Like me. Bob Taylor told me to take everything behind the stumps below waist-high and to take half-volley throws going forward.'

'Why's that? The half-volleys, I mean?'

'It makes both the bowler and the fielder look good. And it's easier with the gloves on. But they used to say of Taylor, you couldn't hear the ball enter the gloves, his timing was so perfect.'

'Anyway, Phil, have you got any tips for me? This is my big chance, today.'

'Ay, lad. A couple. If you get wickets, forget it. If you get runs, forget it. If you're out first ball and take nought for 150, forget it. If you've got what it takes, you'll find out after your second season.'

'Two seasons?'

'Ay. And there's summat else. Watch for my signal. If I don't go down at the start of your run-up, put it in fast and a bit short down leg side. I'll be up behind the stumps by the time you let go and the batsman won't 'ave noticed. We'll 'ave 'im. But that's enough shop, now. Let's get some breakfast.'

We ambled down amiably to the breakfast room, where I was surprised to see Down and Symonds sharing a table with the girls of my brief encounter the previous night, Josephine and her friend who, I gathered from their high-pitched conversation, was known on the cricket circuit as 'Trees'.

'Rather them than me,' said Hills, helping himself to a liberal plate of scrambled eggs and bacon and pouring out coffee. 'They'll regret it by the time the day's through. I don't reckon 'twas too difficult to bowl them maidens over. That was one I heard you telling your dad about, eh?'

I nodded. 'They made me an offer.'

'Good thing you didn't take it up. I'd have paddled their backsides and sent them home to mother if they'd come up to the room. And yours.'

'You and who else?'

'You asked me for a bit of advice. I'll tell you what my old man told me, and he was blunt Yorkshire who played for county for twenty years. Crumpet and cricket don't mix, he used to say. You mark my words. If we field today, those two will be knackered by lunch-time.' He looked across the room at Down and Symonds. He took my silence for agreement.

'And that lot are the worst,' he warmed to his subject. 'They call themselves groupies. My old man would've called them whores. They travel round the counties and talk as if they know it all. They don't know cricket. All they're interested in is what goes into a cricketer's box and what comes out of his pocket. Leave 'em alone, son.'

'I've got my own fish to fry,' I said, and surprised myself to find that I was thinking of Sally Lang, the cool blonde who was learning how to make a cricket bat.

122

We drove the couple of miles to Aigburth cricket ground, one of the more pleasant locations we found ourselves in from time to time. It was quite a change from The Oval, or Old Trafford, Lancashire's home ground in Manchester. Aigburth Cricket Club was a tree-lined circle of brilliant green grass, and its pavilion might have been built as a mansion for a Victorian mill-owner or shipping magnate. Its pile of old red bricks concealed behind curlicues and pillars a wealth of rooms on three storeys, two fine, panelled dressing rooms and some old-fashioned iron baths and two bars already doing a roaring trade at ten in the morning. We did some leisurely warming-up exercises – Carnock did not put in an appearance until they were finished – and then strolled out to examine the wicket. There had been quite a campaign in the press to persuade counties to eliminate these 'out' matches – matches not at county headquarters' grounds – in order to eliminate dodgy pitches, but I was glad to see that this had been resisted by the county authorities and by the Test and County Cricket Board. The campaign seemed to me to be inspired by nothing more than the idleness of cricket correspondents who wished to avoid travelling to and working with the rather limited facilities provided for them at the 'out' grounds, while ignoring the importance of taking the game of cricket to the people in order to keep it alive. There certainly appeared to be nothing wrong with the Aigburth square and I instantly prayed that we would bat first. I had no desire to bowl first on this shaven, bone-hard piece of marl and clay with a comparatively small outfield. It had an ominous air of 'nought for plenty' about it.

Which went to prove my lack of experience and judgement. Smithson won the toss at a quarter to eleven and strode back to our dressing room, not exactly rubbing his hands with glee, but beaming. 'We're fielding,' he said. 'Get your pads on, Phil.'

I sat down on my locker and tried to control my nerves. In a few minutes I would be called upon to bowl my fastest on that twenty-two yard brick strip. No one else could do it for me. My hands were sweating. I wiped them on my flannels. Phil Hills saw the action and grinned.

'Butterflies, young Rodge?' he asked kindly.

'Red admirals,' I said, thankful to joke, however poorly. 'But what's the skip thinking of? That track's like glass. And there's no cloud cover. It won't swing. They'll get a thousand.'

'We'll see. Just keep it on a length. The pitch will do the rest. We've played here before, you know.' I was not convinced. Hills looked at me quizzically. 'It'll seam and bounce. The sea's just over there. I dunno why, but it makes a difference.'

'Hmmm.'

The sun rode high in the sky and already the temperature was in the high seventies, but there was a bit of a breeze, presumably off the sea 'just over there'. On Hills's advice but under protest, I donned a long-sleeved sweat shirt and my white Surrey pullover.

'Surely it's hot enough out there already.'

'Never let your back get cold,' he said. 'Even if you want to. If you sweat and get the wind on it, that way lies pulled muscles. End of career.'

Smithson led us out onto the field, to a smattering of applause and some friendly catcalls. The Lancashire crowd knew its cricket and greeted its opponents from the despised South with tolerant superiority.

'See you've got twelfth man on field,' called one spectator. 'You're going to need thirteenth an' all by time we've finished with you lot.'

This sally was greeted by a round of laughter, drowned as the Lancashire opening batsmen, Tony Johnson and the West Indian test player, Malcolm Morgan, came down the pavilion steps behind us. They passed me on their way to the wicket. They looked what they were: vastly experienced and more than competent cricketers. Both

124

carried bats scarred by many innings, and in the case of Morgan, more than eighty centuries. He had been nicknamed the Pirate, or Cap'n Morgan, by the press, for his swashbuckling style and ferocious hitting. I had never seen him close to before, and it surprised me that he seemed too small, frail even, to have accomplished all that he had done. He had a shock of grey hair which stood out from his head and gleamed gold in the sun like a halo. He disdained to wear a helmet. I felt I might make him regret that. Johnson carried his bat in his left hand, dwarfing the Pirate. He had a large handlebar moustache and a face weathered by fifteen seasons for Lancashire. He had never received a test call, which many thought he deserved, but he was respected throughout cricket as a true professional. The pair held the Lancashire record opening stand of 323, scored against Northants at Blackpool, the county's other 'out' ground.

George Lodge, the statuesque umpire, produced the game ball from his pocket, unwrapped it from its soft polythene cover, and handed it gravely to Smithson. Completing the ritual, Smithson examined it perfunctorily, polished it briefly on his backside and threw it to me. I was so surprised that I fumbled the catch and nearly dropped the ball. It was rock hard, deep blood red and with a sheen that felt both dry and oily, like a polished refectory table. Smithson had obviously decided to toss me in at the deep end to prevent the wait playing havoc with my nerves. Which was all very well, I thought, taking the marker from Lodge and pacing out my run. Behind me Morgan took guard, thumping his bat purposefully into the iron-hard batting crease as the Surrey fielders scattered to their predetermined positions.

'Nine, ten, eleven, twelve.' I scraped the grass with my studs and pressed down the marker with my boot. With my back to the wicket and facing the pavilion I swung my arms alternately to loosen my shoulders, looking round at the field as I did so. I was a bit miffed that Smithson had given me only two slips, but didn't feel confident enough to ask for more. Then I took two more paces away from the wicket, grasped the ball in my right hand with two fingers along the seam, swung round and began my run-up without even looking at the batsman. For the first few paces I had the habit of watching the ground as I gathered pace and balance. It was a mistake.

Half way to the wicket my eyes came up, to see the white-clad arm of the umpire stretched horizontally, blocking my path. Behind it, at what seemed a hell of a long twenty-two yards, Morgan the batsman was stepping away from his crease, his left hand raised like a policeman stopping the traffic. I swore under my breath and pulled up.

'What's wrong, umpire?'

'Wait until the batsman is ready,' said Lodge sternly.

'Sorry, young 'un,' called Morgan from the other end, in mock contrition.

'That'll be the day,' I heard Johnson, his partner, mutter softly to himself. And Smithson came over from mid-off to say quietly: 'Don't let that old trick worry you, Roger. Settle down.'

It was good advice, but I was too angry with myself for falling for the ancient dodge of putting a bowler off his rhythm. 'I'll show the bastard,' I said to myself on the way back to my mark. 'I'll show him.'

I would have done, too, but for one thing. The ball was short and fast and leapt towards Morgan's throat; a near-perfect bumper. Had it hit him, it would probably have killed him, but the batsman never even flinched. He stepped across his wicket, inside the line of the ball and flung his bat around in the classic hook shot. But that early in his innings, his timing was a touch awry and the ball top-edged over the wicket-keeper's head and cleared the boundary by a good ten yards. The first scoring stroke off the first ball of the innings. Off my first ball in the championship. Six.

The bowler's classic answer to a hooked six, even if

it is a mis-hit, is a fast straight yorker, pitching into the block-hole and beating the bat with its speed. My second ball nearly achieved just that. It was fast, straight and on a full length, and Morgan's bat met it perfectly on the half-volley. The ball flashed back past my despairing plunge, straight along the ground, narrowly missing the stumps and rattling the boards of the sight-screen behind me as it leapt up from the boundary rope. Four. Ten off two balls. Not a good start for a young bowler beginning his career. I gritted my teeth and walked back to my mark, determined not to let the situation get on top of me. At the end of my run I stopped, deliberately relaxed my taut stomach muscles and took two slow deep breaths, careless of the crowd watching me.

That was better. I felt the tension leave my body. Deliberately I slowed my run to the wicket, holding the ball loosely in my right hand, concentrating on line and length. As my right arm came over, I felt it brush against my ear, as Geoff Arnold had taught me. Good. The ball looked a better one; on the off-stump, good length. Morgan, who had moved confidently onto the front foot ready to drive again, checked his stroke and jabbed uncertainly at the ball, missing it by a fraction as it floated away from the bat at the last moment. In the slips hands went up involuntarily and I gasped, choking back an appeal as Hills moved quietly to his right and took the ball, chest-high and rising. Hills patted his gloves together approvingly.

'Good ball.' Smithson spoke quietly from mid-off again, and there was a ripple of attention from the crowd. Morgan the batsman nodded his appreciation at me sportingly, and settled down more watchfully to face the next ball. This time I angled the seam fractionally towards the off and was gratified to see the ball swing sharply towards the slips. But the movement occurred too early to worry an experienced performer like Morgan, who merely lifted his bat and watched the ball fizz harmlessly off the pitch into Hills's safe gloves. It seemed as though the atmosphere and the wicket were going to help me, but my surge of confidence was rudely shattered when Morgan picked up my next ball, an in-swinger this time, and clipped it off middle-and-leg on the half-volley, one bounce into the crowd at square leg.

I ground my teeth again, determined that I should not be struck for another boundary off the last ball of the over, but wondering how I was going to prevent it. As I ran in to bowl I saw at the last moment that Hills had not gone into his customary crouch but was walking on tiptoe, quickly and lightly so as not to attract the batsman's attention, in towards the stumps, slightly on the leg side. Automatically my mind registered his instructions and I fired the ball wide of the leg stump, although not short-pitched as I should have. Morgan, coming forward to drive on the on side, reached forward and was beaten for speed, missing the ball as it flicked past him at knee-height, pitching on the popping crease. Hills, in one movement scooped up the ball on the half-volley and broke the wicket, with Morgan's rear foot a fraction outside his crease. Hills and the slips appealed simultaneously. Up went the square-leg umpire's finger, and a burst of astonishment and applause ran round the ground. My first wicket in county cricket.

Morgan marched by me, thrusting his bat under his arm and removing his batting gloves none too gently. But even his annoyance at himself for falling for one of cricket's classic sucker punches did not prevent him from muttering 'Well bowled, son,' as he passed me, for which I was grateful. The Surrey players gathered round, shaking my hand and thumping me on the back. To remove Morgan, a dangerous batsman at any time, so early in the innings was a plus for any bowler. Hills came up grinning and blowing into his left glove.

'Next time do what I bloody well tell you. Nigh broke my hand, that bugger did.'

'Thanks, Phil. That was great. Sorry I didn't pitch it shorter. I only saw you at the last moment.'

'Aye, well you look where you're going in future. We might get a few more of those.'

'Man in.' Smithson's voice broke up the little circle as the next batsman reached the crease. I looked around for the ball, waiting for it to be thrown to me. But something was wrong. A chuckle rippled round the crowd and I realised that the second opening batsman, Johnson, was taking his guard at the wicket at my end of the pitch.

'That was over, Rodge,' said Hills, and I ran off to my position at third man with my face flaming. There is nothing worse than making yourself look foolish in front of a crowd, especially one as knowledgeable as this Lancastrian crowd. They cheered me ironically all the way to the boundary, but there was nothing to do but to grin and bear it.

'Forgot where ye were, lad?'

''E 'asn't learnt to count yet.'

'Brought your nappies with you, Roger?'

'Show us your dimples, Roger.'

I waved, trying to bear no more ill-will to the barrackers than they did to me, and received another small cheer as I turned round to watch Symonds running up to bowl. But it was a relief when Johnson thick-edged the first ball towards me at third man, and I was able to concentrate on picking up the speeding ball cleanly and returning it, flat and hard, to the wicket-keeper.

'Eee, the lad can throw a bit.'

'Learnt it chuckin' bottles out his pram.'

'North!'

A voice cut through the banter. I swung round, but could see no one I recognised in the sea of faces.

'North!'

There it was again; insistent, imperative. I shaded my eyes against the sun, peering round.

'North!'

There, by the sight screen twenty yards away, a black hand was waving, holding something white. As I watched, the hand moved, flicking an envelope towards me onto the outfield. Involuntarily I moved towards it, but as I did so I heard the thwack of bat against ball and a great shout: 'Catch it, Roger.'

Distracted, I tried to take in the scene, peering round for the ball. There were the batsmen, running but with both their faces turned towards me. Hills the wicket-keeper stood, arms wide. The entire field was looking at me. I gazed up, squinting against the glare, searching for the ball against the mottled background of the crowd and the dark trees. I could see nothing. Then, suddenly, there it was! High in the sky, looping down to my right. I took off for dear life and, against the odds, got to within four yards of the ball as it bounced high over my head into the crowd for four. Applause for the boundary mingled with some sympathetic noises for me – 'Bad luck, son' – but I knew that the catch would have been on had I started soon enough, and I tossed the ball back to Symonds with a very contrite, 'Sorry, Sy' and made my way back to my position. The envelope was still there on the grass some twenty yards to my left, but I was determined to maintain my concentration and it was not until the end of the over that I ran to pick it up, shoving it into the hip pocket of my flannels.

Smithson came towards me with the ball.

'Bad luck, you couldn't quite reach it. You didn't seem to get the line early enough. Don't let it worry you. Just keep your eye on the game.'

'Sorry Skip, I know I boobed. It won't happen again.'

'What was that you picked up?'

'Nothing. Just some waste paper that was distracting me.'

He tossed me the ball.

'Get on with it.'

I wondered what profound remarks the spectators would be crediting us with, but the exchange had achieved its desired effect and I ran up to begin my second over in a much more relaxed frame of mind. It was a good one, but I felt unlucky that a couple of balls 'morally' bowled the Lancashire No. 3 and another squirted off the inside edge of the bat, shaving the leg stump and beating both Hills and deep fine-leg, where I felt that Jason might have made a little more effort to stop the boundary.

I was taken off after seven overs, having taken one wicket for twenty-six, with one maiden. Symonds, who took two wickets, kept going, and by the time we trooped off for lunch, Lancashire had progressed to 91 for three. In the crowd outside the pavilion I thought I saw a man resembling Pravisar, and this reminded me of the envelope in my back trouser pocket. I hurried to the loo, locked myself in a cubicle and took out the envelope. It was unmarked and unsealed, and inside was a single sheet of cheap lined notepaper. It carried one word in childish capital letters: 'HAVE'. I looked at it, turned it over, upside down and sideways, but it still said: 'HAVE'. It meant nothing, except a possible promise of more to come. I considered flushing it down the lavatory, but decided against it and took the envelope and the piece of paper back to the dressing room where I buried them in the bottom of my cricket-bag under my pads. I would have dismissed the incident as some kid's trick, but the events of the past few days added up to considerable pressure on my nerves and kept me speculating busily while I ate the statutory ham, salad and baked potatoes that make up a cricketer's staple diet in summer.

'Pass the salt, Rodge.'

'Er, what? Sorry.'

'I said, pass the bleeding salt, for the third time.'

'Sorry, I was miles away.' I scooped up the cruet and passed it over. 'Anything else?'

'You can tell me about the girl.'

'What girl?'

'The one that's on your mind. She must be a cracker.'

'Not this time, Gerry. I'm worried about my father.'

131

'What's wrong with Frank?' Down, like most cricketers, knew and liked him.

'I think he's getting into a deal that he'll regret.' I did not tell Gerry Down that I was deep in it too. 'He's never been so good at the business side since my mother died.' But was I any better? So far my dealings with Pravisar had led to nothing but unpleasantness for the people around me and pain for me. What the hell was going on?

The five-minute bell sounded and the umpires got up from the lunch table and put on their white coats, transforming themselves by the simple action from elderly, ruddy and apparently amiable gentlemen to those anonymous figures of authority upon whose decisions all our careers depended. I shook off the dark thoughts and trooped out with the rest onto the field behind Smithson. He threw me the ball again.

'Length and line, Roger,' he said. 'Forget about the pace. I'm going to want thirty overs out of you this afternoon.'

Actually, he got twenty-nine overs and three balls. I rattled the stumps of the last Lancashire batsman at 5.35 p.m., having bowled unchanged since lunchtime, and Smithson held the players back to give me the honour of leading them off the field. It would be several matches before I took six wickets for sixty-nine in an innings again. It was as good a county debut as I could have dreamed of making, and I relished every sweet, excruciating moment as the Lancashire team and members stood to clap me into the pavilion. As I was going up the steps a little bunch of pushing children barred the way, autograph books and ball-points at the ready. I scribbled a few signatures awkwardly, dripping sweat onto the pages, and as I handed over the last book felt a hand thrust something into my hip pocket. I swung round, too late to see which of the children had done it. I wrestled my way wearily through the throng and into the dressing room. Gerry Down pushed a pint glass of lager into my hand.

'You've earned it,' he said, lifting his own tankard to me and there was a chorus of agreement as the rest of the players followed suit. Even Jason raised a reluctant glass in my direction. I sat on my locker, too tired to shower yet, and felt in my pocket. I looked at the one word in shaky capitals: 'YOU'. It was simple, childish, and somehow frightening. 'HAVE YOU'. Had I what? What would the next message say? A threat was implicit, and yet there was nothing menacing in the content. So far. I stripped off and stood under the shower for ten minutes washing the sweat off my body and some reason back into my mind. I had to do something to gain the initiative, which so far had belonged exclusively to Pravisar, or whoever was behind him. There was something I could do that very evening. It might not get me very far, but it was at least action. I wondered if Gerry Down would help me? Or Phil Hills? Could I ask them?

I dressed slowly in jeans and a loose shirt, and wandered out to watch Smithson and Belfer begin our reply to Lancashire's meagre total of 224. I wouldn't be wanted to bat that evening. We only had forty minutes, and nothing would happen in that time.

Carnock grabbed me by the shoulder.

'Why are you changed? Why haven't you got your pads on, North? What the f. . . d'you think you're playing at? Just because you get a couple of wickets you think you can go all high and mighty, eh?'

I shrugged off his hand, none too gently. I don't like being bullied. I was pretty nervy anyway.

'And what the f. . . d'you think you're talking about? Mister coach?' With the emphasis on the 'Mister'.

'Don't you talk to me like that. I'll . . . I'll report you to the committee.'

'Try it,' I said, knowing that he wouldn't. Carnock backed off.

'Haven't you been told you're night-watchman?' he asked in a milder tone.

'I have now,' I said, undoing my belt and slipping off my jeans. 'Tell them not to get out for a couple of minutes.' I had no desire at all to sit for the next half an hour with my pads on, still less to face the Lancashire bowlers should one of our batsmen be dismissed. The night-watchman's is not a job to covet. But as I changed back into my flannels I felt strangely relieved that I had something to concentrate on, to distract me from the Pravisar problem.

My services were not needed after all. I sat on the players' balcony watching our opening pair cope competently with the Lancashire pace attack, but the back of my mind kept gnawing at the puzzle. Why did Pravisar want 2,500 bats? Why did he not export them himself? And what had that got to do with the death of Persse Grace? Had my father arranged to poison the Surrey captain? If not, who had? If he had, what was I to do about it? And why had I been attacked, abducted and left in my own workshop? And why did Pravisar seem to have such an influence behind the scenes at The Oval? None of it made sense, particularly in the context of the peaceful, traditional scene of the Aigburth Cricket Ground unfolding in front of me. I watched Smithson glance the last ball of the day delicately for four and unhurriedly lead the procession of players off the field to a smattering of applause from the Aigburth faithful. I changed leisurely with the others and carried my bag down to the car-park, chatting to Down on the way. Tucked under the windscreen wiper was a square piece of paper.

'Heck, you can't have picked up a bloody parking fine in here, Rodge,' said Down. I did not reply for some time. I was staring at the one word scrawled in those familiar capital letters. 'CALLED', it said.

'What's wrong, Rodge?' asked Down, looking at me curiously.

'I don't know yet, Gerry,' I said. 'But I'm going to find out? D'you feel like giving me a hand? It may be rough.'

134

Down's eyes sparkled. He loved a scrap.

'Lead me to it,' he said, slapping me on the shoulder. 'Let's find a pub. I'll buy you a beer if you tell me what's going on. The suspense is killing me.'

'Okay,' I said. 'It's a deal.'

6

We found a quiet pub not a mile from the ground and Down flirted with the barmaid while he ordered two pints of lager, while I laid out the three pieces of paper with their incomplete message: 'HAVE YOU CALLED' and wondered for the fiftieth time what it could mean. Call? Call whom? Was I intended to make a telephone call?

'Obviously,' said Down when I had told him the story as I knew it. 'It's intended to scare you. But there's no sense in it. You'll just have to wait until the message is complete. Whoever they are, they're obviously going to complete the message sooner or later, and this is just a way to put more pressure on you. Have you called your dad today, for example? Not since this morning? Well isn't it about time you rang again? You'll never forgive yourself if something's happened to him.'

I had been making excuses to myself for not having done this from the ground, but in response to Down's urging I went across to the telephone in the corner of the bar and dialled Willford. My father's voice answered. He sounded more animated than I'd ever heard him.

'Glad you called, Rodge. Well done. You've just been on the news. With a picture as well. Trouble here? Not at all. I'm going to take Sally out to supper at the Royal Oak to celebrate your debut. We've been fixing the shipping for Pravisar. There's a lot of paperwork. We'll get it done in

136

time. Do you want a word with her? All right. Never mind. She sends her congratulations.'

'Tell her thanks. And look after yourselves.'

'And you keep off the beer. You've got to bat tomorrow.'

'Don't worry, Dad. I've got other things to do. Take care.'

I hung up, thankful that there was nothing to worry about there. I fished out the notepad on which Bob Jason had written down the addresses to which he had delivered cricket bats. He had said one was in Liverpool. Perhaps there was something I could do, after all. I could at least find out if what he had told me was accurate.

'Jackson Bats, Warmington Close, Aigburth, Liverpool,' he had written. I picked up our empty glasses and took them to the bar for a refill.

'Do you know Warmington Close?' I asked the barman.

'Yeah, sure. Couple of blocks away. A few sheds. Light industry, they call it. Huh.' He snorted with contempt. 'Who d'you want? Maybe I can help.'

'Bat-makers. Jackson Bats. Ever heard of them?'

The barman scratched his head, doing nothing for his bald patch.

'I reckon. Jacko Jackson. Had quite a nice little set-up there. Only man who made cricket bats in the north-west. He used to drink here. He shot himself a year ago. I did hear he'd got into money trouble. Cash-flow problems, they say nowadays. Huh.' He snorted again.

'Did anyone take over?'

'I was coming to that. Jacko had a brother, Arthur. They call him Jacko too, now. Bit confusing. About ten years younger. Fancies himself. Does everything – bit of bat-making, bit of guitar-playing, bit of conning. Tell you one thing, though, he's a wiz with cars. Fix anything with a spanner and a piece of chewing-gum, would Arthur. He took over when Jacko topped himself. Funny little bugger. But he must have got some money from somewhere. I hear he's got quite a good business going. Plenty of cash to throw around. Comes in of an evening sometimes with two birds.

137

He probably runs 'em. Oh-oh.' The barman stopped. 'Don't look now. They've just come in. In the corner.'

He broke off and moved along the bar. The man answering the description 'funny little bugger' was beckoning to him, flourishing a ten pound note.

'Ta, John. A couple of White Ladies for the girls, and I'll have the usual with ice. Have one yourself.' He had a harsh voice, much bigger than his 5ft 2in suggested; a jockey's build slightly gone to seed, and light, almost white hair plastered down over a big forehead. His voice sounded youngish, but his lined face could have been any age between thirty and sixty. His eyes were an opaque grey, and when he glanced along the bar I saw that the only colour on his face was provided by light ginger eyebrows. The barman leaned across the bar and spoke to him, indicating me.

'You asking questions about me, son?' The grating voice was unwelcoming.

'Mr Jackson?'

'That's me. Who's asking?'

'North. I'm playing cricket along the road. For Surrey. I understand you make bats?'

'So?'

He didn't seem anxious for business, but I persisted.

'I need a re-blade quickly. Can you fix it?'

'Nah. We don't put our blades on other people's bats. Try one of the sports shops.'

'Thanks for your help. I will.'

'Do that.' He turned away, pocketed his change, and I watched him carry his drinks to the girls across the room. One of them waved to me. It was Josephine, the girl from the bar the previous night.

'So you know her too.' Gerry Down was looking at me quizzically. He was quite unabashed.

'Not really. We passed the time of day, or rather night, last evening in the Apollyon.'

'That's a bit of a coincidence,' said Down. 'Her mate

Trees spent the night with me. She was quite interested in you. Kept asking questions about you. You must have made quite an impression.'

'It doesn't seem to have washed off onto Mr Jackson, of Jackson Bats,' I said. 'He didn't want to know at all. It's not like a bat-maker to turn down a job, however small.'

Mr Jackson still didn't want to know. He hustled the girls through their drinks and escorted them to the door at the far end of the pub. Josephine looked back at us and started to wave, but he shoved her through the door savagely enough for us to hear a squeak of pain.

'Nice character,' I said. 'I think I'd like to have a look at his business. Are you game?'

'I'm with you,' said Down. 'I must warn you that I don't mind a bit of trespass,' he added. 'But breaking and entering's not in my line.'

'Nor mine,' I said. But I didn't mean it that night. Down had mentioned coincidence, and there was far too much of it about for my liking. I asked the knowledgeable barman who the girls with Jackson were, but he professed not to know. He had only seen them a couple of times before.

'Pretty free and easy, I'd say,' he said with a grin.

'Easy,' said Down from experience. 'But not free, man. Oh no.'

'What d'you think they're doing tonight?' asked Down.

The barman grinned.

'On the game, I reckon,' he said. 'They trawl the big hotel bars. There's a Beatles memorial at the Civic Centre, and they'll probably drop in there first.'

The barman went on to say that Jackson drove a silver BMW, two or three years old, so we checked the car-park and the road outside, but there was no sign of any such vehicle and we concluded that they had already driven into the city.

I drove cautiously the few blocks to Warmington Close, which I wouldn't have found so easily without the barman's directions. It was tucked in behind two of the drab red-brick

139

streets with those multi-painted doors which seem to be lower Liverpool's architectural trademark, and consisted of a rectangular area of ground covering a couple of acres sub-divided into plots by six foot pig-wire fences each side of a concrete roadway. Each plot was about seventy or eighty feet square, and contained a large pre-cast concrete structure. There were no windows, but each building had a double door with a single door set into one side, and each plot had padlocked metal double gates wide enough to admit five-ton trucks. Most were pretty derelic.; the wire rusting and the gates broken, but some of the sites were obviously in use, with faded name-plates screwed over the doors. There was a Volkswagen repair specialist, a paint-spray unit, a furniture store and, halfway along the close, Jackson Bats Ltd. A new brass plate on the small door was inscribed: WORLD BATS INC, and the rusty gates were firmly closed with a new chain and lock.

'Not very promising,' said Down. 'In fact, the whole area's bloody miserable.'

It was indeed. Warmington Close at eight o'clock in the evening epitomised the Liverpool of the depression of the seventies. There was no sign of life; not even a security guard. The plot next to Jackson Bats had obviously been deserted for years. I pulled in by the entrance.

'Wait here, Gerry and whistle if anyone comes along.'

'I don't like it, Rodge. This place gives me the creeps.'

I flicked the bonnet release catch.

'Pretend to be fixing the engine. Say you were told there's a repair shop along here.'

'What, at eight o'clock in the evening?'

He grumbled on a bit, but got out of the car and began to poke around among the wires leading to the distributor. I slapped him on the backside. 'Don't worry, I'm only looking around, I won't be long,' I said. I pushed at the rusty gate and the chain fell away. The gate creaked as I shoved it open and made my way gingerly through the debris of rusty oil drums and odd pieces of machinery round to the side. In

140

the blank wall of Jackson Bats was a small metal door, and the smell and state of the concrete wall alongside it made it uncomfortably apparent that the staff were accustomed to using this side exit for relieving the calls of nature. Trying not to get myself covered in grime I lugged a couple of oil drums up to the wire fence and hoisted one over, to give me an exit route. Then I climbed on the other and vaulted over the wire fence. I landed safely and pushed at the filthy metal door. It gave with a reluctant squeak. Hardly able to believe my luck, I tiptoed into the dimness beyond. I wedged the door open with a convenient brick and set out to explore Jackson Bats Ltd.

It took my eyes a moment or two to become accustomed to the gloom after the sunlit evening outside, and I had to feel my way along a short, narrow corridor to another door. The walls were rough to my fingers, untreated breeze-block, I thought. This door too was unlocked, opening inwards, and I sensed rather than saw that I was in the main area of the factory premises. I had seen no windows outside, and the place was only gloomily lit by a filthy fanlight, so I searched around to find a switch on the wall by the door and, holding my breath, clicked it down. A couple of overhead arc lamps sprang to life, but between me and the light were stacks of crates piled on top of each other, almost to the ceiling twelve feet above. I picked my way through a gap and found myself in a typical small bat-making factory. A long work-bench with vices and a lathe ran along one wall. The wall itself was hung with tools, all of them either new or in good condition. In the confined space, pressed in by the crates, were an angled saw bench and a bat press which looked like a small printing press. These were covered with dust, unlike the workbench itself which looked well-used, with piles of shavings curled across it and mounting up on the floor below. A crate that had been broken open stood at one end, and a number of blades were piled carelessly on top of each other alongside handles which had obviously been removed from them. A piece of machinery I had never seen was bolted to another, smaller bench. It looked a bit like a sausage-maker. I had no idea of its function.

I picked up a handle. Someone had ripped it carelessly from its blade. The ends of the bamboo were frayed and bent over, and there was a stress mark midway down the handle as though a pipe lever had been used as a wrench. A blade was gripped firmly in one of the padded vices, with a powerful Bosch electric drill on the bench beside it. An extraordinary steel bit, at least eighteen inches long with a 1½ in cut, extruded from the end. This was obviously the source of the shavings. I picked it up and touched the trigger switch. The drill whirred menacingly. I put it down and examined the bat blade more carefully. Externally, there was nothing to distinguish it from any other bat, but in the V of the splice a hole had been drilled straight down the centre. The bit fitted it exactly. I tried the handle in the V splice. When it was tapped home, there was no sign of interference. A touch of glue, I thought, and no one would know the difference until he picked it up. Then I remembered a story my father had once told me.

In the days before heavy bats became fashionable, one famous Midlands firm had, stupidly in his opinion, experimented by building their bats fatter, but cutting down the weight by drilling a hole like this down the middle. According to him, the bat had not been weakened in any way, but had driven like a beauty. One Test player was alleged to have made a century with a bat 'doctored' like this, and had all his bats deliberately treated in the same way afterwards. There had even been talk of patenting the idea, as the variously sprung handles of the past or the inlaid toes of the sixties had been, but there had been some hitch. My father pooh-poohed the idea on the grounds that the bat would not last a week, but he had to admit that he had never tried it. It seemed a very odd way for Jackson, or Pravisar for that matter, to make money, if that was what they intended. It was odd, but not illegal, though I was pleased to see that bats by Frank North & Son were not included in the pile. Father would not have allowed anyone to tamper with his bats in any way.

I left everything as I found it, switched off the lights and made my way outside. Down was waiting anxiously for me, but he had not been disturbed. On the way back to the hotel I told him what I had found.

'The hell with it, Rodge. That's plain nonsense. Who'd drill a bloody great hole down the middle of a cricket bat? Let's call it a day. I'm starving. Let's get dinner. You'd better freshen up a bit first. You've got oil on your shirt and sawdust all over your blazer.'

'All right,' I said, a trifle wearily. 'Let's call it a day.'

It wasn't as easy as that. When I went to the desk for my room key, the receptionist, immaculately dressed in her maroon uniform with a nameplate on the lapel, passed over a small envelope.

'This was in your cubby-hole,' she said with a bright smile.

I looked at it. I did not want to open it.

'Did you see who brought it, Sharon?'

'I'm sorry, sir. I'm night staff. I've only just come on. You'll have to ask John in the morning.'

'Thanks.'

I opened the envelope in the lift. As I expected, it contained a sheet of cheap lined paper. On it was scrawled, in capital letters, the word I most feared to see: 'HOME?' I looked at it for a moment, and passed it to Down.

'I called them from the pub an hour ago and they were fine,' I said. 'It's got to be a bluff. But why?'

He shook his head, but came with me to my room, where I dialled Willford impatiently. There was no reply. For a moment I panicked, then I remembered that father had said he was taking Sally out to dinner. I called the Royal Oak. Henry Ford, the landlord, was an old friend.

'Roger North here. Sorry to bother you, Henry, but is my father in the pub?'

'Yes he is – in the dining room having dinner with a

gorgeous blonde. Never knew the old chap had it in him. Shall I get him?'

'No, don't worry him. I just wanted to know he was okay. I rang home and he wasn't there.'

'Shall I tell him you called?'

'No thanks, Henry. He'll think I'm checking up on him.'

'Well, aren't you? Seeing the company, I don't blame you.'

'Henry, you're a dirty old man.'

'Have to be, in my business. By the way, Rodge, bloody good show today. You must be pleased.'

'What? Oh, yes. Thanks a lot,' I said belatedly. Cricket was the last thing on my mind at that moment. Henry wanted to chat, but I cut him off as kindly as I could without offending him.

'I want to make another call,' I said to Down. 'Would you like to go down and get a table?'

'Okay,' he said amiably. 'What d'you want to drink? Wine?'

'Just a pint. That's my lot tonight. I've got to bat tomorrow.'

'Listen to the night-watchman.' He dodged the pillow I threw at him and ducked through the door. I dialled the number Detective Inspector Light had given me at Scotland Yard. There was a click and then a series of clicks.

'Light here. What's bothering you? Or who?' I was inordinately grateful to hear his voice, even though it sounded as though he was in a bathtub. The whole thing was getting beyond me.

'I don't really know. But I'm getting threats, or they may be threats. And I've found out something, but I don't know what it means.'

'What do you mean, threats?'

'Well, a series of messages, a word at a time, asking me if I have rung home.'

'Have you?'

'Yes, of course. Twice this evening. Nothing's wrong

144

there. My father's out to dinner at the local with Sally Lang. But it's very worrying.'

'It must be. But last time it all turned out a damp squib, didn't it? Where are you now?'

'In my room at the Apollyon. Just going to have something to eat myself.'

'Stay in the hotel and don't go out. I'll be with you by midnight.'

'Are you flying up, then?'

'Lord bless you, no. The Met can't afford air fares for inspectors. I've been on my way all day. The superintendent wants me to learn something about cricket. I'm on the M6 outside Manchester. Save a beer for me. By the way, Old Bill asked me to congratulate you.'

'How ... ?' But Light hung up before I could ask any more stupid questions. Then I belatedly realised he had been using a car phone. I'd been switched through automatically. I washed the grease from my hands, changed my shirt and went down to the dining room considerably relieved. Down was seated at a corner table, deep in conversation with a blonde and a brunette. The blonde looked up and saw me. It was Josephine.

'Hello,' she said, as though we were old friends. 'Gerry said you'd be down.'

'I'm North. He's Down,' I said facetiously.

She looked blank for a second.

'Oh. Oh yes.' She laughed uncertainly. The brunette giggled. She seemed to be the one with the brains.

'I'm Trees,' she said, holding out a claw with jet-black nails to be shaken.

'Sorry, which trees? I didn't quite catch that.'

Down said hastily and slightly belligerently: 'Therese and Josephine are going to have dinner with us. If that's all right.'

'Trees,' said the brunette. 'I told you so.'

'Delighted, but I thought you were out with Mr Jackson?' I said, slightly bewildered.

'Oh no,' said Josephine. 'We're on our own. Jacko's gone to the Beatles. We don't like the Beatles. They're passay.'

'Pass . . . ? Oh yes. What music do you like?' I asked her.

'The other Jackson,' she said. 'Michael.'

'And Beethoven,' added Therese. I must have looked as flabbergasted as Down, who nearly dropped his lager. She grinned. 'Don't look so blank. We're musicians. Jo's trumpet and I'm clarinet. At the LPO.'

'What's that?' Down asked hoarsely.

'The Liverpool Philharmonic Orchestra,' said Therese. There was a short silence.

'You don't . . .' I said, hesitating.

'Look like musicians?' said Josephine. 'We don't work full-time. We do shifts when someone's sick or away. The pay's lousy and it doesn't come very often. So we work the hotels. Twenty quid a night if you feel like it, and a meal. Nothing fancy.'

This devastating candour was beyond our experience in the soft south.

'I told them,' said Down in a strangulated voice, 'It's the meal only tonight.'

'That's okay,' Josephine told him cheerfully. 'Wore you out last night, did she? Anyway, you must be a better bet for an evening than Jacko. He can only *talk* about how big he is. He prefers boys anyway.' She added under her breath a phrase so lewd that I couldn't believe I'd heard correctly. To cover my confusion I called the waiter over and we ordered our dinner. Judging from their appetite the girls were half starved.

'How did you get into this?' I asked them over the soup.

'That's what we're always asked,' said Therese. 'We had to busk when we came out of music college and he found us in the street and said he'd protect us.'

'That sounds too easy.'

'Oh, we wouldn't at first. But we had nowhere to sleep and then we got beaten up outside the station and Jo was

146

nearly raped. Jacko turned up with a gun and scared the buggers off. Then he took us to this house and gave us a room. Said we could pay him when we earned enough. Then he told us how to earn it.'

'Does he, well, demand payment in kind?'

'No, strictly cash. He's a clockwork orange. He takes his rent from us. Fifty per cent of every trick. He sets the rates, too. Bastard.'

'Why did he tell you to pick us up?' I asked Josephine.

'I don't know what you mean.'

'Yes you do.'

'He said cricketers were an easy touch.'

'Why us?'

'It wasn't him.' She indicated Down. 'It was you. "The young blonde one," he said. His very words were: "He's the one we want". I don't know why.'

'But he said "we". He isn't the boss, is he? He runs you; who runs him?'

'I dunno. It's somebody to do with his business. Cricket bats or something. He's got a very smooth voice on the phone, that's all I know. Foreign. Paki.'

She stopped. 'I've had too much to drink. I shouldn't be talking like this to you. Jacko'd kill me if he knew.'

'What should be happening?'

'You should be getting pissed, and in about half an hour we'd go up to your room and I'd earn my twenty quid. But somebody would come in and take pictures, Polaroids. And that would cost you a hundred if you didn't want to see them in the next issue of one of the girlie mags.'

'I don't think it's money they're after. They're trying to force me to do something I don't want to do.'

'You mean lose a match or something? Wouldn't put it past him. So's he can win a bet.'

'Something like that.' I didn't want to disillusion her. I leaned across the table and took her hands. They were very cold, despite the warmth of the night.

'Have you done this before?' I said, looking into her eyes.

'Only once. With a rich Yank. I didn't mind about him.'
It was a risk, I knew, but I decided to take it.

'Will you help us? Both of you?'

'I dunno. What do you think you're doing?'

'Frankly, I'm not sure. But I do know that your Jackson is mixed up in something big and I'm trying to find out what it is?'

'Why you? You're just a cricketer, aren't you?'

'Yes, but someone's threatening my father and another person. They make cricket bats too. Gerry's helping me. Will you? Please?'

'What do we get out of it?'

I was getting better at this.

'I can't promise anything except your twenty quid. But with any luck you'll get shot of Jackson.'

'You want to watch it. You'll get hurt. Jacko uses a knife.'

'Don't worry about us. We know what we're doing.' I hoped we did. Josephine looked at her friend, who had been following every word of our conversation closely.

'They'll kill you,' she said wearily. 'But that's your funeral. If you see what I mean. What d'you want us to do?'

'Just do what they expect you to do. They won't know any different. We'll have a surprise for them.'

'Let's have the twenty in advance then,' she said. 'Now, where they can see you give it to us?'

'Hang on, not so fast.' Down was reluctant to hand over his cash. 'How do we know we'll get what we pay for?'

'If you don't, you'll still have a bloody good scrap,' I told him. It was a challenge he would find it hard to resist in front of a girl, and in any case he had taken a strong dislike to Mr Jackson. He fished out two tenners and waved them slowly in front of Therese's face. She snatched them and shoved them down the front of her dress and giggled as he tried to find them. I reckoned I could match their amateur dramatics. I folded two notes and made as though to thrust them between Josephine's legs. She slapped my hand away and grabbed the money. I pulled her towards me.

'All right,' she whispered in my ear. 'Take care.'

I lifted her hand to my lips, and kissed it. She tried to twist it away, but I held her wrist without effort.

'Where are they?' I said quietly.

'Four tables to your right and behind you.'

'Don't go away. I'm going to the loo. I won't be long.'

'Don't be.'

She squeezed my hand and for the first time looked frightened. I looked across at Gerry, who was beginning to enjoy himself hugely. He sprawled across in his chair, put his arm round Therese and licked her ear. She pushed him away and giggled. She had a convincing giggle. I got up, helping myself to an obvious and enthusiastic feel of Josephine's thigh on the way and made my way, not too unsteadily, towards the toilets. At the exit, I turned and waved to the table, at the same time getting a glimpse of three large men talking and smoking over some beers four tables away. Taking a chance, I slipped quickly past the toilet and ran down the stairs to the next floor, where I knew there was a telephone in a soundproof box.

I gave the hotel operator my room number and the Yard's London number. Within half a minute I was switched through to Light in his car.

'No time to talk,' I said. 'How long will you be?'

The urgency in my voice talked. He made no fuss.

'Twenty minutes.'

'I'm being set up. Room 760. Midnight exactly. I need reinforcements.'

That gave him half an hour. I hung up and raced back up the stairs. At the top I stopped and leant against the wall, looking vaguely about me. As I did so one of the burly men came out of the toilet. He started as he saw me.

'Where'sh the loo?' I asked him in my best slur. He jerked his thumb without speaking at the notice reading

'Gentlemen' on the door behind him and stood aside to watch me push at the wrong side of the door and lumber clumsily through it, fumbling at my flies. I stood swaying at the urinal in case he should look in, washed my hands noisily and swilled water over my face, splashing my shirt and jeans. All the histrionics were unnecessary as by the time I meandered back into the dining room he was back at his table with his cronies. I kissed Josephine fondly and slumped into my chair. Down was convincingly advanced in his flirtation with Therese, who had hitched a knee up against the table and was displaying a splendid pair of thighs and a very small pair of purple briefs.

I waved to the waiter and ordered another bottle of wine. I hoped my expenses would hold out. They certainly wouldn't stretch to Josephine's twenty pounds as well. I nuzzled her ear and whispered: 'Keep it up for twenty minutes. Do you take credit cards?'

'Strictly cash,' she whispered back into my throat. 'But for you, anything.'

Her hands were beginning to wander intimately, so I feigned embarrassment and sat up, pouring out the wine and spilling it liberally across the tablecloth. A large figure loomed heavily over the table.

'There's a pretty sight. I thought so.' It was Carnock, red-faced and none too sober. 'North and Down out on the tiles. Well, well, well.' He belched slightly and swayed. I stood up and pulled a chair from the next table, swung him round with one hand and sat him down abruptly.

'Hello, Harry,' I said. 'Just in time for a drink.'

I filled my glass with wine and handed it to him. Befuddled, he could not understand why I was being nice to him, and he guzzled at the wine rather like a pig at a trough and belched again.

'Thanks, Rodge,' he said, trying to peer up Josephine's brief skirt.

'Look, Harry, don't touch,' I said. 'She's mine.'

150

'No offence, no offence,' he mumbled, his eyes on Josephine's legs. But after a minute his concentration blurred, his head began to sag and his mouth fell open. To cover the beginnings of a snore I stood up, pulling Josephine to her feet.

'Come on,' I said. 'He doesn't belong to us. Your room, Gerry. I don't think Phil would appreciate being disturbed.'

Holding our partners tightly, we made our way out of the restaurant. I had signed the bill and slipped a five pound note to the head waiter. 'See he gets to bed,' I said, nodding at Carnock's slumped form. 'Carnock. Eighth floor somewhere.' That was one fiver that would not come out of Surrey expenses.

We piled into the lift, arms linked, and rode it noisily up to the seventh floor. It took a little time to get out, as we had to extricate Down and Therese, who were busy swapping tonsils, and generally putting up a fair display of incipient debauchery. The room was made for it, large enough to hold two double beds, its own bath and shower en suite and a little refrigerator tucked beside the big television set. They build things well in Liverpool, and the walls were thick enough to absorb embarrassing noises. I shut the door behind us, leaving it unlocked, and the four of us stood and looked at each other, suddenly embarrassed. Therese broke the tension. She giggled.

'What do we do now?' she said.

'What you usually do,' I said. 'Take your clothes off and get into bed.'

'But that's the man's job,' said Josephine, trying to lighten the atmosphere. The fun had gone out of the night.

'If that's the case,' I said to Down. 'Let's get on with it. You two take the bed next to the window. We've got to make it convincing. I've got one or two things to do first.'

'No problem,' said Down, whirling Therese round and

unzipping her dress. She wriggled out of it and turned round to unbutton his shirt. I fetched a couple of bats from my bag and laid them down between the beds and placed a couple of cricket balls behind each set of pillows. That made Josephine laugh, despite the tension.

'Aren't yours good enough for us?' she said, undoing my belt. In a matter of minutes the four of us were naked and under the sheets, waiting tensely. I switched out the lights at the bedside.

'You don't feel very romantic,' said Josephine, and squealed as I stopped her mouth with a kiss and swung my leg across her body. I had heard the door handle turning.

Suddenly the room was flooded with light and three men were through the door.

I yelled: 'What the hell?' and tried to get off Josephine as the sheet was pulled off us. A flash went off.

'And the other one,' said a voice and I heard Down snarl: 'No you bloody don't!' as the second man reached down to pull the sheet away. I heard a sharp crack and a cry as I rolled off Josephine onto all fours with a cricket ball in each hand. At that range I couldn't miss. The first ball hit the Polaroid flush on the lens, smashing the glass and driving the camera back into the photographer's face. He dropped it and fell back, blood spurting from a cut above his eye and from his nose. The second ball found its target precisely six inches below the second man's belly button, and he rolled down onto the bed, clutching himself, retching and gasping obscenities. I quickly hit him on the chin, which regrettably stopped him feeling any pain but at least halted the language flow. The third man was whimpering on the floor, clasping his right wrist which Down had hit with the cricket bat. Josephine and Therese were sitting up with wide terrified eyes, trying to cover themselves. There was no sign of Jackson. As I got up with the obvious intent to finish the job, the photographer pulled himself together and fled through the open door.

There was a thump, and a scuffle, and the photographer returned head first, bent double and with his arm twisted up behind his back, closely followed by Detective Inspector Light, who took in the shambles in the room in one glance, and said, with some amusement: 'So you've done it again, Roger.'

He dropped the photographer on the floor without ceremony and pulled out his pocket transmitter. 'No bother,' he said to whoever was receiving the call. 'Three arrests, one an ambulance case. I shall need a WPC too. No, I'm no superman. You could say I had a bit of help. Roger.' He turned to us. 'Get your clothes on, the lot of you. Now then, Roger, what happened this time?'

'We were in bed when they broke in and tried to photograph us,' I said.

The photographer spoke from the floor.

'The bastards attacked us. They should be up for GBH. We weren't doing any harm. Just a joke.'

'We'll take your statements down at the station,' said Light. 'At the moment you're under arrest on charges of breaking and entering and conspiracy to blackmail. And the last includes you two,' he said to the girls.

I objected.

'But they tipped us off, which is why I rang you. You can't arrest them.'

Light took me by the arm and led me into the corridor.

'Which is exactly why I am arresting them, you silly young fool, to save their skins. You've probably signed their death warrants, telling those blokes that they'd warned you. Although it must have been fairly obvious that you were ready for them. I don't give a damn what happens to a couple of slags, but if they're going to turn Queen's Evidence I want them alive to go into court.'

I started to speak but he cut in. 'And don't get all uppity with me. You and your mate could well be up for GBH if we don't make the conspiracy charge stick. Neither of you looked paragons of virtue yourselves when I came

153

in. Imagine what counsel will do with four naked bodies in a hotel room. And the press, God help us. They're going to make hay of this anyway, even without a shot of your backside. BRILLIANT YOUNG CRICKETERS IN NAKED SEX ROMP, and that sort of thing.'

I held my head. It was beginning to ache.

'You're not joking?' I asked between my fingers.

'No I'm not. At least you smashed that camera. The defence is sure to ask for the film.'

'You wouldn't . . .'

'Let's hope there's nothing on the film. We'll get the labs to look at it.'

'It's a Polaroid.'

'I know it is, you fool. Even though it may be fogged, there's probably a recognisable impression.'

I groaned. 'Is there any chance of . . .'

'Of holding out the story? Shouldn't think so, unless Ashcroft puts it under wraps. We don't like doing that, because it looks so bad when (that's when, not if) the story gets out. POLICE HUSH UP CRICKETERS' SEX ROMP is even better copy. I can try to persuade him to bottle it up, but I doubt if he can for very long. It's too risky.'

'Oh.'

'I shouldn't worry too much. No such thing as bad publicity. The readers will love you twice as much; all the men will envy you, all the women will want to get you to bed. You can't lose.'

'Except in cricket.'

'Not even there. There are plenty of precedents. Plenty of first-class cricketers have been known to enjoy a little wrestling with the camp followers. You know that. Look at Grace, for a start. Rumour has it he should have been done for having it away with minors more than once.'

I had my own opinion about that, but I said no more. Three policemen and an ambulanceman arrived to take away our captives, and a severe WPC took charge of the girls, who refused to say anything to anyone and were marched away in handcuffs like the men. Down and I got dressed and Light drove us to the main police station, where we made our statements and were allowed to go. Light drove us back to the hotel, where he assured the night manager that we had not been involved in a drunken brawl, but were the victims of an extortion attempt, and were fit and proper customers of his establishment. Light also urged the man, on pain of dire but unidentifiable consequences, not to talk to the tabloid press, but if asked anything by anyone to say that neither he nor his hotel knew anything at all apart from the date.

'That's not to say he won't talk if they pay him enough. And what he doesn't know they'll make up for him,' he said gloomily. 'At any rate Old Bill has agreed that we sit on the story for the time being. You may be lucky.'

It was 2 a.m. and I was longing for my bed, with or without Josephine. But Light, who had driven from London after a full day's work, seemed as fresh as if he had just got up. He insisted that Down went to bed and that I joined him in the hotel lounge for an early morning coffee.

'Sit down,' he said. 'There's a lot you've got to tell me. First, what was all that nonsense about Mr North and Sally Lang? When we investigated they were perfectly all right. A bit vague, perhaps, but there was nothing wrong with them that our chaps could find out. They certainly hadn't been abducted, as you thought.'

Yawning, I told him of the car chase, my curious contact with Pravisar, my subsequent experience of being abducted and dumped at Willford, the strange order for bats and Pravisar's seemingly straightforward instruction to arrange for their export to various countries. I omitted details of how I had discovered Pravisar's London address and my suspicions about Sally's involvement with him. In my tiredness the whole series of episodes took on a dreamlike quality, and I must have rambled, for Light's sharp voice jolted into my consciousness.

'What was that about Jason?' he said. I hadn't intended to mention the Jason episode, but I'd obviously let something slip.

'Jason?' I said. 'Jeff Jason? All-rounder. Nothing between the ears. What about him?'

'You were talking about Bob Jason. In a car. Come on Roger, we know Bob Jason. He runs a dodgy transport business in Millwall. Employs ex-cons. And future ones. We're pretty sure that he was involved in that attack on you in Dulwich.'

I decided it was time to come clean. I was out of my depth.

'Yes, he was,' I said. 'I recognised the family likeness, and bullied Jeff, his brother, into fixing up a meeting. He admitted that he was working for Pravisar, but only straight jobs, he said. The attacks on me were a bit of a side-line. He wasn't to hurt me too much, just enough to make me believe that it would be less painful to do what I was told. He even said he'd feel sorry for me when Pravisar caught up with me. He said he knew nothing about my father or Sally Lang. As for him, his job was picking up and delivering cricket bats all over the country. He took a bit of persuading, but he gave me half a dozen addresses. One is only a couple of miles away from here. Gerry and I went to look at it tonight – last night. It's called Jackson Bats Ltd., at Aigburth. By a coincidence we also saw Jackson himself, in a pub nearby.'

'Did he know you?'

'I told him who I was. Said I wanted a new blade on my bat. He turned me down. I gathered he didn't know a lot about cricket bats. He took over the firm when his brother died a couple of years ago, and put money into the place, or so the barman in the Eagle round the corner told me. It turned out that he's the pimp for Josephine and Therese. He's a nasty piece of work. He's the one who tried to set us up. The girls seemed to like us and gave the whole thing away.'

156

'Have you any proof of this?'

'Only their word for it. And that it did all happen exactly as they said it would.'

'Hmm. It sounds as though you might have been set up in more ways than one. That bunch of thugs didn't give you much of a fight.'

'They didn't have much chance,' I said with some satisfaction.

'No.' He grinned. 'I don't suppose they were expecting quite such a reception. But I wonder, all the same. You're playing with fire, you know. Does Jackson know you went to his premises?'

'I don't think so. I didn't say anything to the girls, and nor did Gerry. We met them by chance when we got back to the hotel.'

'Hmm,' Light said again. 'There are too many coincidences. No matter. What did you find out? I'm assuming you couldn't resist trespassing?'

'The side door wasn't locked. I was looking for a bat-maker.'

'We'll let that pass. What did you find out?'

'Not very much. It's a bat factory all right, though I don't think it's been making bats lately. There are crates of the things, some in wooden boxes and some in card. One box was opened, and someone had been drilling bloody great holes down the splice into the body of the blades. It looked a damned silly way to make the blade lighter. It must reduce the life of a blade, though I was told once that it can even improve its driving power.'

'How's that?'

'I'm not sure. You'd have to ask a scientist that. Something like a hollow brick wall being stronger and warmer than a solid one.'

'Would that make money in the shops?'

'I wouldn't have thought so. It's no cheaper on willow, and more expensive on labour – you'd have to pay skilled workmen to do the drilling without ruining the bats. Then you'd have to advertise – sell it hard if you were to get over public scepticism. You couldn't charge much more than usual, because there's no difference in external appearance. Why should you pay more for an unknown brand name?'

Light had lost interest in the esoterics of bat-making.

'Did you notice anything else out of the ordinary?'

'Only that many of the tools – the bat press and so on – didn't seem to have been used for a long time. They were covered in dust. Oh, and there was a curious sort of machine I've never seen in a bat shop. Looked like a sausage-maker. I couldn't make out what it might be used for. There were a lot of shavings under a big electric drill and some dust around the sausage machine.'

'What colour?'

'The dust? White.'

'Do you know what it was?'

'No idea.'

'Keep it that way, Roger.' He looked at his watch. 'I've kept you up far too late. Better get some beauty sleep,' he said. 'Goodnight. Oh, and don't worry if you see me around tomorrow. Remember, Old Bill told me to learn something about cricket. D'you mind leaving me a comp at the gate? I don't want to flash my ID around too much.'

'Sure. But what do you mean; keep what what way?' I tried to ask him, but he merely waved a hand and walked out of the lounge. I felt enormously weary, as if I'd just finished a ten-mile run. It had been quite a day. I took the lift up to the seventh floor. The room was untidy just as we had left it, except that Down was snoring on the bed by the window. My bed was still rumpled, the sheets and coverlet askew. I kicked off my outer clothes and collapsed onto it, pulling the covers over me. I could not sleep for some time, despite my tiredness. My mind was travelling over and over the ground, seeking answers, and the sheets were redolent of Josephine's Eau de Cologne, or whatever her not very expensive perfume was. I allowed myself the luxury of a burst of anger at Light for calling the two girls 'slags', and eventually fell heavily asleep wondering how right he had been.

I was dragged from the depths by a clamorous buzzing in my ears and Gerry Down tugging at my shoulder.

'For Pete's sake answer the thing,' he was saying. 'That's the third time it's rung and it's bound to be for you.'

I looked at my watch. It said 7.30. I put out a hand, picked up the receiver and replaced it. The ringing stopped. I picked it up again and dialled reception.

'Room 760. We're not here. No calls,' I said.

'Very good, sir,' said a female voice. I replaced the receiver gently.

'Problem solved,' I said, turning over and closing my eyes.

The telephone rang again.

'This is a farce,' I said, cutting it off again and dialling reception for the second time. The pleasant female voice asked me what she could do for me.

'I thought I told you we were not taking calls,' I said, irritated. 'One came through immediately I put down the telephone.'

'No calls came through the exchange, sir', she said. 'It must have been somebody in the hotel, on the internal system.'

'Can't you block me off, or something?'

'I'm sorry, sir, I can't help you.'

I put the phone down again. It began to ring. I contemplated wrenching the wire out of the wall as they do in films, and decided that the Surrey County Cricket Club might have something to say if I was to damage the hotel. I picked up the receiver and said, slowly and distinctly:

'This is Room 760. We are taking no calls until midday tomorrow. Thank you.'

A man's voice said something, but without listening I put the phone down again. I placed one pillow over the instrument and another over my head and closed my eyes again. The telephone did not ring again and my stretched nerves twanged while I waited for it to do so. Gradually I relaxed, and I was almost asleep when three thunderous bangs on the door woke me, quivering, into a fighting crouch. I pulled myself together, seized a cricket bat and pulled the door open, ready to hit the first thing that moved. I must have looked fairly desperate, for the visitor jumped back nearly a foot. It was an anticlimax after all my apprehensions. It was Carnock, looking blotchy and hungover. I groaned.

'Oh, it's you, Harry. Can't you leave us to sleep? We're not due on the ground for a couple of hours. We had a late night.'

Carnock was conciliatory.

'I'm sorry to wake you, boys. Did you have a good night?' he smirked suggestively, trying to peer round me, no doubt hoping for a glimpse of undraped female flesh. He was unlucky. 'The captain wants you down at Aigburth by nine-fifteen. You're to give the batsmen a warm-up in the nets.'

'You must be joking.'

'No joke. He's been trying to telephone your room.' Carnock assumed his business-like voice. 'Nine-fifteen sharp.'

'But I'm not the twelfth man.'

'You are as far as I'm concerned. Anyway, it's captain's orders.' He sniggered. 'I suppose you could say you are flying high with the birds at one moment, and down to earth with a bump the next.'

For once Harry Carnock was right. There was no point in shooting the bearer of bad news, so we showered with bad grace and trooped down to the breakfast room, where Linacre, the twelfth man for the Lancashire match, was already tucking into some very unhealthy-looking bacon and eggs. He grinned at us.

'So Harry caught you two as well.'

'More's the pity.' Down ordered the full works: grapefruit, cereal, bacon, eggs, sausages, mushrooms, toast. I contented myself with toast and orange juice, but when Down's bacon and eggs turned up they smelt so appetising that I changed my mind. I bought a couple of the papers, and was relieved to see that our nocturnal exploits had not so far been picked up. The *Sun* obviously regarded our match as beneath them, as their coverage of the day's cricket was confined to a three-line score in 6-point type, but The *Daily Telegraph* gave us a generous half-column, with the punning headline: NORTH WIND SHRIVELS THE RED ROSES, which was a better reflection of the score-line than the report beneath it. The writer, obviously a Lancastrian, made much of the fact that this was a debut performance graced with a fair amount of luck, and hinted strongly that once my 'easy-paced, obvious seamers' became known to the circuit, I would become easy meat to the experienced county batsmen. It finished: 'We shall see today if the young man's pretensions extend to batting as well as bowling.'

Recalling my father's instruction not to read the newspapers and, if I did, to confine myself to the front pages, I stifled a wish to stuff the article down the writer's throat and reflected that I probably wouldn't get a bat that day, if our batsmen did their stuff. I was certainly not prepared to be greeted in the dressing room by Smithson with the order: 'Get your pads on, Roger.'

'Bit of a waste, isn't it, skipper? I thought I was here to give you and Billy a warm-up. I'm not in until seven down.'

'Oh yes you are,' said Smithson grimly. 'I want you to get your eye in. You're coming in with me. Belfer and Martin have gone down with the screaming squitters and Jayne's dosing them up with something to try to get them fit before lunch. I don't want to put Symonds in while the ball's still new, and Down here will try to belt the cover off it before he gets to the wicket. You've got a good eye and you're not frightened. If you keep your head down and watch the ball you can last out ten overs, or maybe twenty. You made a name for yourself yesterday. You can do it again today. Go on, get your kit on. I'll turn my arm over at you and Gerry here will throw some at you, if he can't bowl fast enough.'

I had been nervous enough the previous day before opening the bowling. Now I had the jitters in spades, and I only remembered at the last minute to leave a complimentary ticket at the gate for 'Mr' Light. Although I knew myself to be a fair batsman with a good eye, bowling was my first love and all my coaching had concentrated on line, length, flight, swerve and seam. I certainly did not share Smithson's optimism that I could see out enough time for our ailing batsmen to recover. Nor was my confidence boosted in the half-hour I spent 'getting my eye in', as Smithson euphemistically termed it. His earnest medium pacers induced three or four 'nicks'; one caught-and-bowled, and he also hit my middle stump twice. I was more comfortable coping with the bullets Down slung at me from five yards into the net, but nothing like sure enough to go into bat against the two fastest bowlers on the county circuit that year.

Lancashire had enticed Jefferson King, all 6ft 5in of him, from Port of Spain, where he was not considered good enough for Trinidad's Shell Shield side. He was a beanpole of a man, all arms and legs and elbows, with the same curving run-in from the boundary that Wes Hall had used in the videos I had seen of him. Some of the older commentators made comparisons between the two. He also fielded in the gully where his spider's arms seemed to cover the whole segment of the field between first slip and cover point. This was his second year with Lancashire, and his best figures had been 8 for 56 in the Roses match against Yorkshire. At the other end Joe Watkinson was coming towards the veteran stage of his career, a left-arm seamer after the style of John Lever, who on any pitch with movement in it could wing the ball like a banana. Either was capable of removing me from the scheme of things, Jeff by sheer speed and Watkinson with more subtle changes of pace and swing. This was not my idea of fun.

162

I ducked under a fast bouncer from Down.

'Haven't you got a helmet?'

'No, skipper. D'you think I should wear one?'

'You'll be a bloody fool if you don't. And a vizor as well.'

'All right, Rodge, you can wear mine,' said Down. 'Make sure you're out before I get in, that's all.'

'There's not much doubt of that,' I said, trying on the helmet and adjusting the webbing fitment. Down fastened the vizor to the clips provided.

'Give you a horse and you'll look like Sir Galahad,' he said.

Already I felt confined, closed in like a racehorse in blinkers. My head felt hot and I felt sweat beginning to form on my forehead and at the back of my neck. I took my guard in the net again. I ducked into the next ball which rose sharply and hit me on the helmet. It did not hurt, but it jarred me and a small spray of stars swam across my eyes.

'Are you okay?' Down sounded anxious. With some difficulty I prised the contraption off my head and handed it back to Down.

'Thanks, Gerry,' I said. 'I'd rather see what's going to hit me.'

Smithson looked worried. 'I wish you'd wear it, Roger,' he said. 'You haven't had much experience of pace. I don't want to answer for it if you get hit.'

'Sorry, Skip, I can't concentrate with that thing on my head. I feel slow and unbalanced. You'll get stick, anyway, for making me bat higher up the order. I'll last a lot longer for you without it.'

'It's your head.' He shrugged, and left it at that. I reflected that if a rookie had defied Grace's orders in a similar fashion, he would probably have been sacked, or would at least have sparked off a tirade of daunting proportions. I preferred Smithson's laid-back leadership. But I meant what I said. No doubt if I did get hit I would have to learn to acclimatise myself to wearing the helmet, but until then I was sure that my eyes and my reactions would protect me. As my father had said repeatedly: 'What the hell have you got a bat for?'

To prove my point I thrashed at Smithson's next ball, which whistled through my stroke with a distinct click as it took the edge. But I connected handsomely with a meaty hook on the next, which bulged the net towards square leg and elicited an ironic clap from Down.

'That's enough,' called Smithson, and I was surprised to find that my hangover had almost vanished, along with my attack of nerves, leaving me clear-headed and alert, and eager for the next half-hour to pass so I could take up the new, unexpected challenge.

7

The early morning crowd hummed with interest, not all of it flattering, as I strode out to the wicket with Smithson, wearing my brown Surrey cap in place of the more customary helmet. I don't remember feeling nervous, though I suppose I must have been. I heard the odd remark:

'He's not wearing a helmet. What d'you think of that?'

'Silly young bugger. King'll nail him, first ball.'

''Tis a bit hard, that, sending a kid in so soon.'

'T'others are wettin' 'emselves, I suppose.'

'No guts down south.'

I glanced at Smithson beside me. His face was expressionless, concentrating. He was to take the first over, from Jefferson King.

After the previous day's success I was cocky and overconfident, forgetting that cricket can be the most unforgiving of games when it is taken for granted. Having bowled well, it seemed only natural that I should bat just as well, if not better. I watched as King marked out his run and limbered up by bending and stretching his elastic torso into excruciating poses. Smithson took his guard meticulously, marking the crease with the toe of his boot. He gave the setting of the field a lingering look, and then settled down to receive the first ball of the day. There was nothing I could do but hold myself ready for a quick single if one was called, particularly towards the end of the over, but all that happened was that Smithson thick-edged an attempted drive past third slip in the general direction of third man, and we took a comfortable second run while the fielder was winding up to throw the ball in. 'Always two to Adams,' Smithson muttered as we crossed. He knew the third man's weakness of old. When the rest of the over had whistled harmlessly past Smithson's off-stump, it was my turn to take guard.

'Centre, please.'

'Hold your bat straight. A fraction away from you. Too much. Towards you. That's right. Centre.'

Umpire Pratt directed the little ceremony much as Simon Rattle might conduct a symphony orchestra. All he lacked was the baton. His body bent forward from the waist, his left hand behind his back, he motioned imperiously with his right forefinger using the whole of his lower arm to alter the position of my bat. When all was to his liking the arm shot forward, the fingers stiffly extended, and the whole movement was completed with a dismissive flick of the wrist. I almost expected him to take a bow, but the ritual had calmed me down and I faced up to the left-arm seamers of the experienced Watkinson with the confidence born of inexperience. I will never forget that over.

To start with, he bowled left arm over the wicket, so he approached from a different angle from the bulk of right-arm bowlers. To the spectator, the difference seems infinitesimal, but the inexperienced young batsman finds his stance opened up even before the ball is delivered, giving him a feeling of vulnerability. Watkinson's first ball seemed to loop into me like a boomerang, missing my defensive prod by six inches and thwacking painfully into my thigh guard. Instantly Lancashire's captain called up a second short-leg, so there were now two fielders in the periphery of my vision three yards from the bat.

The second ball appeared to be heading straight for my box, so I jabbed my bat down at the last moment and felt rather than saw it somehow evade the outside edge of the bat and the off-bail. I heard gasps from the area of the slips, and when I looked round, to my amazement five of them were standing there in a great arc round to gully, each expecting the fatal nick. After an in-swinger and a leg-cutter, what would Watkinson do next?

I found out soon enough. The third ball turned me inside out as it pitched short on the off-stump and seemed to follow me in the air as I tried to get bat and body out of its flight path, eventually falling backwards over my feet and sitting down with a jolt, narrowly missing the stumps. The ball cannoned off my chest into the wicket-keeper's arms and the whole of Lancashire, it seemed, appealed.

'Not out,' said Umpire Pratt, correctly.

Ball number four, a very fast, in-swinging yorker, landed in the block-hole fortuitously at the same time as the heel of my bat, squirting off past my legs and just eluding the stumps and the wicket-keeper's dive on its way to the boundary, much to Watkinson's frustration; the fifth flew unstoppably off the shoulder of the bat and over the slips' heads for four more runs. I never saw the sixth, which took my middle stump clean out of the ground. Punch-drunk, I started to walk back to the pavilion, but the forward of the two short legs stopped me.

'That was a no-ball,' he said, indicating the umpire, who was signalling with one arm extended to the scorers, while Watkinson glowered at me as though I had committed the cardinal sin. That left me to face one more ball, which in desperation I tried to hit into the River Mersey. It pitched neatly on middle-and-leg and hit middle-and-off, flattening all three stumps and an all-rounder's dream debut at the same time.

'Sorry, Skip,' I muttered as I passed Smithson on my long walk back to the pavilion.

'Don't worry,' he replied. 'I wouldn't have lasted two balls of an over like that.' But his generosity did not ease my feeling that I had let him and the side down. In the dressing room, Phil Hills poured some balm on my wounded ego by telling me that Len Hutton and Graham Gooch had both started their careers with two ducks.

'What are you moping for, lad? You got eight in the book, no matter how they got there, and no one can take 'em away from you.'

'But the captain told me to stay there.'

'You did your best, didn't you? You can't do better than that.'

Maybe not, but I was facing, probably for the first time in my life, the unpalatable fact that in some circumstances my best was just not good enough. Why not? I knew I had the will, and I was pretty sure that I had the ability. What I did not have was the technique as a batsman to deal with high-class pace bowling, and to acquire that I needed application and experience. The latter could only come with time, but while I was getting it I could apply myself to learning from the best coaches I could find. That resolution made, I felt better, and was able to turn to the other problem which I had been able to thrust to the back of my mind while trying to make my name as a cricketer.

Perhaps the answer was the same there. So far I had been stumbling along, trusting on luck, a certain natural cunning, and a tough physique to see me through the extraordinary series of incidents of the past few days. Really I was as much out of my depth in trying to deal with Mr Pravisar and his machinations as I had been in facing Watkinson, whose only ammunition had been, let's face it, a cricket ball. If I was to win through, in this, too, I would need the advice and help of experts. Fortunately one was to hand. I went in search of the gateman.

'Did my friend pick up his ticket?' I asked him. 'Mr Light?'

'Aye, he did.'

'Do you know where he went?'

'He asked where the best place was to sit, and I told

him top of the stand, wi' that ticket. Wi' any luck he'll fry oop there.'

I laughed: 'Why?'

'That's where all coppers end oop. In 'ell.'

'How did you know? That he's a policeman, I mean.'

'Smell one anywhere. Specially one from London.'

I thanked him and clambered up the narrow stairs to the top of the stand. Light was indeed there, in the full glare of the late morning sun, but the gateman would have been disappointed by his cool and casual appearance. Light was not frying that morning.

'The gateman thought he'd consigned you to perdition,' I said, squeezing onto the bench next to him. His neighbour made way with bad grace. 'Are you enjoying it?'

'A bloody sight more than you did,' he replied with a grin. 'You didn't know whether you were reamed, bored or countersunk.'

'True,' I said defiantly. 'But I did get eight. Which is eight more than I deserved. But I didn't come up here to talk to you about cricket. I came to ask if I could help you.'

'You can,' said Light. 'Talk to me about cricket. I'll ask the questions. You supply the answers.'

'What sort of questions?'

'You'll see. Let's find somewhere less public.'

That is a difficult thing to do on a cricket ground while a match is in progress, but fortunately there was space at Aigburth beyond the trees that ringed the playing area. We sat down on the grass in the deep shade of an oak and Light lay back and cradled his head in his hands.

'Tell me about the bat-making business,' he said. 'You've been born into it and brought up with it and when you've finished playing you'll probably make your living from it. What's it like? Is it worth it?'

'You'd be better off asking my father,' I said. 'Until he got mixed up with Grace he managed to make a fair living from it as an independent, but that's because he's

169

the best in the business. There must be twenty or thirty people like Dad around the country, but the living's risky. The trade is controlled by five or six big firms, who share a total of about twenty million pounds worth of business each year, and although they all know each other and regard bat-making as a sort of privileged club, it's pretty cut-throat. It's swings and roundabouts. First one gets the edge, then another, but by and large it's the personality at the top that counts. Which is why Stuart Surridge made such a go at Witham and Fearnley in Worcester. And dear old Jock Livingstone with Gray Nicholls at Robertsbridge. My dad used to think the world of him.

'A lot depends on who can afford to set the trends. Duncan Fearnley, who had Vivian Richards and Ian Botham on his books, promoted the big heavy bats so well that all the others were forced to copy them and bring out three and three-and-a-half pounders of their own. Now the trend is swinging back, because most cricketers aren't big, heavy, muscular men like Richards and Botham, and can't handle the weight. So the Aussies produced a new breed of classical batsmen like Waugh and Taylor, who could actually cut the ball, and lighter bats, say two-and-a-half pounds, came back into fashion. Then again, someone will produce a steel-sprung handle and call it by a fancy name, and that will sell well for a season or two.'

'Can the independent bat-makers stand the changes?'

'In general, yes, because their customers are usually local cricketers who have their own idiosyncracies, and they know each customer well. They make each bat individually, so it is relatively easy to adjust to differing standards. It's a bit difficult if your client wants you to add weight to a bat, but I've even known one chap who will let small lead weights into the meat of the bat to add weight and driving power. The problem in changing styles is mainly one for the big firms. If you re-tool the machinery to turn out something which the public doesn't want, there's not much you can do with a three-pound piece of willow and cane except to burn it. And if you set fire to your season's production of five thousand bats, you are kissing goodbye to the best part of half a million pounds.'

'Where are the costs? Timber?'

'Obviously, though it's not timber. *Salix auriculata* is actually grass, not wood, which accounts for its softness and wide grain. And it only grows satisfactorily for bat-making in England. I don't know why. People have tried to import willow from America, Holland, even Russia and Pakistan, but the experts have not found a satisfactory replacement for English White Willow anywhere in the world. It grows mainly in East Anglia, but there are scores of satisfactory plantations in Kent, Sussex, the home counties and the Midlands. There are even some in the north. Bats have been made at Willford (short for Willowford) since the eighteenth century. The plantations are usually on private farmers' land. Willow grows best beside running water in marshland which is not suitable for arable cultivation or pasture. The company manages the plantation and the farmer either takes rent or a percentage of the value at maturity, which for cricket bat purposes is six years. Conversely, the farmer will raise a plantation himself as an investment and sell to a timber company or direct to the bat-maker. The company will split it up into clefts, dry them out and sell them in bulk to the manufacturer, saving the bat-maker the job of doing it himself. My father, who learned his trade from Len Newberry and Walter Warsop, two of the great bat-makers in the first half of the century, selects his willow on site, as it is growing, has it felled and delivered, and cuts and dries it himself. That's one of the reasons he jibbed at taking the Pravisar order. F. North & Son has never bought in pre-dried clefts from the trade, which is how father preserves the quality of his bats and his reputation.'

'Where does Pravisar fit into all this? For that matter, where did Persse Grace come in, too?'

'Pravisar? I've no idea. We've known a couple of Pakistanis in the bat trade, but he's new to me. His order seems to us to be way over the top. It's about equivalent to ten per cent of the entire export market for a year, and he can't hope to sell that number of bats, even if he brings the price down. They're not even first-class quality, so there certainly won't be any repeat orders. And I told you what I saw in his factory along the road. He's mad.'

'I don't think so. Paranoid, maybe. Crooked, certainly. And Grace?'

'Again, no idea. He's been sponsored by my father for years. That's the way county cricketers survive. They get their equipment free. Grace gets – used to get – through about six bats a year. I don't know if it was worth it for us. We got some business through him, but more by word of mouth and dad's reputation for straight dealing. Persse tried to bully us into sponsoring the whole Surrey team, but we weren't in that league.'

'Did your father like Grace?'

'Everything was sweetness and light at first, until Grace began putting the pressure on. For the last couple of years or so he's hated Persse's guts, like most people who knew him.'

'Why did he continue to associate with him, then?'

'I suppose he had no alternative. He couldn't see a way to break out of the debt. Dad's too straight, if you like. He wouldn't try to duck out of an obligation. If only he'd told me.'

'What association did Grace have with Pravisar?'

'All I know is that it was close enough to allow Pravisar to lord it over us in the dressing room. He's a smooth bastard, Pravisar. But Jason – that's Bob Jason, the thug – warned me against tangling with him. He said Pravisar would get me. Well, he did. But he left me in a position to get free, more or less unharmed. I'm sure he also abducted Sally Lang and dad, but he either drugged them or hypnotised them to make them forget. He didn't seem to have harmed them in any way.'

'Perhaps it was to show you his power.'

'But why? Why me?'

He didn't answer.

'Has Pravisar any influence in the Surrey club itself?'

'I don't think so, but he might have. He's a member, of course. Angie, the secretary's bird, showed me the list. But he's very well in with Lord Marcelan, the chairman, who seems to know him well. He was with Marcelan at The Oval the evening Grace was killed. And Angie told me that Mr Allason, the secretary is scared of Mr Pravisar. She looked him up in the computer register of members. He's on a special list compiled by Grace, but no one knows how to access that now Grace is dead, except Mr Thorogood the accountant, and he's away on holiday.'

A quiet but insistent high-pitched bleeping interrupted us. Light pulled a plastic portable radio-telephone from his pocket, extended the aerial, pressed a couple of buttons, and spoke into it.

'Light here.'

He held the telephone to his ear. Although I could hear the metallic cadences of speech, I could not make out what was being said. He listened for a few minutes. Then, 'I'll tell him,' he said. He pushed the aerial in with the palm of his hand and returned the radio to his pocket. He did not turn round, so I could only see his face in profile. The muscles beside his mouth were taut.

'I have to tell you,' he said, 'that your father is missing.'

I could not speak for a moment. Then I seized his arm and swung him round to face me.

'What the hell d'you mean? I thought you stupid buggers were keeping an eye on him. How can he be missing? When did he go missing?'

Light's eyes were motionless on mine. Without moving, he said: 'Steady, Roger. We're doing what we can. We've been watching Willford twenty-four hours a day. At three o'clock this morning a minicab pulled up at the house and your father got into it. Our chap was not told to stop him going anywhere – he's not under arrest – so he took the car number and waited for the car to move off before reporting by radio. While he was waiting he was hit on the back of the head and left in the road outside the house. He didn't recover consciousness until Miss Lang found him at eight-thirty this morning. His radio was broken and the phone in the house ripped out. He was concussed, but she propped him up on her bicycle and pushed him into the village. Sergeant Tapp was out on his morning round, so Miss Lang went to the shop next door to the police house and persuaded a Mrs Boswell to put our man to bed and call the doctor while she telephoned county HQ in Lewes to raise the alarm. It wasn't until eleven o'clock that our man came round sufficiently to find his notebook with the number of the minicab written in it and was able to tell us what had happened.

'The car belongs to George Hansford, a local man, and he and it are missing as well. His wife says he was woken by telephone at 2 a.m. and told her he'd been called out on a long trip. She thought he said something about a two hundred mile job, but didn't say where. She was half asleep and didn't register very much, except he said he'd be back at about midday today. It's gone that and he hasn't turned up yet. There's an all-cars alert out for both of them and the car, but we've had no luck so far. We'll find them. But its forced our hand. We'll be raiding all those addresses tonight. Where are you going, Roger?'

He stopped me in mid-stride.

'To find my father, of course.'

Light gripped me by the arm. 'Don't be an idiot, Roger. That's a job for us.'

'You haven't done much of a job so far,' I said angrily. Light sighed. His eyes were concerned. He seemed to come to a decision. His grip tightened on my arm.

'All right, I'll take a chance. He's your father. Find

him, but for God's sake keep in touch. You've got my number. And make it look good. It's my job on the line and you're supposed to be under arrest. Old Bill won't be too pleased.'

'To hell with Old Bill.' I shook off his hand and stormed off to the dressing room, Light following closely behind. I stuffed my kit and my clothes into my cricket bag without bothering to change out of flannels.

'What are you doing, young 'un? You can't leave the ground without permission during a match.' It was Phil Hills.

'Look, Phil. This is Inspector Light, of Scotland Yard. He'll tell you. My father's been abducted in the night. I've got to go and find him.'

My desperation must have got through to him.

'Ay, lad, but they won't like it.'

'Too bad. Tell the skipper, will you. And Carnock. I'll be back as soon as I can.'

My arms were seized from behind.

'You're going nowhere, North,' said Light. 'You're under arrest.'

'What the hell?!' I struggled fiercely, forcing him to grab me even more tightly. Hills started to cross the room towards us.

'Knock me out!' Light whispered fiercely in my ear as we wrestled. His grip slackened and I broke loose, swinging round and stiff-arming him on the point of the jaw. It was a neat blow, given the circumstances. He collapsed limply backwards, eyes closed, into Hills's arms, while I grabbed my cricket bag and bolted through the door and down the stairs two at a time.

No one stopped me. Fortunately the Alfa was parked with a clear road to the exit and the man on the gate had enough sense to lift the barrier and step out of the way as I zoomed through into the main road, tyres spinning and spitting gravel. Within two minutes I was on the motorway and heading south, travelling fast but taking care to move

175

with the stream of traffic so as not to be too noticeable. With one stop to buy an Ordnance Survey map of Essex, a tankful of petrol and a quick sandwich, I rolled into the quiet Witham High Street just before six o'clock in the evening, five-and-a-half hours after leaving Aigburth.

Sitting in the car, I studied the map. I found the village of Totham easily enough, but even the minute detail of the map could not give me Fairbridge Farm. It could have been any one of a number of tiny dots down any number of hair-like lanes. I would have to ask the way. I looked around. Witham, bypassed by the A12 and seemingly by life itself, dozed in the early evening sun. Immediately across the road from the car a little red-brick building displayed a Victorian blue glass lamp with its neat white printing: POLICE.

It was then that the stupidity of the chance I was taking struck me so forcibly that I almost gave up. I was working on the slimmest of hunches. Although I was sure that my father had been kidnapped by, or on the orders of, Pravisar, I had no proof that he had been taken to Fairbridge Farm, near Totham, nor was there any logical reason why he should have been. My only clue was that this was where Bob Jason had told me that he had taken most of the cricket bats Pravisar had bought. It was also a rough two hundred mile round trip from Willford, which fitted with what the taxi-driver's wife had mentioned. I had no idea what I was going to do when I found the farm. Taking the map, I strolled across the road and into the police station.

There was no one at the white, scrubbed reception counter or at the three desks in the small room behind. The only suggestion of life was a grey plastic box beyond the farthest desk which gave out an irregular buzzing sound. Beneath it I could see a large pair of well-polished black boots. I tapped the small brass bell on the counter and it gave out a musical 'ting'. Then I remembered that I had assaulted a Detective Inspector of New Scotland Yard (albeit with his

176

consent) and that I was on the run, having resisted arrest. I was also still dressed in white cricket flannels, which in itself should have alerted any policeman in the country to the fact that something was wrong. On tiptoe, I prepared to creep out. It was too late. The black boots had moved, slowly but inexorably, and their owner had hauled himself ponderously to his feet from behind the grey telephone exchange and was coming towards me. He was a massive man with gentle eyes in an almost circular face burnt the colour of a new cricket ball. He was in shirt-sleeves, but with three chevrons on his right biceps, held in place by a rubber band and a large safety-pin.

'What can I do for you sir?' he said politely but un-curiously in the broadest East Anglian. I became conscious that I was holding the map.

'Er, thanks, sergeant. Can you tell me where Fairbridge Farm is on this map? I can find Totham, but not the individual farm.'

'Let me see, sir.' He turned the map round with massive fingers. 'You see, sir, there are two Tothams, Great and Little. Fairbridge lies between them. Shall I mark it for you?'

He took a ball-point from his breast pocket and ringed a dot on the map. For good measure he placed a cross within the ring and handed back the map.

'There you are, sir,' he said in a slow Essex drawl. 'Been playing cricket, sir?'

'Er, yes, a charity match at Chelmsford,' I said too quickly. 'I was asked to go to Fairbridge. I understand they've got some cricket bats for sale.'

'I wouldn't know, sir,' the slow voice pondered. 'You could ask in the White Hart in Totham, sir. They're sure to know. Landlord's name is De'Ath, same as mine. He's my cousin. Spelt De, apostrophe, Ath. Good old Essex name. You're not from these parts, sir?' The brown eyes in the red, flat face held nothing more than polite inquiry.

'Er, no. I live in Sussex. And, er, in London.'

I thanked him and walked, as casually as I could, back to the car. I had no idea whether he had recognised me or not, whether he was at that moment on the telephone to Essex CID. I looked back. The door was still open. Police Sergeant De'Ath (with the apostrophe) was still standing at his counter. I waved, and he lifted a heavy hand in response as I let in the clutch and drove off towards the villages of Great and Little Totham. Then I realised that I had not asked him which Totham his brother's pub was in.

The lanes were narrow, but the hedges were bright with honeysuckle and dog-roses on the fifteen minute meander through the Essex countryside, and I spotted two or three promising stands of willow, four or five years old, along the banks of a stream. The White Hart stood red brick and four-square on the edge of a small cluster of houses that presumably comprised Little Totham, and a carbon copy of Sergeant De'Ath, in braces and shirt-sleeves, was leaning against the door jamb.

'You'll be the gennulman looking for Fairbridge?' he inquired as I pulled up gently on the gravel frontage. 'Tom just phoned me through from Witham. Well now . . .' And he launched into one of those interminably embellished lists of ultimately quite straightforward instructions, punctuated with sweeping gestures and assurances that I couldn't miss it. I turned left by the double oak with the branch torn off by last winter's storm, carried on past Yew Tree Farm with the crooked chimbleys, forked left past Old Ebenezer's thatched cottage with the roses over the porch, negotiated without incident the dry water-splash which flowed something terrible last spring, found the sign board half-hidden in the uncut hedge and turned into a narrow, rutted, muddy farm track which was not intended for a low-slung Alfa Romeo coupé. The track had been used heavily recently, by a van or a lorry, for the muddy ruts were wet and fairly deep. Occasional gates on either side allowed glimpses of open, flat fields and grazing cattle and the occasional stand of willow. The Alfa grounded hard a couple of times, but I scraped through without getting bogged down, hugging the hedgerows and trying to keep the wheels out of the ruts. The overhanging hedges had been broken, battered and spattered with mud, and scraped dirt along the Alfa's glossy painted sides. Round a sharp bend the track broadened out into a lane and gravel had been used to fill in the ruts. After another hundred yards or so a new five-bar metal gate blocked the way, and beyond was a concrete yard in front of a big old barn with a rounded corrugated-iron roof and new corrugated-iron sides.

A six-foot barbed wire fence ran round the whole property, which as far as I could see was surrounded by open country. A line of poles brought electricity and telephone wires across the fields to the barn, but there were no other buildings on the concrete yard. It was a lonely, forbidding place after the warmth of the lanes. There was no lock on the gate, so I pulled back the latch to open it and drove the Alfa through, parking on the rough concrete which had seen better days. There was no sign of another vehicle, but a number of dried-out wheel tracks led to the only entrance to the building; a set of huge double sliding doors, large enough to allow a thirty ton transporter through. These were locked, and so was a small inset wooden door with a brass plate on, similar to the one I had seen in Soho, saying WORLD BATS INC.

I pressed a white bell-push and set up a harsh jangle of sound inside the barn. No one appeared, so I thumbed the bell again, pressing my ear to the door in an endeavour to hear any movement inside. Nothing stirred. I tried the handle of the door. It would not budge. I put my shoulder against it, and shoved. I felt the door move a fraction under the pressure, but it was still solid. Searching around for some sort of lever, I found a foot-long screwdriver in the Alfa's tool kit, so I jabbed it into the jamb of the door and tried to use it as a jemmy, hauling on it to force the lock to give. The wood splintered, but the door held fast. In desperation, I backed off a half a dozen yards and ran at the door, jumping horizontally straightening my legs and slamming both my feet into the door with the whole weight of my body behind them. The lock still held, but the door burst off its hinges and sagged open. I picked myself up, rubbed a bruised shoulder and went inside. There was no light, so I felt along the wall until I found a switch.

The arc lights revealed a similar set-up to that of Jackson Bats in Aigburth, only on a larger scale. There were three large containers and scores of wooden crates. Each crate was labelled: Cape Town, Sydney, New York, Karachi, Amsterdam, Buenos Aires. Closer inspection revealed the name of a company, sports shop or club. I looked at some of them. Woollebarra CC, New South Wales. Ahmed Faisal and Sons Sports Emporium, Jalalabad. The Kowloon Sports and Social Club. Van Hoogen Sports, Delft. Sun Valley CC, California. P. R. A. Visar Cricket Bat Co, Islamabad. They all looked genuine addresses.

One smaller container stood apart. It was labelled 'Bamboo cane' and was addressed to World Bats Inc., Fairbridge Farm, and was obviously an import from Mexico. It had been broken open and I was tall enough to peer inside. Six-foot lengths of seasoned bamboo had been thrust aside, and between them showed glimpses of something white. I dug my hands in and grasped shiny plastic. With some effort, I dragged out an oblong packet weighing 20lb or more, professionally heat-sealed. For the first time I began to realise just what I had tangled with. The stuff had to be cocaine, or some such drug. I wondered how I had not cottoned on before.

I turned my attention to the long work-bench. There was a rack of tools, looking pretty new, and a sheaf of invoices held together by a bulldog clip. I leafed through them; they looked familiar. Then I realised that the names coincided with those in the scorebook I had found in Grace's cricket bag. I was willing to bet the amounts would coincide too. The discovery would definitely link Grace to the drug shipments. This was the jackpot. I switched my attention to the tools. They were the same as those in Aigburth, including the curious sausage-maker. But this one was attached to an inch-wide nylon band which led from a reel to the rear of the machine. A three foot hopper was suspended above the machine, leading into its funnel, and the whole affair was wired to a switch screwed onto the bench beside it. I touched the switch, and the machine began to hum. As it did so a white sausage extruded slowly from the front of the machine until it was about 8 inches long. There was a sharp click and the sausage dropped into a bucket hung below the machine. The machine carried on producing the curious sausages at the rate of about one every ten seconds. Each had been sealed at both ends with a little metal tag. I picked one up. It weighed about a pound.

I switched off the machine and inspected one of the sausages closely. Just as in Aigburth, there was a padded vice at the far end of the bench, and beside it a drill with the same, curious, foot-long bit. I picked a bat from a pile on the bench and clamped it in the vice. The V-shaped splice had been forced open and replaced, but it did not appear to have been re-glued. A sharp tap with the heel of my hand broke the bat in two. A hole had been drilled down the centre of the blade and there, nestling in it, was one of the white sausages. I shook the blade and tapped the end, and the sausage slipped out easily. I used a chisel to slit it open and examined the white powder it contained. It had to be cocaine.

I sat on the bench and worked it out. Pravisar was turning the drugs trade inside out; importing the stuff in bulk and using the bat exporting business to redistribute it worldwide. Assuming that all the 2,500 bats on our export order carried their pound of cocaine, this meant he was shifting well over a ton of the muck at one shot. I had no idea of the 'street value', as the newspapers put it, but it had to be worth hundreds of millions of pounds. My anger rose. The bastard was using our firm, my father's name and reputation, to further his filthy business. He had to be stopped. It was time to tell the police everything, whatever the consequences.

I looked around for a telephone. At first I couldn't see one, but at the end of the work-bench was a waste bin. For no particular reason I glanced inside. To my amazement, there was an FNS cricket bat, the handle stripped down and a tiny syringe let into it. Gingerly I lifted it out and studied it. The syringe still held some dried red matter. Ink? This was the joke bat that my father had made for Grace; the model for the one that had killed him. Here was proof indeed that my father had been telling the truth. And more information for the police. Where was that telephone? I had seen the wire coming into the barn, so it had to be somewhere. As I prowled around, I heard a noise, as though someone was breathing with difficulty.

I froze. There was no other sound in the huge barn. I moved a few paces forward, then to the left. The breathing seemed to be coming from a crate in the corner; one of those destined for Jalalabad. The top was nailed down firmly. I could not shift it with my hands. I found a big screwdriver and a claw hammer on the bench and ripped the lid off the crate, tearing the boards away with frantic speed. There, on a bed of cricket bats, was my father, lying on his back with his mouth wide open and his eyes closed, his voice rasping softly in short sharp gasps. His face scared me the most. It was bluish-grey, the skin drawn tightly over the cheek-bones and away from the eyes, creating great black saucers in which the lids stretched paper-thin over the eyeballs. His jacket had been thrown over him, and one shirtsleeve had been pushed up. A thin trickle of blood had run down from his upper arm and congealed dark brown. At its apex was a small puncture, as though he had been injected with a hypodermic syringe. Frantically I felt for his wrist. His pulse was weak, but now the top was off the crate his breath seemed to be coming slightly more easily. I held his ice-cold fingers, my mind racing.

All my instincts told me to telephone the police and get my father to hospital straight away. But there were a number of things that militated against that. Although Light had connived at my 'escape', it would be his word against mine. The evidence would be strongly against me if I was found in a barn full of cricket bats stuffed with cocaine patently ready to be smuggled all over the world, on export dockets provided by my father. Pravisar could not avoid the fact that he controlled World Bats, but he would certainly claim that Frank North & Son were running the drugs racket for themselves. I had very little concrete proof of his involvement that would stand up to cross-examination in court, and in any case Pravisar or his henchmen could return at any moment and find us both while we were waiting for the police to arrive. I did not fancy our chances of coming out of such an encounter alive.

I made up my mind. An old friend of my father lived only a few miles away, in Little Baddow, near Chelmsford, in an old weather-board house on the banks of the River Chelmer. He had retired from general practice a few years ago to live on the land he had acquired when he had run a prosperous practice in Danbury, and for several years he had supplied F. North & Son with perfectly matured willow from the stands my father planted for him each year. Dr Waring, Julian to his friends, had lost his wife twenty years before during the birth of his only son, and had never remarried. The son had died two weeks later, and the doctor had recovered from the double tragedy by indulging in a two-year, round-the-world trip which was still talked about in cricket circles, and then devoting every spare minute of his time to cricket. He had been chairman of Essex CCC, an MCC committee man, captain of I Zingari and vice-president of half a dozen lesser clubs. He took his holiday every winter to tour with the England team and delivered scathing judgments on everything from the state of pitches in Bulawayo to the catering in the members' bar

183

at Lord's. He was irascible, entertaining and knowledgeable, and I thought he was just the man to turn to for advice and help. I had no way of knowing whether he would be at home. I took one more chance on that day of chances, praying that my luck would not run out just yet.

I found the telephone in a side office and Scotland Yard put me straight through to Ashcroft. He did not interrupt as I spoke as urgently as I knew how, telling him of all that I had found adding merely that I was rushing my father, who was unconscious, to a doctor. He said police would be there in fifteen minutes; they had already been alerted by Witham. I hung up fast, and carried the inert body of my father as gently as I could to the Alfa, and made him as comfortable as possible on the back seat, wrapping him in two of my cricket sweaters and cradling his head on a third. I went back for the joke bat my father had made. There seemed no point in trying to cover up the traces of my visit so I did not bother to close the crate in which I found him or to disguise the smashed door. Instead I went to the work-bench and in the cocaine dust by the sausage machine I wrote with my fingers two words: 'Oval, Saturday.' I felt I owed Pravisar something for those threatening notes. An idea had formed, incomplete, reckless and probably unworkable. But it was better than nothing.

It was past ten o'clock and dusk was falling by the time I turned into the short drive by Dr Waring's house. No lights were on, and I suffered a moment's qualm that he might be away, but as I got out of the car the porch lit up and the front door opened. The unmistakable barrel of a shotgun poked round the lintel, followed by a red face with bushy white moustaches and a voice which rasped out: 'Who goes there?'

'Roger North, sir. Frank's son. I'm sorry to bother you at this time of night, but I need your help. My father's in the back, and he's very ill.'

'Frank North. Ill? What's the matter?'

He threw the gun with a clatter into the umbrella stand by the door and bustled out to the car. He was wearing slippers and, in spite of the heat, an old woollen cardigan with leather patches at the elbows.

'Show me! Show me!'

He pushed me out of the way and bent into the back of the car.

'Torch. Inside the door.' The order was accompanied with an imperious gesture behind his back. I ran to fetch the miniature searchlight he kept for just such emergencies. He shone the light full on my father's face, turning up the eyelid with a thumb.

'Hah!'

The torch illuminated the puncture and dried blood on my father's arm. Dr Waring thrust his hand inside dad's shirt to feel his heart.

'Is he all right?' I asked anxiously. He answered my question with two of his own.

'Who did this? What is it?'

'I don't know positively,' I said, answering both questions at once. 'But I think it's cocaine.'

'Hmmm. You're probably right,' he said gruffly. 'He'll live. He should be in hospital, of course, but you've probably got a good reason for not taking him. Bring him inside and we'll put him to bed. Then you can tell me all about it. You look as though you could do with a drink, too.'

Between us we carried my unconscious father upstairs. Waring produced a pair of pyjamas three sizes too big and a syringe, which he stuck unfeelingly into my father's buttock.

'That'll help reduce the reaction to the drug,' he said. 'He'll wake up in the morning with a monumental thirst and the worst hangover he's ever had. He'll also have a craving for another fix. A dose like that can make a junkie overnight. Leave him here and I'll see it doesn't. He'll be right as rain by Saturday.'

He waved my thanks away.

'Don't be such a bloody fool. Do the same for any of my friends. I'll get you some coffee and a bite to eat. Better than alcohol, though you can have some if you wish. Come into the kitchen. You talk. I'll cook.'

In the next ten minutes, while I gave him an abbreviated account of what had led me to his door, he rustled up two huge omelettes with mushroom fillings and fried potatoes, one of which he wolfed down with as much enjoyment as I did, washing it down with a big mug of strong black coffee. He listened in silence as I completed my story. He showed no surprise at any of its more outlandish aspects.

'What do you intend to do now?' was all he said.

'Well, sir, if you really mean I can leave dad here in your care, I'll drive back to Liverpool tonight. I'm supposed to be playing cricket for Surrey. Then I'll figure out what I should do.'

'Yes, you are playing for Surrey.' He seemed to think that was the most important thing. 'Your lads did all right today, after you were out. They finished with 386 for 7. Smithson got a hundred and there were a couple of long fifties. I pick up the commentary on the telephone cricket lines. Costs me a fortune. You'll be needed in the morning. Take care on the roads.'

I thanked him from the bottom of my heart and drove away profoundly relieved that my father was in safe hands, and that neither the police nor Pravisar could have the slightest idea where he had been taken. They would assume from the brief message I left scrawled on the bench that it was from me, but they would have no inkling of my intended course of action. I wasn't much better informed myself, except I knew that the longer I could keep him guessing the safer I would be. Pravisar had the sort of mind that might even assume that, as I hadn't gone immediately to the police, I might be tempted to join him if I was offered sufficient incentive.

I set out from Little Baddow just before midnight and

picked up my key from the Apollyon reception desk at a quarter past three in the morning. The speedometer touched 120 on occasions, and I was very fortunate not to be pulled up. There was a message in my pigeon-hole, but I left it there unopened and went straight up to our room. Phil Hills turned over sleepily and inquired where the hell had I been, but it didn't sound serious so I threw my clothes on the floor and crashed onto my bed.

The sun was shining through the rain that was choking me in my dream as I woke up to a brilliant morning with Hills standing over the bed with an upturned glass in his hand. My nose, eyes and mouth were full of water and there was a grin on his face.

'I've always wanted to do that,' he said with vast satisfaction. 'I couldn't wake you by shaking you. You must have had a helluva night.'

'I did,' I said, spluttering and lifting my head from the soggy mess that was my pillow. 'But I can't elaborate just yet. Have they missed me?'

'There was a bit of moaning, but that copper you laid out didn't seem to mind. He told everyone that the message he'd brought you was that your dad was dangerously ill. He thought you'd gone a bit crazy with worry and he'd tried to stop you haring off and hurting yourself.'

'That was good of him. I hit him pretty hard. I've still got the bruise.' I rubbed my elbow.

'How is your father?' said Hills. 'What was wrong with him?'

'He's fine now,' I said truthfully. 'When I found him he was unconscious. But he's being looked after by a doctor friend of the family, who has said there's nothing to worry about.'

Such a skimpy version of the truth was as far as I could go, but the details seemed to satisfy Hills and nearly everyone else to whom I gave them during the day and I learned, in the tradition of the British Civil Service, that

187

the best way to lie was to tell as much of the truth as possible and leave out as much of it as necessary. The exception was Detective Inspector Light, who was very angry indeed when he caught me on my third piece of toast in the breakfast room.

'Don't you come any of that bloody Armstrong rubbish about being economical with the truth with me,' he said. 'This isn't *Spycatcher*. I let you go deliberately because I thought you would lead us straight to them and we'd have nabbed the lot. We would have done, too, but that country bumpkin in Witham didn't report that he'd spotted you. At least he did, but he wrote it all in his handover report to the night duty sergeant and only gave it to him when he came on duty at ten o'clock last night. We nearly lost the lot, and we haven't got Pravisar yet. He's as slippery as an eel.'

'I'm sorry,' I said. 'I took a chance on being able to find father. I didn't know how much you knew, or were prepared to tell me, and I was scared out of my mind that they would kill him.'

I told him how I had found my father drugged unconscious and locked in a crate, apparently destined to be shipped to Pakistan with a consignment of doctored cricket bats. 'I still don't know why he wasn't guarded and how I was able to break in and get him away without being caught.'

'That's easy. There were only four of them at Fairbridge, and they were called away to meet a truck from Tilbury with a fresh container of cane and cocaine. They did the switch just off the A12 at a place called Galleywood Common. They reckoned your dad was quite safe where he was. Customs had been working on the whole network from the other end, and we watched the switch and compared notes. Then we got the Witham report and things fell into place. You must have missed bumping into them head-on in those lanes by about five minutes. Lucky for you that you did.

'When we got there the place was in uproar. Two

trucks were loading, one for Gatwick, the other for the continent. No sign of you, or your father. And of course Jason and his pals swore blind they knew nothing of either of you, but they'll turn Queen's Evidence to save their skins. There was no sign of Pravisar. We laid on simultaneous raids at all the other addresses you'd given us. Four were empty, but in Aigburth we picked up Jackson and three others, plus about a quarter of a ton of cocaine and five hundred prepared cricket bats. We haven't totted it all up yet, but the Customs first estimate is that we've picked up twenty-five million pounds' worth of cocaine.'

'That sounds pretty good.'

'Yes, but so far we've bagged only the minnows. We're after Pravisar and his associates: the men with the money who organise the system. We don't think Pravisar's the top man either, but he must be fairly high up.'

'Surely there's enough evidence to arrest him now. It's his firm, World Bats, which is doing the smuggling.'

'We can hold him for twenty-four hours on suspicion without a warrant, when we find him. If he hasn't skipped the country by now. And you and your father are the shippers, on paper and in law. We've only your word for it that you were acting under duress when you signed those papers. Pravisar will laugh in your faces. You also have to remember,' he added grimly, 'that you and your father are the prime suspects in the murder of Persse Grace. Which is my priority.'

I had forgotten the precariousness of our position.

'There's something else to tell you. I found the bat Dad made for Grace in a waste bin. Syringe and all. With the remains of red ink. It was the model for the one that killed Grace. It's in my car.'

That made Light even more angry, but somehow his threats had lost some of their potency. My father was safe and Light would not have acted as he did in letting me go in search of my father had he believed either of us to be guilty. But it was time for me to be getting to the

Aigburth ground. Life, and particularly cricket, had to go on. I looked at my watch and said as much. There was no mirth in Light's smile.

'At least you'll be somewhere I can keep an eye on you,' he said. 'Me and a couple of thousand others.'

'I think I may be able to help find Pravisar,' I said. 'I'm pretty sure he'll be at The Oval tomorrow, provided you don't put out a warrant for his arrest.' I explained about the message I had left in the cocaine dust on the work-bench at Fairbridge Farm. 'I think he's arrogant enough to believe he can bluff this out, even now. I might even be able to persuade him to talk to me. Would you be interested?'

Light sat up. 'So long as I can be there to listen to the conversation.'

'I think that can be arranged. I've an idea.' I said. Light groaned, and I sketched out my plan and he groaned again. 'Certainly not unless Ashcroft sanctions it,' he said. 'He won't. It's totally against regulations, and you're not even a member of the force.'

'Ask him,' I said. 'Couldn't you swear me in as a Special Constable or something for a day. I'd promise to resign immediately afterwards.'

'You must be joking,' he said gloomily.

'I'm not. Promise you,' I said, and left him sitting contemplating a table full of dry toast and cold coffee.

8

My welcome at Aigburth was cool, to say the least. Smithson and Carnock both made it perfectly clear that I had transgressed all the rules by leaving the field without permission, no matter what the circumstances.

'We can't have people pissing off for any reason at all,' Smithson said toughly. 'To teach you a lesson, you'll be twelfth man again tomorrow against Worcestershire. I know you did bloody well here with the ball, but you'll not dictate terms to Surrey while I'm skipper, d'you understand?'

I nodded. 'Sorry Skip,' seemed the only reply. In fact his proposed punishment might suit me very well, if my plans worked out.

'How is your father, anyway?' he added more kindly.

'He'll be okay now. He's in good hands.'

'Good. You can't play cricket with a load on your mind. Get changed now. You've got a job to do. I'll leave you to Harry's tender mercies.'

Carnock was anything but tender. He laid on his imitation Persse Grace manner.

'I'm told you didn't get in until three o'clock in the morning,' he said in a hectoring tone. 'We'll have to see if you're fit enough to pull your weight today. We don't like slackers at Surrey. It's a matter of discipline. Not to say self-discipline,' he added pompously. 'You'll be docked fifty quid for that, and another fifty quid, with Down, for having nude women in your rooms. The hotel has complained.'

A hundred pounds was not much less than I earned in a week, but there was nothing I could do about it. As coach and manager, Carnock was completely within his rights, although I thought his punishments excessive. It would not do me much good to hit him, so I contented myself with the comment: 'Jealous?', knowing full well that that was exactly what he was. The days when Harry Carnock could entertain a girl in his room, in any state of dress or undress, were long past.

'Don't worry about my state of health, Harry,' I said. 'The girls don't,' and ran down the steps to follow the rest of the team onto the field. Don Smithson threw the new ball to me.

'It'll be harder work this time,' he said. 'But if we can get them going we might just roll them over. It's all a question of pressure.'

With all his bombast, this was an area of cricket at which Grace had excelled. He had exercised pressure by shouting and pointing, mouthing comments in the slips and switching fielders in mid-over. If a batsman looked as if he were ready, Grace would ostentatiously query the shape of the ball with the umpires, examine an imaginary defect in the pitch, ask the batsmen unnecessarily if they wanted the sight-screens moved, and generally try to disturb their rhythm and concentration. The ploys sometimes failed to work, because the more experienced county batsmen knew Grace too well of old, and so concentrated on ignoring him, or because his own bowlers and fielders were quite as often given the jitters themselves by his performance.

Smithson applied pressure more subtly. By the end of my first over he had increased the number of my slips from three to five without once raising his voice, but making a point of studying the wicket closely between my first two deliveries. For Symonds, at the other end he told Hills to stand up to the stumps, risking the occasional four byes for the effect of having the wicket-keeper breathing down the batsman's neck. Next he set two deep fine-legs and told me to bowl bouncers until warned by the umpire, and the opening batsman was caught off a top-edged hook off the second ball by Symonds in a position best described as long-stop.

'These West Indians can't resist a hook,' he murmured to me, pleased as Punch. 'Now try to bowl a slow, swinging yorker – a low full toss will do. It might surprise Da Silva. He always tries to play across his legs.'

I managed the slow, swinging yorker pretty well, relaxing my wrist at the last moment and letting the ball loop from my hand. But the rest was not quite as intended. Just as Smithson predicted, Da Silva played across his front pad, but instead of being trapped l.b.w., the middle of the bat met the ball sweetly on the full toss and sent it streaking to the mid-wicket boundary. So I tried a fast, out-swinging yorker which Da Silva drove fiercely into the covers. But his head was not quite over the ball and, though it was struck hard, Belfer held on to the catch at ankle height, left-handed and at full-stretch thirty yards from the bat. He rolled with the catch like a circus tumbler, came up with a leap and tossed the ball forty feet into the air in jubilation.

'They either stick or they don't,' he said as we crowded round to congratulate him. At ten for two wickets it looked as though we did have Lancashire on the run. But it wasn't to be as easy as that. The bite had gone out of the wicket after two days of blazing sun, and, try as I might, I found it almost impossible to get the ball to rise more than stump high. At least I had the extra pace to keep the batsmen on their toes, but Symonds' seamers went placidly onto the bat without the slightest deviation. Down did a little better, taking a couple of wickets with the aid of Hills, one caught behind and one stumped, as we chipped away at the innings. But by lunch-time Lancs were 150 for 4, within 20 or so of our total, and the match looked as though it would end in a draw.

A couple of overs after lunch, with the luck that makes one captain a genius when another remains merely pedestrian, Smithson decided to switch the bowlers over, transferring Symonds to the pavilion end while I was to take over bowling from the sea end. To accomplish the switch, he gave Taffy Evans, our very occasional leg-spinner, an over from my end and told me to take a breather for an over or two. Evans, a chirpy optimist, beamed with delight, rolled his wrist over experimentally, and proceeded to take two wickets in his first over. The first came from a skied drive to deep cover-point where Down had been stationed as a sort of sweeper to patrol the boundary and stop fours. I never did get back on to bowl. By tea-time Evans had mesmerised the Lancashire batsmen into an extravagant array of false strokes and had taken five of the six wickets to fall in the afternoon session for thirty-odd runs, his career-best return, and Surrey were left needing 121 runs to win the match in ten minutes plus twenty overs.

'No bother, just take it calmly,' Smithson told us all in the dressing room. 'It's a Sunday doddle, provided we keep things steady.'

And so it should have been, on a wicket that was still playing true, but when I went in to bat twenty runs were still needed in three overs and only two wickets were left intact. King, the big West Indian, was at one end with four wickets to his credit and my tormentor of the first innings, Watkinson, was at the other with three. I had to face King, and his first ball whistled past my nose before I even had time to focus on it properly. The second snicked off the inside edge for one of those fours which really infuriate the bowler. I negotiated the next three balls in some style and managed a perfectly respectable on-drive for a single off the last. Hills, my partner, came down the wicket to speak to me.

194

'Well played, Roger. Fifteen to win. Keep your eye on the ball. This left-hander's full of tricks.'

'I'll try,' I said doubtfully, remembering how Watkinson had dealt summarily with me in the first innings.

'Just watch his third ball,' said Hills. 'Be ready for a fast yorker. That's his style.'

'Thanks,' I said. 'How will I recognise it?'

'When it knocks your middle stump out of the ground.' Hills grinned at me. 'Unless you stop it first.'

Perhaps Watkinson was tired, or the wicket had truly lost its venom, or perhaps the ball was older and not so hard. Whatever it was, this time I had no difficulty at all with him. The first two balls were innocuous enough, medium-paced and short, and I played them both easily and as correctly as I could back to the bowler. The third was well pitched up, but short enough of a yorker length to become a full half-volley. Automatically my left leg went forward to the pitch of the ball, the bat came down in a full arc and, with the sweetest of clicks and a minimum of effort, the ball soared up and away, over the bowler's head and clean over the sight-screen into the pavilion stand. The umpire was signalling a six long before it clattered in among the spectators, to a mixture of cheers and boos from the Lancashire crowd. Nine to win now. Watkinson glared at me down the pitch before stalking back to his mark. I could read his intentions with startling clarity.

His next ball was short and fast, swinging in to my body. But there was no lift off the pitch, no cut off the seam, and I anticipated it exactly, pulling the bat round inelegantly but effectively to dispatch the ball to the square-leg boundary. Five to win now. The fifth ball eluded both bat and wickets, but the sixth I snicked and the wicket-keeper, in his excitement, snatched at it and put down the catch, while Hills, with a great shout, 'Come ON!!!' came lumbering at full-speed down the pitch. Frantically I took off for the run, while behind me the wicket-keeper, furious at dropping the catch, flung off his glove and raced to pick up the ball and

195

shy it at the bowler's end. Had he kept his head, I would have been run out by yards, but he aimed at the stumps instead of into the bowler's hands and the ball struck me on the backside half-way up the pitch, adding considerable impetus to my run to the great amusement of the spectators. Four runs to win, and Jefferson King to bowl the last over.

He was a great team man, and he bowled his heart out in those six balls. But when luck is with you on a cricket pitch it can frustrate the greatest, and although he beat me with five balls out of the six, the last flashed off the bat past the only slip and beat the diving fielder to the third man boundary. It was Surrey's first win of the season and the maximum twenty-four points we earned for it lifted us from thirteenth to eighth in the table. The whole team cheered us off the pitch, and Jefferson King put his large black hand on my shoulder and said, quietly: 'Well batted, young-un. I thought I had you there.'

'So did I,' I said truthfully, thanking him. 'I didn't see one ball of that last over. I owe you a beer for not getting me out.'

'I'll take you up on that. It'll cost you, you'll see.'

'The win's worth it. I'll see you in fifteen minutes.'

We walked on amicably together into the pavilion. Joe Watkinson caught us up and added his congratulations, saying that he'd also be in the bar for a beer after he had changed, especially if Surrey was paying.

'Good match, that,' he said. 'Last ball win. Should do you lot some good. How are you all gettin' on without Grace? Makes a difference, I bet. That was a shockin' thing, dyin' like that. Don Smithson seems to be doin' all right.'

'Yes, he is, I think. Most of the chaps seem to be much happier. A few more wins like this will help us all to settle down.'

We split up, and I clumped up the wooden stairs in my kit which suddenly seemed to weigh a ton. I remembered that I hadn't had more than four hours sleep, and there was still the long drive back to London to be faced that evening. I showered and dressed, splashed aftershave on my five o'clock shadow, and made a quick call to Essex. I felt refreshed enough to go down to the bar and stand my promised round. They were both waiting for me.

'What are you having? It's your last chance.'

'Oh, just ask Joe behind the bar there to fill up my usual. He knows.' King grinned hugely. Watkinson laughed.

'You're young. You'll learn. Mine's a pint of Special, please.'

I parked my bag behind the door and pushed my way through to the bar to give the order.

'And a pint of shandy for me. I'm driving. And one for yourself, Joe, on the winners.'

'Ta.' The barman nodded his thanks. He pulled a couple of pints and lifted down a vast pewter tankard from a special hook behind the bar. There was a shout of laughter from behind me.

'This is Jeff's,' he said, grinning. 'Fill it right up? Takes a quart and a half.'

'Sure,' I said. 'Why not? Win some, lose some.'

With some difficulty I carried King's huge mug in one hand and the two pints in the other across the bar without spilling them. We sat down at a small table and toasted each other. King lifted his tankard and knocked back at least half of it in one mammoth swallow.

'Ah,' he said, belching. 'That's better. What's all this I hear about nude orgies and fightin' at midnight? You Surrey boys will be gettin' a reputation. First you kill off de skipper – good riddance – an' then beat up half of Liverpool. I hear de hospital was full up.'

'It wasn't as spectacular as that,' I protested. 'We just beat up two pimps and then the cops arrived.'

He looked at me shrewdly.

'An' now de cops have shut down de cricket bat factory an' got dis creep Jackson inside. What d'you know about dat?'

'Nothing.'

The answer was too bald.

'Hey,' said Watkinson. 'Frank North's your dad, isn't he? The bat-maker?'

'Yes, he is. Why?'

'Hang on.'

He leant out suddenly and twitched a folded newspaper from under the arm of a man drinking and laughing in a group. The man didn't notice, and Watkinson unfolded it and handed it to me. It was the late edition of the *Liverpool Echo*, and its banner headline read: HUGE DRUGS BUST IN AIGBURTH: BAT MAN HELD. I ran my eye quickly down the story. It detailed the raid on Jackson Bats and the arrest of four men, attributing it to the sterling work of the Liverpool CID. Halfway down it mentioned, almost in passing, that several other premises had been raided in different parts of the country and a total of twenty-two people held, including two women. A police spokesman had said: 'Our inquiries are continuing, and we hope to make more arrests in the foreseeable future.' The reporter said that 'sources' believed that the kingpins of the drugs ring had escaped arrest and that ports and airports were being closely watched.

Watkinson pointed to a subsidiary headline down the page: CRICKET STAR'S FATHER SOUGHT. It said that the Sussex police were anxious to trace Mr Frank North, the well-known bat-maker, who had been missing from his premises in Willford, Sussex, since the early hours of Thursday morning. There was a suspicion that Mr North had been abducted. The police were questioning an unnamed minicab driver who was believed to have driven Mr North to an address in Essex. The driver had been found unconscious in his cab in a field four miles from Witham. Mr North was the father of Roger North, Surrey's rising cricket star now playing at Aigburth, etc. He was also the maker of bats for Persse Grace, the Surrey cricket captain whose mysterious death at Lord's was still under investigation.

A loud guffaw in my ear made me jump. Watkinson had been reading over my shoulder, and now he stabbed his finger at a third story, neatly dovetailed between the other two. It was a brief panel saying that a number of Surrey cricketers had been involved in an 'incident' in the Apollyon hotel the previous night involving a fracas over two nude women. 'Full story, page 2'. The juxtaposition showed that the editors had recognised the coincidences in the articles, if nothing more, although they dared not hint at anything further. I turned the page, and there right across the page, ran the headline: CRICKETERS CAUGHT OUT IN HOTEL ORGY. Underneath were photographs of Down and me, side by side walking out to field that same morning, with the caption: 'Roger North (right) and Gerry Down going into a different kind of action this morning'. There was enough truth in the story to make it believable, but it was cleverly slanted to make it appear that we had been caught *in flagrante delicto*, had tried to fight our way out of a hotel bedroom, and had been rescued from more indiscretions by the courageous actions of Mr Harry Carnock, the Surrey manager/coach. It added, correctly, that we had both been disciplined and fined, and Carnock was quoted as saying, magnanimously: 'As far as Surrey is concerned, the incident is closed. They won't do it again.'

'I wonder you found the energy to play cricket at all, man,' said King. 'Some people have all de luck. Who were de women? Anyone we know?'

I could not be bothered to defend myself or them.

'I expect so,' I said. 'Josephine and Therese, better known as Trees.'

King guffawed again.

'You and de rest of de Kop!' he roared. 'Dem two's de Liver bicycles.' He rolled helplessly in his chair, and just as suddenly sat up, cold sober.

'Hey,' he said, dropping the Caribbean twang. 'They're Jacko's girls.'

'And that was the night before the drugs raid,' Atkinson chimed in. He looked at me closely. 'You know a whole lot more than you're saying. What d'you know about this drugs business? And what's all this about your old man gone missing?'

I looked him straight in the eye. 'I have no idea,' I said. 'I'll find out tonight when I get home. Like the rest of it, it's probably just newspaper exaggeration. When I saw him last night, he was staying at a friend's house. I've got to go. Thanks for the drink. I've got a long drive ahead.'

'Who are you playing tomorrow?'

'Worcestershire, De Kok and all,' I said. After Graeme Hick, De Kok was Worcestershire's latest wonder import. 'But I won't be playing. Twelfth man. Discipline, you know.' And I pointed at the newspaper story. 'That's the only bit they got right.'

'Surrey must be bloody mad,' said Watkinson. 'Carnock's a four letter word. Still, with De Kok playing, it might be better to miss Worcestershire. You'll be back soon enough. Good luck. But any bowler who can hit me for six doesn't need it.'

They shook me warmly by the hand, vowing vengeance in the return match at The Oval later in the year, and waved me off. I slipped the Alfa into gear, and drove off reflecting that this was what cricket was all about, and why I had chosen it as a career. They were the first friends I had made outside Surrey on the circuit, but I was certain I would find plenty more. I hugged the warmth to me all the way down the M5 as far as the Knutsford service station, where I pulled in for a wash, a sandwich and a tank of petrol. The car-park was not crowded, and I drove into a space on the far side and strolled across leisurely to the restaurant, enjoying the softness of the evening. I had just taken the first bite from my excellent salmon and cucumber sandwich when a smooth voice said: 'May I join you?' and a tall, thin, dark-suited figure sat down at the table opposite me. My feeling of contentment melted on the instant, and

200

the salmon in my mouth tasted of ashes, but I continued to pay attention to my meal as though there had been no intrusion. Pravisar lit a cigarette and blew expensive smoke across the table in my direction.

'You have cost me a great deal,' he said. Beneath the suavity, he was very angry. 'I gave you the opportunity to join me. Now you will pay.'

I ignored that. 'Did you get my message?' I said coldly. He did not reply directly.

'I doubt if you will be able to keep the appointment,' he said. 'I shall be at The Oval tomorrow. You may not be.' He got up and strode out, tall and elegant, and with menace in every movement of his body. Through the window I watched him climb into the back of a black Mercedes, which drove off with a roar of exhaust, back wheels spinning on the tarmac in the best melodramatic tradition. I was becoming accustomed to his threats, and with my father safe and Sally under guard I felt there was not a great deal to worry about, provided I remained vigilant. I finished my sandwich and washed it down with weak black coffee which resembled dish-water more than anything else, and went out to the Alfa, a hundred yards or so across the car-park. Perhaps the encounter with Pravisar had set my nerve ends a-quiver, for although there was no outward sign of danger, some atavistic sense prompted me to bend down and glance under the car.

I froze. Clamped onto the metallic floor under the driver's seat was a flat round object about the size of a movie film canister. When I gingerly put my ear closer to the car I thought I could hear a faint ticking. Sweat broke out on my forehead and my back as I straightened up. A car drove into the park, its driver seeking a suitable space. He turned towards me. I ran forward, waving my arms to stop him. He pulled up, winding down his window irritably. I ran to it. He was a middle-aged man with an indignant expression behind a military moustache.

'What the hell? . . .'

'Look. There's a bomb under my car.' I pointed. 'Go and dial 999. Get the police. I'll try and stop anybody else coming in.'

Fortunately the military man knew an order when he heard one, even from someone half his age. He didn't quibble. All he said was: 'Good God! Wilco!', swung open his door and ran for the telephone. Then he roused the security guard and within a minute I heard the loudspeaker broadcast: 'This is a security alert. No one is permitted to go back to the car-park for the time being. Stay where you are. Do not panic and listen for further announcements.' As the voice boomed out two security men ran to block the car-park entrance with a 'Closed' notice.

The military man returned and took command with practised authority. He introduced himself as Major Faulkner, (retired), Parachute regiment, demanded to know who I was and what I did, and ordered me out of the car-park too. He knew the ropes, all right. He had seen service in Ulster and the Falklands, and he handled the situation with the minimum of fuss until the police arrived five minutes later, sirens screaming. The competent major herded the twenty or thirty members of the public into the restaurant and commandeered the restaurant manager's office and sat me down in it to cool my shaking nerves. The manager, understandably indignant at such cavalier treatment, was told to serve everybody whatever they wanted, without charge and when he protested was told, simply: 'Do it!'

He did.

'You stay here,' said the major to me. 'I'll go and keep the car-park clear until the bomb boys get here. You haven't had anything to do with Northern Ireland, have you? They don't play much cricket over there, as I recall.'

I said as far as I knew I had never had anything to do with the Irish problem, and he grunted and went out to stand guard, keeping well away from the Alfa and making sure he was sheltered by other cars. After half an hour or so a police helicopter roared down to land on the

202

grass plot in front of the restaurant and decanted two Army officers and two men in civilian clothes. The officers, from the Bomb Disposal Unit, set about their dangerous task with quiet competence, and after half an hour were able to pronounce it safe for the public to take their cars away and get on with their lives. The civilians turned out to be Detective Chief Superintendent Ashcroft and Detective Inspector Light, who had been at Liverpool Police HQ when the alarm call came through and had heard my name involved. They spent the next half-hour grilling me about my meeting with Pravisar to find out precisely what he had said.

Then I put forward the proposition I had been working out while I had been waiting. They heard me out, Ashcroft expressionless but Light showing increasing signs of impatience.

'It's impossible,' he said forcefully, breaking in to my exposition. 'Surely you can't go along with such a crazy scheme. It's out of the question. Let's put out a call for the Merc right away.' He started to get up, but Ashcroft flapped a placating hand at him and he subsided.

'It's the sensible thing to do,' said Ashcroft. 'But if North here agrees to carry on being the guinea-pig, I'm inclined to take a chance and let things ride until tomorrow. I like the idea of a confession, if you can squeeze one out of him, Roger. We'll let it be known that tonight's little episode was a hoax, and as the thing hasn't gone off Pravisar will wonder just what the hell's going on. He's sure to turn up at The Oval to find out, and I think Roger here can make his scheme work. There's just a chance we can wrap the whole thing up tidily tomorrow.'

He turned to me.

'It means sticking your neck out one more time,' he said. 'Will you do it?'

I shrugged. 'I'm getting used to it by now. But after what he's done to my father I'll do anything I can to stop him. I won't be playing tomorrow. They're disciplining me for leaving the ground yesterday. I'll be twelfth man, but that will give me the chance to get Pravisar on my own.'

'Try and make it somewhere in the open air,' said Ashcroft. 'Otherwise the radios won't work properly.'

'Oh, it'll be in the open air all right. I've got just the spot.'

'Where's that?'

I told them. Ashcroft laughed.

'Well, you won't get more open than that,' he said. 'But be careful.'

'I don't like it,' said Light gloomily. 'Something's bound to go wrong.'

'Provided he turns up and provided he doesn't see you, I'm sure I can handle him,' I said. 'How soon can I have the Alfa back? I want to go to bed tonight. I didn't get much sleep last night. In any case, it's not my car.'

'As soon as forensic have finished with it,' Ashcroft said. 'In about a week. We can give you a lift in the helicopter, if you like. What are you moaning about, Amber? As a Special, he's staff, more or less.'

'When did we swear him in, sir?'

'Oh, haven't we?' said Ashcroft. 'Never mind. We must have forgotten. Just as you did when you let him go yesterday, Amber. By the way, young man, where *is* your father?'

At that moment the Bomb Disposal officers came in carrying their spoils. One placed a round film can carefully on the desk.

'It's all yours. Two pounds of Semtex,' he said cheerfully. 'That would have made quite a mess of you, sir,' he said in an aside to me. He was no older than I was. The second officer was holding a small cardboard box in his gloved hands. He opened it gently and showed a small contraption looking like a tiny balance with wires leading from it. There was also a torch battery and a brass tube half the size of my little finger.

'Trembler,' he said, rocking it to show the contact.

'Were there any fingerprints?' said Ashcroft.

'Not so far as we could see, but that's a job for your forensic chaps.'

'Thanks very much,' said Ashcroft.

'Piece of cake,' said the first officer. 'Glad to oblige.'

'What about the ticking sound I heard?' I asked.

'Oh, I nearly forgot.' He pulled a tiny alarm clock from his pocket. 'It's a back-up system in case the trembler didn't work for some reason. That would have gone off just about when you'd have reached Spaghetti Junction. It's also a bit of a booby trap. It makes you believe it's on a timer, so you set the trembler off looking for it. Pleasant people, these terrorists.' They saluted and left the deadly objects on the table. Ashcroft ignored them and repeated his last question about my father to me.

'He's safe, Mr Ashcroft. Why do you want to know?'

'There's still the little matter of the murder of Persse Grace to be resolved,' said Ashcroft. 'There are some more questions to be answered. You'd better tell me. Avoidance is one thing. Evasion is another. And obstruction is an offence. I want to question your father, who is still a suspect in a murder case. Please tell me where he is. I have been very patient so far.'

I was left with very little option. Ashcroft had removed the velvet glove and shown the steel hand wearing it.

'He's being cared for by Dr Waring in Little Baddow, Essex,' I said reluctantly. 'He was heavily doped with cocaine and I thought he was going to die. I took him there last night after I got him away from Fairbridge Farm. But he had nothing to do with killing Grace. He told you all he knew. He may have been a bloody fool about that syringe, but he didn't kill him.'

'Maybe not,' said Ashcroft. 'But if he didn't murder Grace, then who did?' He looked at me keenly as he spoke. 'You? You were the one with the opportunity. You knew which bat to give him.'

'But he chose the bat himself,' I said. 'And anyway, I had no reason to kill him, I didn't know about his financial

205

dealings with Dad. I didn't know Sally then either. He was a bastard to work for, but that was no reason to kill him. I didn't dislike him that much. And he was a wonderful cricketer.'

'Why do you say you didn't know Sally then? What d'you mean?'

This had turned in a moment into a hostile cross-examination.

'You'd better ask her.'

'Why are you defending her?'

'I'm not. I've no reason to defend her.'

'Was it something she told you about Grace?'

'No it wasn't. It wasn't.' I sounded like a guilty school-boy. I said, 'You'll have to ask Sally.'

'Listen Roger, at one moment you're trying to hide your father, at the next you're shielding Miss Lang,' said Ashcroft, gently. 'If you want to protect her, you're not making a very good fist of it. We can't use hearsay as evidence, but it might help us to understand the case. It might even save us from having to ask her ourselves and embarrass her further.'

'Even . . . even if she had a reason to . . . kill him?'

'It's possible. Let us be the judge of that.'

'She . . . he . . . he was her stepfather, and he . . . tried to interfere with her when she was a kid. I *would* have killed him if I'd known.'

Ashcroft seemed satisfied for the moment.

'All right. We'll leave it at that, for now. Why are you so certain your father didn't kill him? He had a motive. A very good one.'

'You don't know my father. He would never kill a thing. He would even release a mouse caught in a trap. He's physically incapable of doing anything like that.'

'I think you're holding something back, Roger.'

'No I'm not. Why should I?'

'Only you would know the answer to that.'

I had nothing more to say. But Ashcroft had not finished.

'I have one more question. Did you have charge of Grace's car for the whole of the Lord's match?'

'Yes, I did.'

'And did you take it back to Dulwich with you on the Friday night?'

'Yes, I did.'

'And parked it in the garage?'

'Yes.'

'Did you lock it?'

'Of course.'

'And what did you do with the keys?'

'What I always do with my own keys. I put them on the cup hook in the kitchen.'

'Thank you,' said Ashcroft.

'Do you still want me to go ahead tomorrow?'

'Certainly, if you wish to.'

'I thought I was under suspicion.'

'Everyone is under suspicion,' said Ashcroft. 'Until we make an arrest. You are not under arrest. And I know for certain that you're not a drug-runner. Will you help?'

'Try and stop me.'

'Good. Then meet Light at The Oval at ten o'clock. He'll brief you on exactly what to do.'

'All right.'

'I shall be there,' said Ashcroft. 'After I've spoken to your father. I want to see this De Kok in action. I'm told he's better than Hick and Botham put together.'

'I don't know,' I said. 'I rather wanted to find out. But I'll be watching too.'

'Oh yes. Twelfth man again, you said. I think Surrey have made a mistake. But I hope it works in our favour tomorrow.'

'So do I.'

I telephoned Dr Waring to be told that my father had beaten him at chess and was now sleeping peacefully, with the aid of half a bottle of vintage claret. I warned him to expect Ashcroft early the next morning. Then I called Mrs

Marchbanks, and explained that I would be very late that night. I did not tell her why. She was coy, which was unlike her, and when I told her so she laughed.

'There's someone here to see you,' she said. 'I've put her to bed in the spare room. She said she was scared to stay at Willford after your father went missing. She didn't know what to do, so she came here. She's a very beautiful young lady. You mind you take good care of her, or you'll have me to reckon with.'

'You old matchmaker, Mrs M. There's nothing between Sally and me. I only met her the other day.'

'Oh yes? And another young lady, Angela from the office, has been trying to get hold of you. She says she rang Aigberth after you left. Mr Thorogood's home from his holiday, is the message. You *are* in demand these days.'

'Thanks, Mrs M. Don't wait up for me. Goodnight.'

'Goodnight, Casanova.'

'You're not an old matchmaker, Mrs M, you're an old witch.'

'I hope I heard you correctly, young man.'

I grinned and fetched my cricket bag from the Alfa, watched suspiciously by two constables guarding it, who had to be reassured by Light that it was in fact my car. The flight was something else. I had never been up in a helicopter before, and the first thing that struck me was the sheer noise, which wrapped around me and pressed my skull down onto my brain so I could hardly think. The only comparable sensation to the lift-off was the Sky Ride at Southend, but once I regained control of my head and stomach I began to enjoy myself. It was a bright night with a full moon, and the landscape was continually touched by silver, especially the streams and rivers. I passed the time matching my limited knowledge of geography to the names of the places as we flew across the heart of England, the ribbons of moving lights on the roads merging into great sparkling clusters of gold, spangled here and there with red and blue. London from the air by night was a stupendous sight, and I was almost disappointed when the ninety-minute flight came to an end and my stomach hit the roof of my mouth again as we dropped swiftly, checked, and landed like a feather. I had no idea where we were, but Light cupped his hand and yelled in my ear: 'Dulwich College playing fields. You go thataway.' The glass bulb slid open and I dropped to the ground and followed the direction of his finger to find myself a two-minute walk from Mrs Marchbanks's establishment.

It was one o'clock in the morning, but my landlady was still bustling about in the kitchen like a mother hen. She greeted me with a steaming cup of cocoa and a flurry of concern.

'You must be worn out, Roger. How did you get back so quickly? I didn't expect you for another hour or more.'

'I was given a ride in a helicopter, Mrs M.'

'Was that the dreadful noise I heard just now? I thought the roof was coming in. It reminded me of the doodle-bugs when I was a child.'

'How's Sally?' I asked her, getting a word in between scalding mouthfuls.

'I think she's better now she's here. She was very frightened, poor girl. A good sleep will do her the world of good.'

'Why was she frightened. Did anyone hurt her? I'll . . .'

'There's no need to get all hot and bothered. No one's touched her. She's fast asleep. I put her to bed with a paracetamol. It's time you were in bed, too, young man. But first you must tell me all about the game.'

It took me half an hour to satisfy her curiosity, and my eyelids were beginning to droop by the time I was able to drag myself up the stairs to my room. I noticed the smell as I put my hand to the door knob and began to turn it. I paused, and sniffed. It was as though someone had been smoking scented exotic tobacco; sweet, sickly and sticking at the back of the throat. Cautiously, I pushed the door ajar and sniffed again. The smell was stronger, and the shaded lamp beside the bed was switched on, giving the room a warm glow. On the tiny table a saucer held the source of the odour: a burnt, brown, tarry substance still emitting a thin wisp of smoke. I thought I was going to vomit, so I covered my mouth and nose with a handkerchief. The figure on the bed did not move as I trod softly across the carpet, picked up the warm saucer, took it to the window and flung it as hard as I could into the garden. I left the window open and went over to the bed.

'Hello?' I said quietly. The figure stirred under the sheet that was its only cover. Two hands pushed the sheet down and a golden head emerged. The blue eyes opened slowly and Sally Lang smiled and said in a slurred voice: 'Shoo . . . I've been waiting. Come in.'

She thrust the sheet aside with one hand and lay spread-eagled on the bed. She was naked. She was also smashed. I sat down on the bed and tried without success to ignore her body. She was a natural blonde, which blended perfectly with her tan. There were no bikini marks.

'What is it?' I asked. 'Grass?'

'Mmmm.' She shook her head dreamily. 'Crack.' She moved her hips and ran her hands over her breasts, caressing the taut nipples. 'Want some?'

I managed somehow to cover her gently with the sheet and sit down chastely on the bed. I bent over her and kissed her softly on the forehead. She whispered something I did not quite catch.

'Suri? What about Suri?'

Her lips were against my ear, confidentially.

'Do what Suri does.'

She looked up at me sideways under an indolent arm. The drug was still working. She spoke as if she was dreaming.

'Nobody could do it like Suri,' she said.

I sat up slowly, trying not to disturb her mood.

'What do you mean, "do it like Suri"?'

'Suri,' she whispered, her lips tickling my ear. 'He's always made me feel like this. Persse gave me to him.'

'What do you mean? When did he give you to Suri?'

'When I was thirteen. As a birthday present. Suri taught me. I always do what Suri says.'

'Did he teach you to smoke?'

'Mmmm.' She moved her hands again, sensually.

'What else did he teach you?'

'Oh, everything. This.' Her fingers caressed her breasts and travelled downwards across her stomach. I caught hold of her hands.

'What about Persse? Didn't he stop it?' Tired as I was, I couldn't suppress the anger in my voice.

Sally giggled. It was an unpleasant sound.

'God, no. He did it too. But not as well as Suri. You try.' She sighed deeply, wriggled in my arms some more, yawned and fell asleep. With an effort, I managed not to emulate her. I dragged myself off the bed, picked her up and carried her, naked as she was, to the spare room. I laid her on the bed, fetched a pair of my pyjamas and dressed her in them gently, unable to resist stroking the velvet skin as I did so. She lay as innocent and beautiful as the Sleeping Princess. I returned to my room, and flapped a towel vigorously in the direction of the open window to rid the room of the stench. Then I straightened out my dishevelled bedclothes as best I could, badly shaken by what I had just learnt and wondering where it would lead. It confirmed the depravity of Pravisar and Persse Grace but did not resolve the mystery of who killed Grace or why my father and I had been attacked and abducted. I wondered if Sally would remember anything in the morning. It was obvious that Pravisar had exercised some form of hypnotic and sexual power over her for years, aided and abetted by Grace.

There wasn't much left of the night, but I set my alarm for 6.30 and crashed out, so tired that I could not even think. The alarm brought me up from some black velvet depths with my head aching viciously, but with my mind instantly alert I forced myself to shower and shave, pulled on a T-shirt and some jeans, made a jugful of strong black coffee and took it to Sally's room, barging in without ceremony. She lay half covered by the sheet but I steeled myself to ignore her beauty and shook her awake.

She threw herself away from me on the bed, covering her face with both hands and groaned. 'Oh, my head. My head. Go away. Go away. Leave me alone.' The sheet slid up her back as she rolled over, exposing her bottom. It was an irresistible target. I slapped it very hard, once, and the sound of the blow echoed off the walls to be instantly drowned by her scream of pain and genuine rage as she scrabbled around on the bed, kicking, biting, slapping, scratching and screeching. I thanked God for Victorian workmanship on the doors and walls of the old house as, with some difficulty, I managed to catch both her hands and fold them round her body, holding her tightly to my chest in a bear hug so she had no room to do any damage. Surprisingly, she didn't scream.

'Sorry,' I said, none too truthfully. 'Nothing personal. But I must talk to you. If I let you go, will you shut up and get some clothes on? And talk?'

She made one frenzied attempt to burst free but, realising that I was far too strong for her to break my hold, she nodded. 'All right,' she said resignedly. Cautiously, I loosened my grip and, making no attempt to cover her nudity, she pulled on a pair of slacks and a blouse. When she turned and faced me, her eyes were clear and focussed, but with tired rings round them. She took a long gulp of the coffee and passed a hand across her eyes.

'Don't be sorry,' she said. 'I deserved that. What did I tell you last night?'

'Enough,' I said. 'But not enough.'

'I'm a junkie,' she said suddenly. 'At least I thought I *was* a junkie. I thought that working at Willford I had

212

kicked it. But then Suri gave me a fag at The Oval and I was gone again. You said he took me to the Savoy. I only remember pinks and greys. And Suri. He screwed me again. He always does. He calls me his little slave girl.'

She caught her breath, leaving the words hanging in the room. I controlled my voice with an effort. 'He won't do it again. Ever. I promise you. But how did it start?'

'He's evil,' she said. 'Evil. He bought me from Persse on my thirteenth birthday. Persse couldn't control me, but Suri did. He hypnotised me. He gave me a little gold charm on a chain as a birthday present and used it to put me out. When I was under he . . .' she faltered '. . . he . . . had sex with me and started me on drugs. He switched me on and off like an electric light. I'm no good for you, Roger. I'm . . . I'm used goods. Worn out.'

I gripped both her hands, tightly.

'Will you do what I tell you? Exactly?'

Sally nodded, but her eyes were miserable. 'I thought I could break away, but I can't. Suri proved that.'

'Look at me, Sally.' She tried, but her eyes were full of tears. I kissed her, full on the lips. 'Go to Mrs Marchbanks and tell her exactly what you've just told me. She probably suspects most of it, anyway. Stay with her today. After that I'll take you back to Willford and get you well. Then you'll marry me. You'll never see Pravisar again.'

From the door, Mrs Marchbanks said: 'And a good thing too. You don't have to tell me anything, Sally, that you don't want to.' Neither of us had heard her come in, and I had no idea how long she had been standing there. 'And as for you, young man, that's no way to propose to a girl. It's not romantic at all. I'm going now, to make a nice cup of tea for us all. That coffee's no good for anybody. So you just shut the door behind me and do the job properly.' She fumbled at her left hand. 'And here's something to help you.'

She pressed something into my hand, and went out, shutting the door briskly behind her. I looked down;

nestling in my palm was a ring; one dark blue sapphire in a cluster of diamonds. I sat Sally down on the edge of the bed, went down on one knee, and said, as firmly as I could: 'Now young lady. Are you going to do what you're told, or am I going to spank you again?'

Sally looked at me, her lips trembling.

'I'll try,' she said, and held out her hand for the ring.

Afterwards, I crept downstairs and bypassed the kitchen, where I could hear the homely sizzle of bacon and the rattle of china, and crept into Mrs Marchbanks's sitting room. I went to the drawer in her desk and took out the old army-issue Browning 9mm automatic I knew she kept there 'in case of burglars'. This was a little item of persuasion that I hadn't told Ashcroft and Light about. I slipped the magazine to make sure the gun was loaded and checked that the safety catch was on, then I put it in my cricket bag under my flannels. Then I went out into the road and flagged down a taxi to take me to The Oval. For the umpteenth time, I sent up a little prayer of thanks to my mother for leaving me able to afford little things like taxis.

9

It was only nine o'clock when I arrived at the ground, although the mowers were already out putting the finishing touches to the green carpet. Ken Knobbs, the groundsman, was marking out that day's pitch with his usual meticulous attention to detail and the rest of his staff were out and about at their various duties, so it only took a matter of moments to dive into his shed and 'borrow' a groundsman's overalls, a stout screwdriver and a pair of pliers. Carrying the overalls over my arm, I slipped out of the main gate and round the peripheral wall until I came to gates leading in to the old gasworks, site of the famous Oval gasometers. They had ceased to be used for their original purpose years ago, and seemed to be just left there as one of cricket's traditional landmarks. As I expected, the locks had rusted over the years, and it was the work of a moment to don the overalls and prise open the lock. Even at this early hour spectators had begun to trickle along the road, but no one paid me any attention.

Back in the ground I returned the overalls and screwdriver, changed into my flannels and began the twelfth man's chores to which I had become accustomed: tidying up the dressing room, taking a box of balls out to the nets in front of the pavilion for the pre-match practice, fixing up the elastic catching-net and chatting to the odd spectator. A few members congratulated me on my performance against Lancashire and inquired about the morale of the team in the wake of the captain's murder, but most were more concerned to know if Worcestershire's De Kok would be playing. They all wanted to see the young Australian with the South African name, and such was his advance reputation that they were fearful for the fate of Surrey's bowlers. As one elderly spectator put it to me: 'You should thank your lucky stars that you're out of this one, North. We're lambs to the slaughter if we lose the toss.'

The press had made us well aware of the new phenomenon Worcestershire had imported from the outback somewhere east of Alice Springs, or, to be more accurate, the sheep-station manager's son from the sixth form of Cranbrook, one of Sydney's more expensive private schools. De Kok senior, himself a Currie Cup cricketer of some renown and a farmer with literary leanings, had emigrated from the Eastern Cape in South Africa when his son Byron was three. He had coached Byron himself since the boy was four, beginning with a bat made of a eucalyptus branch, until the boy was sent away to school. There he was found to possess a precocious talent which propelled him into the first XI by the time he was thirteen, when he made one thousand runs in a school term. In that sports-mad nation, the fact that young Byron De Kok had a reading age of eight when he was fifteen, and had still to pass the secondary school entrance examinations for boys of eleven when he was sixteen (the age at which Worcestershire signed him up) did not prevent the media labelling him a 'genius', and the 'second Bradman'. When interviewed, it appeared that he could talk knowledgeably of sheep and adoringly of his father, but of not much else.

This was quite good enough though, since Byron's bat spoke for him. Already that summer he had struck five hundreds and a double century, and his average of 142.25 verged on the superhuman. His secret, like Bradman's, as was said every week and twice on Sundays, lay in his superlatively quick eyes and footwork. He 'saw' the ball

216

seconds sooner than anyone else. His timing was instinctive, his driving savage, his cutting exquisite and his leg glance pure perfection; and it mattered little to him whether the ball came fast or slow, short or full, swerving, spinning or cutting. In short, he was God's gift to the tabloids, a new model for the television pundits, an instant hero to the cricketing public and a pain in the backside to the rest of us mortal cricketers, whose task it was to try and contain this natural phenomenon and prevent Worcestershire from running away with the championship (and all the other pots) for the third consecutive year.

When I met him as he got out of the Worcestershire manager's car he looked like an ordinary young man – a bit younger than me, slightly taller and slimmer – and none of the things he'd been reported to be.

'Gee, is this The Oval?' he said, gazing up at the grimly forbidding curve of old concrete and older red brick which form the ground's exterior. 'You don't see this bit on television.'

'It's better on the other side,' I said. 'All pastel plastic. Very modern. I'm North. Welcome to The Oval.' He shook hands. 'Roger North? Great. You're Frank North's son, eh? I'm dying to meet your old man. I want him to make a bat for me. They tell me he's the best. Say, you had a bloody good game against Lancs. Is the buzz true? You won't be playing today because you've been a naughty boy? That's shit, man. No wonder English cricket's going down the pan.'

'If it is, what are you doing over here?' I said, taking one handle of his bag. He looked me straight in the eye.

'Money,' he said. 'My old man said if I wanted to be a professional cricketer I should earn my keep. Everyone over here thinks because he farms sheep he's a millionaire. But I know he can't afford to fork out ten grand a year to keep me going with the world wool price on the floor. Worcester made an offer I couldn't refuse.'

'You're doing them proud,' I said. 'I'd give my eye teeth

to bowl against you. Good luck, but not too much. A beer you don't get a ton today.'

'You're on,' said De Kok, swinging his bag through the door of the visitors' dressing room as I went out onto the field to bowl at our openers warming up in the nets and to bat catches to the outfielders. At 10.30 the sun was already high in the sky, and the shade temperature was beginning to approach the eighties. Several thousand spectators were already in their seats, attracted partly by the publicity following Grace's death, but also by the prospect of a batting spectacular. The chance of that was enhanced at 10.45 when the two captains strolled out onto the emerald turf. Smithson tossed, the coin flashing silver in the sunlight. 'Tails,' called Bruce Woodward, and as the coin landed he added with satisfaction: 'We'll bat, Don.'

'Damn,' said Smithson with a straight face as they strolled back together to the pavilion. 'I thought that was my double-headed coin. Now I can't claim any credit for putting you in.'

Woodward gazed at him open-eyed. 'You can't be serious,' he said. 'On a track like that?'

Smithson grinned. 'You'll see,' he said mysteriously, and came into our dressing room chuckling at having put one over on the opposing skipper. Unfortunately it was just about the only round he won in the whole day's contest, for after Worcestershire's opening batsmen had knocked up a swift seventy in an hour, De Kok came in at the fall of the first wicket and proceeded to give the Surrey attack a clinical thrashing similar to that administered by Grace to Middlesex at Lord's the previous weekend.

Where Grace had been all crude power, De Kok wielded the rapier of a Woolley, a Compton or a Gower. In the whole of that magnificent innings, there was only one six; but De Kok was hitting fours at the rate of three an over from the moment he came to the wicket. Symonds was the first bowler to come under his lash. His first ball to De Kok hit the seam off just short of a length and lifted sharply away from the bat. De Kok, on the back foot, simply turned his defensive straight bat into the most delicate of cuts, played so late as to be almost posthumous, and bisected the slim space between wicket-keeper and first slip. He had obviously never heard of Hobbs's, or was it Sutcliffe's maxim: 'Never cut before lunch'? The next ball he glanced, equally delicately, inches wide of Hills's diving glove to beat fine-leg's right hand; the third, off the full face of the bat to take account of the fielder's ten-yard shift in position, beat fine-leg's left hand by exactly ten yards. He played the next two balls with easy respect and contented himself with a subtly-placed single off the final ball of the over to take him to the other end to face Gerry Down, whom he drove exquisitely to off and to leg, and then square on both sides of the wicket. Gerry said afterwards that it was like bowling to a robot, programmed in advance to play any ball you could produce to maximum effect. Down even tried a high donkey-drop, designed to bamboozle the batsman into a childish mistake. De Kok hit it onto the second tier of balconies in front of the pavilion for the one six of his innings, endangering ITN's expensive video camera and even more expensive cameraman.

It was magic to watch, and although the Surrey bowling was being torn to shreds, the crowd, already several thousand strong, sat nearly silent in admiration. The ripples of applause for each boundary ebbed and flowed through the overs like waves on a restless sea, every now and then a large surge marking a particularly delicious shot. The lunch interval broke suddenly on the ground, like an unwelcome awakening from a dream. The players stood back to applaud De Kok as he led the way from the field, undefeated with 105 on the board.

Light's hand on my shoulder was a clap of doom.

'I've been trying to attract your attention for half an hour,' he said. 'Where can we go for some privacy?'

I shook myself back to reality. I had forgotten Light, and Pravisar, and the rest of the rotten business. 'Hang on. The team will be off to lunch in a couple of minutes. We'll use the dressing room then. It's the only place on the ground where you can get a bit of peace and quiet. I'm supposed to look after the kit as well as the drinks tray.'

Inside the dressing room Light looked at me speculatively. 'We shouldn't be doing this,' he said. 'Old Bill must have a lot of faith in you, or in your lucky streak. For God's sake watch Pravisar. He's a slippery customer. And dangerous. Are you still game to go ahead?'

'Of course. You know what he's done to my father. And to Sally.'

'I understand. But don't get angry. Keep your cool. Have you seen him yet?'

I had to admit that De Kok's innings had totally engaged my senses for the past hour – the best way of keeping calm I could have devised.

'We're keeping an eye out, but we haven't spotted him either. I don't think he'll try to come into the ground. He must know that we're after him. Particularly after last night's little effort. Anyway, let's kit you out.'

He produced a cardboard box, which contained a small metal tube with fine wire mesh at either end. It was about half the size of my little finger and was attached to a thin silver chain. Light hung it round my neck. A plastic-covered wire ran down under my shirt to a flat box, held in place by light nylon tape round my waist.

'Microphone,' he said. 'It's the same as the ones they use on telly, but it would usually be hooked into a lapel or to the top of your shirt. The chain's less noticeable. If you don't fasten your jacket over it or wear a woollen sweater, it'll transmit for half a mile or more. It will pick up a voice within a ten-yard radius, provided the speaker's facing you. How will you get him outside the ground?'

'You can see for yourself there's nowhere here we could hold a private conversation. This is the only time all day the dressing room will be empty. He'll come, don't you worry about that.'

In fact, it wasn't until mid-afternoon that Pravisar came, and then, as I had half suspected, he did not try to enter The Oval himself. I was watching De Kok nearing two hundred at about three o'clock when one of the gatemen approached the little balcony.

'Letter for you, Mr North. The gennulman gave me a fiver to make sure you got it right away. He's waiting for an answer.'

The note inside said merely: 'Mercedes at gate.'

'Tell him I'll be down, thanks.'

I had arranged for one of the youngsters on the ground staff to stand by in case a substitute might be needed on the field (with Smithson's permission this time) and it was easy for me to slip away. I donned my blazer, and tried to stuff the Browning into the pocket. Eventually I had to thrust it into my belt and buttoned the blazer over it, shoving my hands into my trouser pockets to conceal it.

I was glad to see the Mercedes parked outside the gates, facing the way I wanted it to go. Pravisar was waiting behind the wheel, his face expressionless. He did not seem to care if he was under observation or not. I took no chances. I made sure that he was alone in the car, opened the door and slid into the passenger seat, at the same time ramming the nose of the Browning into his thigh. He did not move.

'Drive round to the blue gate a hundred yards away. Get out of the car and go through the gate. I shall be right behind you. We can talk there.'

Pravisar did not seem surprised, nor did he try to resist.

'Very well,' he said, starting the engine. 'There are a number of things I wish to say to you.' He seemed resigned, apparently accepting the fact that his grandiose schemes had ended with the police raids. But he was still dangerous, even in defeat. He drove slowly along the road, looking for the gate. His utter calmness made me suspicious, and I looked round to see if we were being followed but there was no sign of any pursuit.

Emphasising the point with the nose of the Browning I said: 'Mr Pravisar. If you try to get away, or if anyone tries to rescue you, I will shoot you. Do you understand?'

'Yes,' he said. 'But this is unnecessary.'

'I don't think so.'

He braked the car gently into the kerb and got out.

'If my car is clamped, I shall expect you to pay the fine.' Even with a gun at his back he retained his curious arrogance.

'Keep going.'

He pushed through the broken gate as I followed, feeling like a Hollywood gangster, my left forefinger in the small of his back, the gun in my right hand. I realised that it was not cocked, but it did not seem to matter. I marched him across a waste-land of cracked concrete, with shrivelled weeds growing through the gaps, up to the giant steel wall of the nearest gasometer. An iron inspection staircase ran diagonally up its side. The metal was burning hot, reflecting and doubling the heat of the sun's rays. It was a giant oven.

'Start climbing,' I said.

For the first time fear touched his face.

'What are you going to do?' he said.

'I am going to listen,' I said. 'You are going to talk. Otherwise . . .' I gestured with the gun. 'Climb.'

He put his hand on the rail and pulled it away sharply. It was burning hot.

'Climb,' I said.

He shrugged and sighed, as if humouring an idiot, but all the same he began to climb the steep steps. I followed him, keeping my distance in case he tried to lash out with his feet. By the time we had passed twenty steps I was wringing with sweat, and great dark patches were showing on the back of his grey suit and under the arms. I unbuttoned my blazer and felt the little microphone under my shirt.

'Take your jacket off,' I ordered him. 'Keep climbing.'

He obeyed, and trudged on upwards, carrying his jacket in his right hand. As we rose above the level of the walls round the old gas plant, the noise of the crowd from The Oval itself rose to meet us. Soon we were above the roofs of the intervening blocks of flats, and the applause grew clearer. A glance showed me that De Kok was still batting, now one of the miniature figures in a toy Subbuteo set far down below. The Browning was weighing down my arm, and sweat was pouring into my eyes and down my face, but I forced myself to keep Pravisar climbing until we came to a small inspection platform about eight feet square, where the dome of the gasometer rose like a giant green mushroom fifty feet or so above us. Pravisar gripped the rail and turned a grey face covered in perspiration to me.

'Why do you drag me up here?' he said. 'We could talk anywhere.'

'We can't be overheard up here,' I said, hoping the microphone was doing its stuff. 'Besides I wanted you to see that. That's what you've been trying to destroy.' I pointed down to The Oval, hundreds of feet below us, an emerald Fabergé egg with tiny white figures dancing in their shifting patterns as the waves of applause rose up at us and fell away again with almost rhythmic regularity.

'Why?' he said again, this time with a pleading note. 'I . . . I . . . can't stand heights. I have vertigo.' And indeed, the knuckles of the hands gripping the rail showed white with strain. Under the tropical brown of his skin, his face took on a shade of grey. This was a totally unexpected weakness.

'The sooner you talk, the sooner we can go down,' I said. 'Start talking. Turn round and look at me. You can't fall over.'

He did as he was told, and slowly the tension lessened in his face and in the muscles of his body, though he still

223

gripped the rail tightly with arms stretched out on either side behind him. When he did begin to speak, the words came out in a stream so fast that I had difficulty in following them. I took a glance down below. Two more minuscule figures were standing on the concrete, close together, their faces little white pin-heads as they strained to look up at us. Pravisar was talking. He was doing more than that. As Light said later, 'he was singing like a bird.' Possibly the drama of the situation went to his head. He took a deep breath.

'For centuries my ancestors were great princes in India,' he began. 'During the Raj, the Princes of Pravi continued to flourish. In many ways they protected the Raj rather than living under its protection. Clive himself signed the treaty guaranteeing my family's rule in perpetuity. But when the British left everything changed.' His voice took on a vicious note. 'Our power, our authority was removed from us, and taxes took away our wealth. Many royal families became governors or even took menial jobs under the Congress Party to preserve a semblance of their former influence, but the Pravis refused to compromise like that. I am the last of the line. I shall have no heirs, but I shall never die a pauper.'

'So you turned to drugs.'

He continued as though I had not spoken. He was rapt by his own story, almost hypnotised by his sense of the injustice inflicted on him by circumstances. I did not want to interrupt the flow. He continued in that meticulous, over-precise English adopted by many foreign products of Oxbridge.

'My father, the Prince of Pravi, made me promise that. He sent me to Eton and Oxford to educate me in the ways of the Western world. "Go where power is," he said, "and you will find power for yourself." It was there that I met Marcelan and others like him, and I found that these young lords and sons of lords were frightened, frightened of losing their inheritances and their ancient rights just as we had done in India. At Oxford were Marcelan,

224

Fitzjohn, and Walbrook, and Clemency de Woolf and two or three others. We sat up night after night in our rooms analysing our prospects, and came to the conclusion that the only way to ensure that we could maintain our position in the world was to ensure a substantial and regular flow of income. We called ourselves the Society of Excellence, but unlike many of the effeminate societies of our contemporaries we were not playing at success. Our analyses covered mining, manufacturing industry, financial management, stock-exchange speculation, space-age technology and computing. At Oxford we had the best brains in the world to help us, though even they were not clever enough to know how they were being used.

'In all these fields we calculated that success, if achieved, could only be temporary. One only has to study the newspapers to understand that. Politics? Too dangerous, and even more impermanent. Permanence was the essence of our requirements, and we calculated that the permanent growth industry of the twentieth century had not been heavy or light engineering, coal or steel, shipping, or even gold and armaments. They are all too volatile, subject to war, depression, natural phenomena. No, the permanent growth industry since 1945 has been the supply of narcotic drugs to an ever-increasing market. There are risks in it, that is true, but we set about minimising the risks for ourselves.

'One way of doing that was to cultivate respectability. No country could be more respectable than Britain? What could be more *respectable* than the British aristocracy? What could be more *respectable* than cricket? We devised a way to wed these respectabilities to the cocaine trade. Britain exports cricket bats to some of the richest countries in the world. And what could be more innocent and respectable than a cricket bat? We could place a kilo of cocaine into every cricket bat we exported and all that would be registered to the authorities would be a healthy increase in Britain's exports of cricket bats.

225

'Marcelan had little difficulty in getting himself elected to the Surrey board in due course, and when his predecessor died he became president. He found that Grace, the captain, was as hungry for reward as any of us. Cricketers do not earn much of a wage in today's society, and he quickly fell in with our plans. We supplied the money. Grace began building a corner in the bat-making industry, though when his gambling got out of control and placed our scheme in jeopardy he had to be disciplined. Thorogood, the club accountant, was invaluable. He kept Grace's extravagance in check, as well as setting up the computer control network.

'My task was to control the operation and to organise the bulk supply, which was more simple than I thought it would be, once I had discovered that Marcelan's father's old regiment was a principal recruiting ground for mercenaries for the Colombian cartels. The British soldier is a natural target for anyone who wants a dirty job done. It all went well for two or three years as we built up the export orders steadily. But then Grace tried to entice Frank North into his consortium. He committed himself too deeply there. Then he tried to bully your father, which failed to work, and we had to increase the pressure through you. That was a mistake as well. We should have eliminated you instead of treating you with kid gloves. We were about to achieve our biggest success yet. Two hundred and fifty million pounds of export orders. We could not afford to have it interfered with.'

'You mean that the bully-boys, the beating-up, and the rest were kid gloves? And what did you do to Sally Lang? Hypnotise her? Drug her? Rape her?' In my rage I could have picked him up and thrown him over the rail. Keep your cool, Light had said.

'Ah, that was another mistake, sending her to Willford. I lost control of her. She has a very strong will. But it is not as strong as mine. I got her back. It will break. I will have her again, and you will not,' he sneered.

226

Once again I had forcibly to restrain myself from assaulting him. 'Why did you drug my father and kidnap him?'

'There was a chance that it might keep you quiet until the bats were out of the country.'

I remembered how my father had been nailed down in that crate, packed and labelled for export too. I said: 'There must have been more than that. You intended to kill him.'

Pravisar looked at me. His dark eyes were contemptuous. His hands gripped the railing at his sides. The knuckles showed white. He spoke with a new intensity, preening himself in his own cleverness. This time, I thought, I was getting the truth.

'I knew for months that I had to remove Grace from my scheme. He was too greedy, too unreliable, he drank too much and he knew too much about me. He had begun to make mistakes. He could ruin the whole enterprise. I made my plans months ago. Grace had told me about the trick bat your father had made for him, and I asked him to lend it to me. I had it copied, exactly. My cousin in Australia obtained the poison from an Aborigine who milked it from the Queensland toads. He sent it over as a present in an after-shave bottle. I filled the syringe in the bat and then all I had to do was to give it to Grace as a present at Lord's. I said I had had it made specially for him by Frank North to celebrate five years of our partnership. He suspected nothing. He was preoccupied with Surrey's bad performance and he merely thanked me and pushed it in among the bats in his bag. He said he would try it out later. It was fate that you took it out to him at the wicket. I never suspected that it would happen like that. Sally. . .'

'You bastard. Sally what?'

'Sally told me that you and your father had discovered the fake bat and that the police had been told. He wasn't important, but you were, with your nosiness and good fortune. I thought if you went looking for him I could catch two birds in the same net. But you moved too fast. I never thought you could leave Liverpool while the cricket match was taking place.'

I gestured with the Browning. 'Turn round,' I said.

Pravisar flinched. 'I . . . I can't,' he said. 'My vertigo.'

'Which would you prefer? Vertigo or a bullet in your balls?' I jerked the gun towards his groin. He flinched again, genuinely this time. He turned round, gripping the iron rail, despite the heat. Under his brown skin, the face was the sickly grey of blotting-paper. He swayed and would have slumped forward over the rail had I not gripped his left wrist, wrenched his grip from the rail and twisted his arm up behind his back.

I swung him round again and stood back, still holding the Browning. I said as calmly as I could. 'You're finished, Pravisar, and so are your fine friends. But there are one or two other small matters to be taken care of first. Like turning Sally Lang into a junkie and raping her when she was thirteen. Like kidnapping me and my father. Like shooting him full of dope. Like murdering Persse Grace. Like trying to blow me to bits last night.'

For the first time in that extraordinary dialogue Pravisar showed something approaching human emotion. His face contorted and his lips curled back, showing his white teeth. I pressed on. 'You threatened me at Knutsford Service Station last night. Ten minutes later I found a limpet bomb fixed to the underside of my car. The bomb squad defused it. It would have blown a house down.'

Pravisar regained control of himself.

'That idiot Jason. Typical British inefficiency,' he said, not bothering to deny the charge. I looked at him with a contempt that neutralised the hate in his eyes.

'It's no good, Pravisar. You corrupted Grace, and killed him. You corrupted Sally Lang and you tried to corrupt my father. When that failed you kidnapped him and tried to turn him into a junkie. And you tried to murder me. Now you're finished. As you say, there is nothing left. Look down there.' I pointed down the side of the gasometer to where Ashcroft and Light stood, ant-like on the concrete far below. He shuddered, and once more his knuckles whitened as he swayed as though he would faint.

I reached out with my left hand and swung him round to face me again. His face now was mottled grey and brown and streams of sweat ran down his cheeks, soaking the front of his jacket and tie. He couldn't speak.

'They're policemen. They're waiting for you.'

I broke the slim chain round my neck with a savage tug of the wrist and held out the little microphone in the palm of my hand.

'They've heard every word.' I threw the mike away. 'This is from me, alone. I promised Sally I would kill you myself. But I can't. You're going down there, and you're going to court and you're going to be disgraced and humiliated and you're going to spend the rest of your life in jail. A fine end for the Prince of Pravi. Murderer, drug dealer, paedophile. I'll give you one chance to avoid all that – not that you deserve it.'

I extracted the magazine from the Browning and unloaded the bullets into my hand with my thumb. Leaving one in the magazine I replaced it and slid back the sleeve to push the lone round into the chamber. I held out the gun, butt first, to Pravisar. Like a man in a dream, he shook his head and stood, staring at the gun. I placed it on the floor of the little landing and turned to descend the iron ladder. Even if he used the single bullet to shoot me, there was no escaping the policemen waiting there below. I walked down the iron ladder step by step, taking them one at a time and forcing myself not to look back. To steel my nerves I looked down at the cricket match still in progress on The Oval. Even from that height I could distinguish the elegant movements of the young De Kok. As I watched, he leaned back and square cut the ball to the Tenison School boundary and a huge wave of applause broke out, crashing against the stands and surging up into the air to engulf me. That thunderclap of sound swallowed the single crack of the shot above me, but as I watched the hordes of spectators invade the pitch to chair the Australian round the field to celebrate his three hundredth run, something wet spattered on my head and a body whisked noiselessly past me to shatter itself on the ground below. There was blood on my jacket and on my hand when I wiped my face.

Feeling very sick, I descended slowly to the ground, holding onto the rail for support, to where Ashcroft and Light were waiting. Light carried a tape recorder on a strap round his neck, and he came forward to help me off the last step.

'Come and have a wash,' he said. 'You needn't waste good vomit on that.' He jerked his head towards the object I could not look at. 'You did a fine job. Good riddance, that's my private opinion. But the Super here isn't best pleased, I must warn you.'

That was an understatement. Ashcroft bore down on me with a face like thunder.

'You bloody young fool,' he said, the only time I heard him swear. 'You've no licence to carry a gun; you've enabled a murderer to commit suicide and you've left us with a bloody mess to clear up. You've concealed evidence and you're guilty of breaking and entering, as well as resisting arrest and assaulting a policeman. I could send you down for five years, and I've half a mind to do just that.'

'You got what you want,' I said defensively.

'And I'll be lucky if I'm not back on the beat tomorrow. And there's one more thing.'

'What's that? Don't tell me you don't have enough proof?'

'Oh no, we've plenty of proof,' said Ashcroft. 'But did you have to choose the moment of that young man's three hundred to stage your dénouement? I've always wanted to see three hundred runs scored in a day.'

'So have I,' I said.

EPILOGUE

Four months later Surrey ended the season at The Oval with a resounding victory over our old enemies, Kent. I took six wickets in the match and my thirty-two in the second innings included the winning hit. We came fourth in the championship, high enough to swell the team kitty by a few thousand pounds and certainly reason for a raucous celebration in the Long Bar at the end of the game with a couple of hundred of our supporters. One of them, pint tankard in hand, clapped me on the shoulder. It was Detective Inspector Light.

'Congratulations,' he said. 'A good clean finish this time. I'm beginning to get hooked on cricket.' And then he added, more seriously, 'When are you getting married? I'd like an invitation to the wedding.'

'Next Saturday,' said Sally squeezing my arm. 'Do come.'